"Quiet, you two!" "We've got worse things to worry about than your petty little paranoia."

Kane pointed to one of the unconscious hooded men. He knelt and tore the man's cowl back, revealing a dark, meshlike covering that, in the shadow of the hood, would render the upper part of his face above his lips completely invisible. It was a cheap effort that produced an unnerving effect, and Kane himself had experienced a momentary pause as he was dealing with the shadow-faced opponents. Only encounters with equally weird and terrifying opponents had given him the ability to act despite the distracting nature of their appearance.

"That doesn't look right, even with that cloth over his head," Demothi said.

Kane reached out and took a handful of the meshy sack and tore it off the unconscious man. It was soaked through, which was strange as he had fallen on dry ground. But as he tugged, stringy mucus stretched between the fabric and gangrenous gray tumors that ringed his skull, the tumors themselves riddled with wires and circuits. The downed man wasn't bleeding from his head trauma, but the crushed growths where he'd been struck were oozing translucent yellow pus that seeped into the grass under his head.

"What... Oh, God," Suwanee began. She clamped her hand over her mouth, trying to fight off the urge to vomit.

Other titles in this series:

James Axler
Outlanders®

INFESTATION
CUBED

A GOLD EAGLE BOOK FROM
WORLDWIDE®

TORONTO • NEW YORK • LONDON
AMSTERDAM • PARIS • SYDNEY • HAMBURG
STOCKHOLM • ATHENS • TOKYO • MILAN
MADRID • WARSAW • BUDAPEST • AUCKLAND

Recycling programs
for this product may
not exist in your area.

First edition November 2011

ISBN-13: 978-0-373-63872-7

INFESTATION CUBED

Copyright © 2011 by Worldwide Library

Special thanks to Doug Wojtowicz for his contribution to this work.

Where ere we tread, 'tis haunted, holy ground.
—Lord Byron, acclaimed poet and
founder of Romanticism

World's full of ghosts. They ain't real, but they're
everywhere. Maybe learn from 'em. If we do, maybe we
don't make their mistakes again.
—Domi, survivor, pragmatist and fighter for a rebuilt future

The Road to Outlands—
From Secret Government Files to the Future

Almost two hundred years after the global holocaust, Kane, a former Magistrate of Cobaltville, often thought the world had been lucky to survive at all after a nuclear device detonated in the Russian embassy in Washington, D.C. The aftermath—forever known as skydark—reshaped continents and turned civilization into ashes.

Nearly depopulated, America became the Deathlands—poisoned by radiation, home to chaos and mutated life forms. Feudal rule reappeared in the form of baronies, while remote outposts clung to a brutish existence.

What eventually helped shape this wasteland were the redoubts, the secret preholocaust military installations with stores of weapons, and the home of gateways, the locational matter-transfer facilities. Some of the redoubts hid clues that had once fed wild theories of government cover-ups and alien visitations.

Rearmed from redoubt stockpiles, the barons consolidated their power and reclaimed technology for the villes. Their power, supported by some invisible authority, extended beyond their fortified walls to what was now called the Outlands. It was here that the rootstock of humanity survived, living with hellzones and chemical storms, hounded by Magistrates.

In the villes, rigid laws were enforced—to atone for the sins of the past and prepare the way for a better future. That was the barons' public credo and their right-to-rule.

Kane, along with friend and fellow Magistrate Grant, had upheld that claim until a fateful Outlands expedition. A displaced piece of technology…a question to a keeper of the archives…a vague clue about alien masters—and their world shifted radically. Suddenly, Brigid Baptiste, the archivist, faced summary execution, and Grant a quick termination. For Kane there was forgiveness if he pledged his unquestioning allegiance to Baron Cobalt and his unknown masters and abandoned his friends.

But that allegiance would make him support a mysterious and alien power and deny loyalty and friends. Then what else was there?

Kane had been brought up solely to serve the ville. Brigid's only link with her family was her mother's red-gold hair, green eyes and supple form. Grant's clues to his lineage were his ebony skin and powerful physique. But Domi, she of the white hair, was an Outlander pressed into sexual servitude in Cobaltville. She at least knew her roots and was a reminder to the exiles that the outcasts belonged in the human family.

Parents, friends, community—the very rootedness of humanity was denied. With no continuity, there was no forward momentum to the future. And that was the crux— when Kane began to wonder if there was a future.

For Kane, it wouldn't do. So the only way was out—way, way out.

After their escape, they found shelter at the forgotten Cerberus redoubt headed by Lakesh, a scientist, Cobaltville's head archivist, and secret opponent of the barons.

With their past turned into a lie, their future threatened, only one thing was left to give meaning to the outcasts. The hunger for freedom, the will to resist the hostile influences. And perhaps, by opposing, end them.

Chapter 1

Cerberus redoubt had repelled the invasion by Ulli-kummis and his cult, but at great cost. Brigid Baptiste was missing, and Manitius base scientists such as Clem Bryant, Daryl Morganstern and Henny Johnson were dead.

Mohandas Lakesh Singh took another step, his breath coming raggedly in the relentless New Mexican heat. Ahead of him, the feral albino outlander girl Domi scouted, pausing to look back over her shoulder every few moments, concern etched across her porcelain features. The wild woman had already fashioned a head wrap from the scientist's shirt, tying the sleeves around his forehead, then flipping the tails of the shirt over like a hood. Lakesh felt like something out of *Lawrence of Arabia,* but he had to admit that the cover kept him from sweating too much, and what moisture he lost was wicked away by the garment.

Domi stopped and crouched low, her ruby-red eyes sweeping the edge of the scruff ahead of them. Back before the nukecaust, engineered by the Annunaki overlords, the ground they covered had been a highway that cut through the desert. Now Lakesh was getting his kicks on the cracked and centuries-worn Route 66. Ironically, thanks to the desertification of "the Mother Road," it had not been considered a vital target for Soviet nuclear missiles, and long stretches of the old interstate highway were relatively intact and easily traveled.

Lakesh pulled a map from his pocket, feeling the tremors in his hands. Of late he'd been growing increasingly tired, and he realized that the gift of returned youth was being stripped from him by Enlil. As the imperator, Sam, had once cured Lakesh of the effects of two and a half centuries of cryogenic sleep and cybernetic organ transplant. With but a touch, a horde of nanites had descended upon his cellular structure, turning bionic life systems into the matter necessary to reconstruct his slowly aging and failing organs.

What Enlil had bestowed, he could take away, and Lakesh hadn't noticed that until he physically passed the age of fifty a while back. Now his knees popped and crackled with each step, and his back couldn't stand the burden of even a small backpack. The subtle shake of his fingers as he fumbled to unfold the map was an indication that everything was failing him. His genetic code had been laden with a deadly little bomb. Whereas Lakesh had previously been able to maintain control of his body, even at his advanced age of 275 years, two hundred of which had been negated by suspended animation and cloned organs, Lakesh knew that this time, as his body continued to collapse at Enlil's will, his brilliant mind would be quick to go.

Domi had twice complained in the past couple of days that she couldn't understand what Lakesh was saying. Lakesh grimaced, knowing that those lapses in communication were caused by memory lapses and he was speaking his original Hindi. Those brain farts were something that Lakesh could recognize as the beginnings of Alzheimer's disease. Most people only displayed signs of the dementia in their mid-sixties, though he was aware that subjects could manifest symptoms eight years before they reached the point of easy diagnosis for Alzheimer's. Memory lapses could have been brought on by stress, especially with the horrific events of Ullikummis's conquest of the redoubt and taking its staff prisoner. The sight of the son of Enlil forcing a stone seed into the broken skull of Morganstern would itself have been more than sufficient to break the sanity of a less experienced person. As it was, the young mathematician's demise had been sickening. His fight against the assimilation by Ullikummis's seed ended with his brains burst on the floor, crushed to a pulp.

Lakesh tried to picture that event, but nothing came to mind. Lakesh knew his brain too well, and he knew his coping mechanisms. He'd seen the world he'd known destroyed in a rain of atomic fire and had withstood the shock, retaining details of the annihilation. His ego didn't sublimate terrible memories, and it especially didn't do that this quickly. Something had happened to him, and self-analysis told him that he'd obviously reached a point in time where he was being destroyed from the inside by neurological degeneration.

Of course, that now meant he was in his late fifties if he was experiencing the inability to retain recently learned information or recall current events in his short-term memory. He looked around, and wondered where Kane, Brigid and Grant were on this road.

"Where are the others?" he asked out loud. "Didn't they make the jump with us?"

Domi frowned and gently took the map from his hand. "We didn't jump, Moe."

Lakesh looked into her crimson eyes and saw a flicker of recognition in them. "Domi... I'm sorry."

"Not your fault. Told me an hour ago," she said. She rested her hand on his cheek. "Hour before that, too."

"How long have I been telling you?" Lakesh asked.

"Past half day," she answered. "Told me you're getting tangle brain. Not remembering stuff."

Lakesh swallowed hard. "I'm so sorry."

She kissed him gently on the forehead, stroking his thinning silver hair. "It's okay, Moe. It'll be all right."

"We're still going to Vegas, correct?" Lakesh asked.

"To get away from Rocky," Domi replied.

"Rocky..." Lakesh repeated. It took everything to drag up the image of Ullikummis. The stone-fleshed giant had swept through Cerberus like a deadly storm, had driven a stone through Daryl Morganstern's forehead, calling for him to submit. "I've been losing my mind for half a day, but how long—?"

"We've been away from Cerberus for four days," Domi told him, slowing her speech down, speaking clearly and fighting not to drop words. Lakesh knew that was a struggle for the wild-born creature who had learned to talk while fighting for her life tooth and nail. She was going above and beyond for his sake, and he could see the exhaustion in the form of gray-and-pink wrinkles under her ruby-red eyes. "We're almost to Vegas."

Lakesh closed his eyes. Old information was something he always would have access to. Route 66 swung up north for a bit before crossing just south of Las Vegas from New Mexico to California. The road they were on was as good as any paper map he carried, and there would be a turnoff that would direct them the rest of the way to the deserted city of sin. "About twenty more miles, right?"

Domi smiled, nodding in agreement. "Right."

Lakesh returned her grin. "I'm not completely simple yet."

"Never will be," Domi replied, cupping his cheek once more.

The ancient scientist swallowed, wishing that he had some water to remove the dried gunk from his tongue. As if on cue, Domi handed him a small canteen, and Lakesh took a sip. Domi turned and continued her role of leading him to a promised land.

Lakesh's heart ached. He knew he was going to forget her as Enlil's destructive genetic code tore through his intellect. The overlord had found a way to torture the Cerberus founder—attacking his mind but leaving him sufficient cognitive ability to realize what his fate would be. The New Mexican heat and desert winds had dried his eyes out too much for the tears he wished he could bring.

Enlil was stealing Lakesh, dismantling his brain by bits and pieces, almost as if he had been strapped down to a buffet table and forced to watch as carrion birds tore at his flesh and not allowed to die.

"Damn you, Enlil," Lakesh growled under his breath. He continued to follow Domi, trying to count down to the moment when he forgot this exchange.

After fifty minutes, Lakesh wondered why he had been counting.

THE YOUNG WOMAN HAD stalked ahead of the two men, acting as a scout but also to get away from the stifling feeling of being the outsider among the pair. Though she was beautiful—a shapely, curvaceous vixen with flowing dark hair, tanned olive skin and bright, attentive hazel eyes—she felt a resistance to her presence, despite their asking her for her allegiance. Kane and Grant, the rebel ex-Magistrates and fabled warriors who had taken on the hybrid barons and foiled them in battle after battle, were missing their third counterpart, the tall, flame-haired and brilliant Brigid Baptiste in the wake of an all-consuming battle that had shattered the defenses of Cerberus redoubt. There had been loss of life, but the mastermind of the assault and takeover, Ullikummis, had been repelled.

Now Rosalia found herself alongside the pair as they did what they could to find leads on the stone giant, the spawn of an alien overlord that had been forged by science and cruelty into a living weapon. The trouble with seeking out information on Ullikummis was that they lived in a world where cross-country communication had been severely curtailed. Sure, the Cerberus redoubt had done its best to spread globe-crossing comms to its allies, enabling them to keep close ties to New Edo in the archipelago that used to be Southern California, but as of now, the Tigers of Heaven were on lockdown, preparing for Ullikummis's attempts to lay siege to them. On the other side of the planet, there was radio contact with New Olympus, but they had been told to lay low, as well.

Ullikummis's power was simply too big a threat right now. Taking over the minds of war-honed samurai or armored mobile skeletons would mean that the Annunaki prince would become unstoppable. Ullikummis sought the tools to reforge the Earth, to destroy his father, Enlil, and to take his place as a cruel master of human life.

There were friends and allies scattered across the

face of the planet, but calling them in against a mind-controlling god who was hewed from living, lava-blooded stone would be folly. Firepower and technology, martial skill and courage, these would only lead to the slaughter of Ullikummis's thralls.

Rosalia was practical enough to value her life over those sent to attack her, no matter how innocent they were before the stony prince commanded them. She herself had carried the seed of the Annunaki prince within her; it was no secret from either Kane or Grant. At times, she'd feel the tickle of Ullikummis's thoughts, but her will had proved too much to be kept tamped forever, not when the half-god was working to coordinate the New Order, his rapidly growing cult that had proved mighty enough to breech the walls of Cerberus and leave it in ruins.

Right now Kane had directed them toward the swamplands of what used to be the southeastern United States. Rosalia wasn't happy with this mission, a run through a dangerous, treacherous terrain that was filled with inbred, crazed outlanders and the remnants of genetically altered species that strove to endure in the freshwater marshes and waterlogged hammocks at the southern end of what used to be called the Wiregrass Region.

This was a running feint by Kane. He and the others had left a trail that even the blind could follow. Her mongrel dog, padding stealthily beside her, turned his attention toward her.

"I don't like being a target, either," Rosalia answered him.

A soft whimper escaped the dog's throat, and it turned its dark eyes toward the shadowed canopy that left the sinking marsh ahead of them in eternal dusk. Fingers of sunlight managed to penetrate, so the swamp wasn't pitch-black even at noon, but the shadows were long and prevalent, providing hiding places for people or things. Rosalia rested her hand on the hilt of her knife, knowing that with the trail they'd left behind, it was likely that they could have been anticipated.

The New Order might be waiting ahead of them, ready to pounce. Though she still had the alien seed that linked her to Ullikummis's will, she wasn't certain if she, or her companions, would be taken alive for reprogramming or outright killed.

Either way, Rosalia didn't want to press her luck. There were too many enemies in this world for her to let down her guard. Even if Ullikummis wasn't in wait, there were rumors of vampiric raiders to complement the normal bandits and cold-bloods who stalked the corners of postapocalyptic America. Kane might have enjoyed drawing the ire and fury of Ullikummis's machinations, but Rosalia had signed on to assist in resisting the godling.

Rosalia's brow wrinkled as she looked in the shadows of the cypress trees sticking out of the slowly deepening water. There was movement flickering between the trunks, and it took her a moment to categorize them as birds and other small mammals flitting up and down bark, or leaping among the rare "low" branches of these waterlogged trees.

She looked back toward the two men who had been left behind, tending the boat that they had bought a few miles back when they were still working their way along a river toward the wetlands. Rosalia had volunteered for this stretch of scouting, scurrying across the length of spongy, muddy land that was only covered by an inch of water, rather than dipped down into two to three feet depths, teeming with leeches or microbe-laden mud that literally burned skin on contact.

Rosalia dipped her head in disbelief. Here she was, in a place filled with alligators, poisonous snakes, even bull sharks who had swum through the river delta as far as five hundred miles from the ocean to seek prey. Even the river mud seared the skin so that boots immersed in the mush had to be pried off so that bacteria and microscopic fauna could be scraped away from the skin. Rosalia wasn't sure if such a concoction would eat even through the shadow suit she wore beneath her clothes, but she wasn't willing to risk that. She was too experienced with swamps to think anything was bulletproof, self-contained environment or not.

Bandits and pirates were known qualities of this region, as well, and there were rumors of beast-men, both apelike and reptilian, who haunted the forested wetlands. The creatures could have been related to the so-called scalies, who had been hunted into extinction once the remnants of humanity in North America had been consolidated in the nine baronies. She'd never heard of any furry muties, but it hadn't been something outside the realm of possibility. Kane also had delivered a warning about the swamplands of Louisiana, where there were small colonies of the nigh unkillable mutants known as "swampies." If one pocket survived, then it was likely that the difficult terrain of intermixed marshes, ponds and hammocks would protect the swamp dwellers.

Rosalia turned back to see if the others were in sight. Between the long grass and the fifty-yard stretch of spongy ground she'd crossed, and the fact that the two men were seated in the scull to maintain a relatively low profile for now, she couldn't spot her companions.

"Sure, Magistrate Man, hide when I'm checking for my backup, but not when a stone god's hunting for your ass and mine," she grumbled. She returned her attention to the cypress swamp ahead. Something was in there, and even her dog could sense the ominous stench of wrongness coming out.

There was a rustle behind her and she whipped around, dagger out of its sheath and lashing toward the figure's throat.

Only Kane's lightning reflexes prevented her from opening a deadly gash from ear to ear. His fingers locked around her wrist while the blade was still inches from his neck. "I know you're mad about me being out of sight, but that's no reason to take my head off."

"Not funny, Magistrate Man," Rosalia said with a sneer. "This stretch of river stinks worse than the rest. And not in the traditional sense. This...has a weirdness to it."

"I feel it, too," Kane said. "We'd heard about something going on here, something strange, even amid all the stuff we've been doing with alien overlords, extradimensional conquerors, even a tribe of dimension-hopping hackers."

Rosalia shook her head. "Anyone else said any of that, I'd have called them a fused-out tangle brain."

"Before or after you met Ullikummis?" Kane asked.

Rosalia nodded. "Before. I have to say, the weirdness really took off after I ran into you, Magistrate Man."

"Don't blame me," Kane answered.

"So, you brought us here, leaving a trail of breadcrumbs for the New Order to follow, even when you knew that there was trouble already waiting for us?" Rosalia asked.

"I've been at this long enough to know that when you're on the menu for two enemies, they'll end up taking bites out of each other to get to you," Kane said. "And since I'm still here, having two enemies at each others' throats seems to be a good strategy."

"Seems, Magistrate Man," Rosalia answered, her hazel eyes scanning the shadows amid the cypress trunks and roots, "this won't be just two opponents. We'll be an open buffet for anything with teeth, and there's lots of them in there."

"This isn't my first dance in a swamp," Kane replied. "If anything, the terrain is on our side, in that it's on its own side. It'll eat anyone and anything that stumbles in."

"What was the weirdness you'd heard from this stretch of swamp?" Rosalia asked.

"People disappearing, and reptilian creatures," Kane said. "Sad thing is, we can't narrow down what kind of lizard men we're dealing with. A colony sent by Lord Strongbow, a missing detachment of Nagah, maybe even an overlord and his Nephilim followers."

"Nagah?" Rosalia repeated, hoping for an answer.

Kane shook his head. "Want nothing to do for you. Or me. Or any human for that matter."

Rosalia's full, soft lips pursed in frustration, then she looked back. "Dog doesn't like this."

"I know. Neither does Grant," Kane added.

"So, you promoting the mutt or demoting me to animal sidekick?" Grant rumbled over his Commtact. Kane repeated the comment of his grouchy friend since Rosalia couldn't hear anything broadcast by the implanted communication device.

Rosalia looked down at her belt, noting the conventional radio that she'd had clipped to it. While small and handy, it was nowhere nearly as convenient as a cybernetic transmitter installed in the mandible, capable of transmitting words even if the speaker was whispering. The vibrations of the voice through bone were translated by the small, solid-state technology residing along the bone, pintles connecting the contact plate to the jawline. Kane and Grant could hear everything the other said or even heard, while she had to fumble with even the slim transceiver unit.

It was part of their link that made Rosalia feel so alienated. Of course, since she hadn't wanted to get rid of the Ullikummis stone inside her, she couldn't utilize the Commtact, as had been proved with Edwards when he had been infected. The shard had produced interference with the body's energy flow and disrupted the miniaturized cybernetics. The point was made moot for her, as the field surgery to implant the stone was not possible in the wake of the New Order's attack. The redoubt had to be put on total lockdown, now that its location was known. To preserve the store of supplies and technology within the underground facility, Lakesh had engaged blast doors and emergency locks. Nothing short of a bomb could cut through the doors of the compound, and explosives that powerful would also collapse tunnels.

The storehouse of vehicles and weaponry alone had to be secured to prevent bandits from suddenly expanding their capability beyond those of their traditional victims.

"So, lizards to the front, stone men to the back and

a hungry swamp all around," Rosalia said. "Can't say you don't know how to impress a girl, Mag Man."

Kane's lower lip twitched, as if the smile her quip had inspired had hit the brick wall of reality.

This was not going to be fun and games. Kane and Grant no longer had the backup of Cerberus redoubt, and Rosalia, despite her fighting ability, was not capable of the same kind of brilliance that Brigid Baptiste could provide.

Outnumbered, hunted and cut off from their usual support, the outlanders returned to the boat, each oar splash bringing them closer to the dangerous mysteries within.

Chapter 2

Domi could tell that something was in the air as they got closer to the half-buried city in the sand. Somewhere beyond what was once named Las Vegas lay a sprawling facility, heavily guarded and shielded on all sides by nothing but inhospitable desert. The feral girl had been kept there once as a prisoner, taken along with Kane, who was pressed into stud service for the genetically deteriorated hybrids in the months before the barons' ascendance to the demonic Annunaki overlords. It was there that Domi had overcome her hatred and bigotry toward hybrids, learning that the actions of a few powerful leaders did not paint the total picture of the whole race.

While they were barons, the nascent overlords were cruel and petty, but their health depended on transplant surgery and blood transfusions from unwilling donors. Now the reptilian giants sneaked through the shadows of the world, their minds and bodies complete but their support system shattered with the destruction of *Tiamat,* the living space leviathan who had awakened the genetic coding within the barons and their Quad V hybrid minions alike.

Domi remembered rows and banks of young hybrids, babies actually, soft and vulnerable, so fragile that they were placed in lexan boxes in sterile, airtight rooms lest an errant microbe strike their nonexistent immune system and kill them where a normal human would shrug the infection off after a few days of sniffles. Domi herself had known the hardship of a less than optimal physiology, though she didn't think of it in terms of biochemistry, anatomy or genetics. She was an albino, so her fair skin was prone to burning unless she kept herself wrapped, and her ruby eyes— so keen at seeing in the dark—needed to be hooded by a ball cap and sunglasses lest the brightness burn out her pupils.

While she could have made use of a shadow suit, one of the high-tech field uniforms worn by Cerberus personnel, the skintight, advanced fabrics would stick out. Domi already had enough trouble, being a tiny, slender albino traveling with an enfeebled, aging Lakesh. The shadow suit would attract too much attention, something she couldn't afford when the elderly scientist was slowly losing his brilliant faculties as well as his physical vigor.

It was little things that Domi noticed. Even the mind that had endured centuries of existence and treachery under the barons was slipping, memories fading after only an hour, and he grew tired far more quickly than before.

They looked like prey out here in the desert, a hunter-plagued landscape of cold-blooded bandits, robbers, psychopaths and other killers. Domi knew that there was little she could do to make herself seem larger and stronger, even though she was one of the deadliest fighters who called the Cerberus redoubt home. Behind her wraparound shades, her ruby eyes swept the desert, looking for signs of trouble. Stuffed in a tied-off belt around her hips was a powerful, small-framed .45 automatic, and on her denim-clad calf was a long, wicked fighting knife. She had a back-pack with water, food and extra supplies for the long journey, and cradled in the crook of her right arm was something she'd rarely carried, though she'd trained with it.

Domi, through the redoubt's supply stores, had access to hundreds of weapons of all manner and make. Domi was more feral than tame, and while she was deadly with the semiautomatic Detonics .45 in her belt, the hand blaster wasn't something she'd need on a long, dangerous loop through the desert. Crucial was something that could reach out across the sands and take down attackers long before they got too close. Because of that, she had a Winchester Model 70, in 7 mm Mauser. The choice was simple for Domi, who had seen fellow outlanders in roving bands dealing with human problems and meat acquisition with equal ease using this caliber. While she'd have to adjust for rise and fall with a .30 caliber, like the .30-06 or the 7.62 mm NATO, the 7 mm shot flat, making it perfect for long-range work.

At close range, the 7 mm would smash through a human torso like the horn of a rampaging bull, some-thing she'd also been familiar with, having seen raid-ers dropped with their rib cages crushed to splinters when hit at only a few yards. Domi had a box of one hundred rounds in her backpack, as well as spare rounds stuffed into a collar wrapped around the rifle stock, and a few more stuffed into belt loops. There were five in the rifle's magazine, and Domi had learned long ago that it wasn't the number of bullets you threw at a problem as much as it was the shots that stuck to an enemy. She wouldn't spray as fast as she could shoot, and once things got even closer, then it was time to let her Detonics Combat Master speak in its earthy bellow.

"What's happening?" Lakesh asked. Like her, he was wrapped head to toe against the desert sun, a loose hood drooped over his evermore gray hair. His blue, transplanted eyes looked across the horizon that Domi was watching.

"Nothing," Domi answered. "Time to sit and rest. Have a sip."

Lakesh glanced at her, his full lips turning downward in a frown. "You don't have to baby me, love."

The albino girl caressed his cheek, soft and wrinkled, and managed a smile. "In the desert, remember?"

Lakesh managed a snort through his large nose. "My mind isn't completely addled."

"Keep your strength up," Domi urged. "We're almost to the city, and who knows what's waiting inside there."

Lakesh nodded. "How long have we been traveling?"

"Couple days," Domi answered tersely.

"There's trouble," Lakesh muttered. "I know you."

"Didn't say you for—" Domi began.

"I mean, I know you drop unnecessary wordage when you're worried about something," Lakesh said. "Under stress, especially ready for combat."

"No fight yet," Domi promised. "But it's quiet. Too quiet."

Lakesh took a deep breath, then glanced down at the rifle she cradled in her delicate-seeming hands. He reached out and rested his fingers over hers. "Why did we come here?"

"Fix your tangle brain," Domi said. "Might find someone."

"It was a year or two ago, right? Surely they abandoned Area 51, especially with the ascension," Lakesh said. "Why make any use of a facility for breeding hybrids when—?" He paused and winced. "*Tiamat* is gone. Right?"

Domi nodded somberly. "Happened a year back."

Lakesh's brow wrinkled. "I wasn't sure."

"Remember old things pretty good. Now, more fused out," Domi muttered.

Lakesh sighed. "Enlil giveth. Enlil taketh away."

"Enlil built 51," Domi said. "No more *Tiamat,* no more snake-face council, might wake up old labs."

"Canny reasoning, except that Enlil is operating on the far side of the globe," Lakesh said. His face twisted in concern. "I can remember that, but everything else—"

"Not natural," Domi interrupted him. "Tangle brain caused by something different."

"I figured that much, probably once an hour for the past several days," Lakesh lamented.

Domi hoped that her ball cap and sunglasses hid the concern in her eyes, but the scientist still retained sharp senses, even if his memory wasn't as keen as usual. He cupped her cheek. "You made a smart decision coming here, darling."

"Maybe," Domi answered. Her attention was drawn by the flicker of a shadow.

Downtown Vegas had shifted much when Sky Dog's convoy blasted its way through, past a pitched ambush. Many of the buildings not wrecked in the explosive firefight, or by the tower collapsed to block pursuit of the convoy of Sandcats, looked about ready to collapse in on themselves. The sands had crawled over the cityscape in an effort to reclaim the territory that once belonged. Hardy scrub grew close to where underground streams still sluggishly rolled through old sewer systems, the southern Nevada reservoirs long ago shattered and deteriorated by the earth-shaker bombs that destroyed most of California.

Vegas was empty, but far from devoid of life. It was the signs of movement, the leftovers of habitation, that had left Domi on high alert. Someone was still present, or more likely, had been released in the wake of the devastating battle where she had nearly died, plucked instants from death via implode grenade and pulled to safety on Thunder Isle's remarkable time trawl. Domi was aware that the laboratories in the depths of what used to be Area 51 had churned out a colony of hybrids; she'd seen the nursery, seen the babies.

What if it wasn't merely hybrids that lived there, or what if the infant hybrids who'd somehow survived had been altered, changed by *Tiamat's* awakening signal? Domi wished she could pose these questions to Lakesh, but she didn't even have a quarter of the vocabulary necessary to convey those thoughts to him when he was at his sharpest, let alone when he was halfway to full tangle brain.

Domi advanced from cover. "There's a hotel. We can stay there. The sun's going to hot."

Lakesh nodded. Where she used to look to him as a source of learning, of protective affection unlike the grim, competitive existence she'd engaged in while growing up, now he seemed much less confident, weaker. Domi loved him with all of her heart. This was a man who had done what he could to teach her, giving her the ability to read at what he called "a third-grade level" and treating her as an adult, a woman who was an equal, despite her relative youth and her wild nature.

That love was still there, evidencing itself in the form of trust in her, trust in her ability to cut through a torrid, hostile desert and into the ruins of a dead city that wasn't so dead.

Domi couldn't give voice to many of the thoughts racing through her mind, but she had one clear message.

"I will *not* let you down," she whispered.

PRISCILLA STAYED VERY STILL, the eternal shadow of a collapsed casino interior forming its protective cocoon over her as the grunts and snorting inhalations of the hunters resounded on the other side of a barrier of light Sheetrock. The dark might not have been good concealment from her "brothers," but so far their noses were not keen enough to follow her spoor, even through a thin wall. She was also glad that even if their ears were sensitive, they made too much noise sniffing the air, trying to find her.

She knew all she had to do was wait. Soon enough their interest would fade and they would go elsewhere, seeking some other form of prey. She cursed herself for a fool, allowing them to spot her when she'd assumed they would be snoring heavily during the rising heat of the day. Nighttime had been the cool period, when they could exert themselves without tiring under the blazing gaze of the sun. It didn't help them much that daylight seared their sensitive eyes, especially in such a sandblasted environment. Priscilla was glad she had the intellect and calmness to make use of items left behind by the humans, like sunglasses. She'd read somewhere of a condition called snow blindness, and it was readily apparent that there could be sand blindness, as well, when the eye is so washed in the reflection of icy white or pale yellow that even the strongest contrasts couldn't penetrate their vision. Her days of effort, leaving the great dead lake and its abandoned buildings behind, had made her aware of the need to protect her own sensitive eyes.

She'd adjusted her schedule to the daytime thanks to the use of polarized lenses, knowing that the primitive creatures she'd struggled to escape had been forced by experience to adopt a nocturnal hunting pattern. The day was when she could forage, to escape, to breathe and not feel like a stalked animal.

That was the source of Priscilla's pride. She was not an animal.

She wasn't human except in the broadest sense of the term. Her limbs were no longer as slender as they once were, and in place of the silky-smooth flesh that covered them, she was adorned with a layer of scales, shimmering, partly erupted in a night of agony that had awakened her and torn her from the protein "womb" she'd been stored in. Gasping for breath, clawing at agar-slicked floor tiles, she'd made her first few steps, brain assaulted by waves of images, body tingling as it tried to grow, but something shorted out her transformation, much like what had happened with the others.

Priscilla was the least affected. Many of her brothers and sisters had changed into the placid beings who, she assumed, were the final result of "the change." From the thoughts that rained down upon her from *Tiamat,* she knew that the still, stolid reptilians were known as Nephilim, and they were the end result of a powerful psychic signal that flipped a switch at the genetic stage.

Priscilla floundered in the underground complex, just strong enough to hold off her half-formed brothers one-on-one when they tried to rape her. For some reason she hadn't descended into a savage half state, but from the behavior of the Nephilim, she realized that they were in a stage of evolution, or rather devolution, from human to alien servant drone.

The hungry savages grew tired of the quiet ones and fell upon them, developing a taste for flesh.

The weak, the infirm, the wounded all became easy pickings for the others, and despite herself, Priscilla found that she preferred when the hunters returned at night bearing meat from some unknown source. She forced herself not to concentrate on what had been killed to fill her stomach, but she had not become deranged enough to enjoy the flavor of raw, torn flesh.

Slowly the hunters were learning to work as a team, and there was no way Priscilla would be able to hold off more than one rapist, no matter how much her intellect guided her nascent fighting abilities. She'd run far, all the way to Vegas, finding this little corner in the eternal shadows of the once neon-lit city. Here she'd managed to locate food, clothing and other necessities. Sitting just inside the shade of a looming section of roof, she was able to organize her thoughts better, reading and putting thoughts and descriptions to abstracts that had tumbled back and forth in her brain, scrambled images and concepts that had been implanted via infodumps as she floated in a nutrient bath, growing to full size, and the competing telepathic awakening given to her by a godlike alien mind.

Something had given her the ability to be more than a mere savage when the others were snarling predators.

Most of the books had decayed, their ink fading from two centuries of sitting, but there was still more than enough surviving text and information that she was able to make use of the vocabulary that burbled across from the extraterrestrial identity that had wanted to turn her into a mindless servant.

What had failed?

Even here, in the dark, with the grunts of her hated brethren behind a mere inch of brittle stone, she asked herself what had made her so different. Why had she resisted *Tiamat's* call so well when they couldn't?

There was a change in the noises her pursuers made. Perhaps the sun had grown too much for their nocturnal eyes, or the heat had grown too much for them to do more than slump onto their bellies in a few inches of shade. Whatever it was, there was a sudden explosion of breathing and footsteps.

Something had caught their attention, and they were on the move.

Priscilla was tempted to follow them, at least to see who the poor creature was that had drawn their ire.

Whatever or whoever it was, Priscilla felt a pang of regret as she hid in the pitch-black.

At least, she thought, whatever was out there wouldn't suffer for long.

LAKESH HAD HEARD DOMI stalk away from him, and even in his compromised memory situation, he knew that she was planting the seed of a trap. Born in the wilderness, the slender, pixie-haired albino girl could move with the silence of a cat. If she was obvious enough that Lakesh could locate her by hearing alone, that meant she was baiting someone she had sensed, risking her existence by making herself a target.

Lakesh clenched his eyes shut, squeezing the skin between his brows. Only a few months ago he had the physique and endurance of a man who was less than a fifth of his current chronological age of two and a half centuries. And while he knew that he'd crossed the Nevada desert, deposited there by one of the interphaser units he'd built, he wasn't certain how much of a liability he had been across the hot, arid sands. Domi wasn't one to keep her mouth shut about Lakesh acting like a baby, but she was unusually taciturn now.

He was out of breath, and if it hadn't been for the layers of clothing he wore, his naturally dark complexion still would have burned in the blazing sun. One of the advantages of the multiple layers that were loosely bound around his torso and limbs was that they allowed for pockets of cool air, as well as absorbing sweat and whisking excess heat away. Domi didn't look as if she had been in a recent conflict even past the hour or so he'd retained his memories for, so there was no other reason for Lakesh to assume that it was anything other than a walk in the sand that had so exhausted him.

"Useless," Lakesh lambasted himself. He took a quick inventory of himself and found that he had a pistol in his belt. She hadn't left him defenseless, and since it was only his short-term memory that was failing him, he made sure the weapon was locked safe, but still had a round in the chamber. Unfortunately he had to click off the safety lever to retract the slide enough to see there was a bullet in place. He closed the action and flicked the switch. "Don't shoot by accident."

There was the distant sound of grunts that distracted

him from the heavy chunk of steel in his hand. It took everything in his willpower to keep from calling out to the feral girl to warn her.

Again, if Lakesh could hear them, there was no way her wilderness-honed senses missed them. He did roll over and peer over the berm of sand Domi had tucked him behind. He spotted a pair of big, bestial creatures. The last time he'd seen anything similar to this was when Quavell, the Area 51 hybrid who had befriended the Cerberus redoubt and Domi especially, resisted the clarion call of *Tiamat* so that she could give birth. Their skins were mottled with scaly, fine armor, and their limbs had swollen from the usual hybrid spindles to something slender and tightly corded. They were nowhere nearly as bulky and powerful as the Nephilim, but neither did they seem to be something Lakesh could best in a fistfight.

Both appeared to be about six feet in height, and their faces, still looking like those of the original Quad Vs, were twisted in anger. Each bore a length of steel with a hooked end, a bent L pipe that had been made into an improvised hatchet by hammering the tube shut with a rock and scraped to sharpness. They were tool users, and able to improvise, but that was where their civilization and advancement ended. Lakesh was reminded of cavemen, down to the tattered dark sheets that hung around their waists like loincloths.

Lakesh lowered himself behind the sandy berm, his thumb sweeping the safety off on the pistol. The gun felt so heavy, he wondered how he could keep it steady and on target if he had to shoot.

There was a gruff bark, and Lakesh lifted his head again. Domi was nowhere to be seen, and the pair of savages appeared confused. A smile crept across his fleshy lips.

The albino could disappear in plain sight. He didn't envy the creatures.

Then two sets of black, teardrop-shaped eyes swiveled toward him. Their slitlike mouths curled up, revealing sharpened teeth awaiting inside.

They had seen him!

Lakesh started to lower back down, in the hope that they hadn't, but the two beasts exploded from a standstill, legs pumping as they rushed to fall upon the former Cerberus redoubt leader.

Chapter 3

There had been two of them, stuck halfway between the snake-faced drones that served the Annunaki over-lords and the odd, bigheaded spindles they had grown from. Domi made enough noise to alert the pair, and she continued to stomp until they had nearly gotten into sight. With deft quickness, the feral girl nestled herself in the shell of what used to be an automobile, shadows covering her like a blanket.

These freaks reminded Domi of Quavell in her final, suffering moments, a tormented beast tearing itself out of what used to be a gentle, delicate friend. She remembered the exponentially increasing strength that the hybrid woman had applied to her hand as she held it, lending emotional support to her. She remembered the final promise that she'd made, to protect her baby, the fragile little life for which she fought biology and alien technology to free from the prison of her body before it transformed into a sexless drone.

There was a brief jolt of pain, as Domi recalled when Balam had taken the child, disappearing so that neither the Annunaki nor the Cerberus rebels could claim control of the ninth overlord, which was what the infant had become. Domi had hoped that in the days since the apparent death of the orbiting dragon ship *Tiamat,* they would have the chance to locate Quavell's child. Things never went according to plan.

One menace had faded from the center stage, and dozens more popped up. Domi had done her best to bury those feelings, but the monsters who reacted to her baiting were just too similar to her dead friend to pass from her thoughts quickly.

"Waiting for more," Domi whispered to herself, seeking an excuse to deflect her recriminations. So far, despite the long moments she waited, there were no more of the odd, alien hunters stalking in the open. Satisfied that she wasn't going to be blindsided, she drew her wicked combat knife from its sheath. Just because only two had come to the sound of her footsteps didn't mean others would ignore the discharge of a firearm.

The two of them would die quietly, and then Lakesh could be taken to shelter in the half-collapsed building they had emerged from. With nearly boneless ease, she slithered out of the derelict car's window, crawling onto the sand, ruby eyes locked on the monstrosities even through her protective goggles. The rearmost creature would be her first target, and she already envisioned herself clamping a hand over its slit mouth, keeping it quiet as the saw-backed blade tore through the blend of scales and hybrid skin.

The hunters suddenly turned, and Domi's plans disappeared. They'd spotted something, and out of the corner of her eye she recognized the steel-gray shock of Lakesh's hair. He'd pulled his hood and cap off to maintain a lower profile as he spied upon the mutated hybrids, and he'd pushed his luck too far. They noticed him, and the swiftness of their response changed the albino's plans in the blink of an eye.

Domi burst to her feet, tossing the knife from her right hand to her left so that she could reach her Detonics Combat Master. The need for silence had disappeared with the luxury of the hunters' ignorance of their surroundings, and she brought up the locked and cocked little pistol, thumb snapping down its safety. Her arm was an ivory rod, corded muscles spearing the gun ahead of her as her legs shoved against the sand beneath her. She waited until the thumbnail of a front sight was almost swept toward the head of one of the two half-breeds before she applied force to the trigger. With a thunderous crash, the .45 spit out its deadly message. Her aim was off—she had meant to core the skull of her first target, but the fat bullet merely ripped a crease in the side of the beast's head, missing a dead-on hit to bone and causing the slug to only split skin with a glancing impact.

The blast had done its job in protecting Lakesh, however, despite her miss. The two creatures skidded to a halt. The one that was clipped curled into a ball and rolled toward the cover of a chunk of masonry. The other spun on its heel, letting loose a strange keening wail as it wound back and sent its improvised pipe-ax whirling toward Domi. The albino girl jerked her head out of the path of the cartwheeling scythe. Its crudely sharpened tip ripped a long furrow through the side of her hood, cloth flapping away from the side of her face.

Had it not been for her catlike reflexes, Domi knew that she'd have suffered at least a shattered cheekbone, and perhaps worse given the strength of the hunter's throw. She adjusted her aim, only a few degrees of movement as she continued her charge to meet the enemy, and pulled the trigger again. At this range, there was no finesse with the shot. She was going for center of mass, the mutant's broad chest making a relatively easy target to hit. With a squeeze, she pumped the second round in her Detonics, and the half-breed stopped in his tracks, eyes flinching and squeezed shut in pain.

Domi had no illusions about the debate about the stopping power of handgun bullets. The end of a fight was the end of a fight, and she wasn't about to turn her attention from an opponent until it was down and not struggling to kill her. With a kick, she launched herself through the air, whipping her knife around in a savage arc. The monstrous mutant lifted one of its brawny arms, blocking the swing of her knife, keeping its razor edge from its throat.

One shot to the chest, and the thing still had the speed to block her neck slice, but luckily, Domi intended to bring down the six-foot reptilian with more than just a bullet and a blade. Even with the knife blocked, she slammed both of her knees into its chest, bowling it backward with her weight and momentum. She knew that she wasn't big enough to win a fight with the half-breed with just her brawn and muscle, but her deadliness came from far more than even the remarkable strength of her steel-cable muscles.

The creature let out a roar as it fell, and its chest seemed to sag a little under one knee as they sailed toward the ground. She'd managed to nail the ribs that her .45 bullet had gone through, and with her mass focused behind the joint, she'd caused the mutant even more damage. Broken ribs parted as they both hit the ground, shards of bone making its chest sag as she landed on top. The teardrop-eyed predator's face was a mask of pain and fury, and though one arm wasn't working thanks to skeletal trauma, it whipped its fist toward her face.

Domi's sun goggles went flying as she barely had

a chance to roll with the punch, cheek and forehead grated by scaly knuckles that left her porcelain skin red and raw. The bright sun intruded, searing her eyes and distracting her for a moment. That gave the enemy a chance to shove her off and roll away from her. Domi tumbled and got her legs beneath her, springing to her feet in an instant. The half-breed was on its knees, one gnarl-fingered hand pulling a second of the bent pipe-axes from its belt, ready to continue this battle on more even footing.

Domi snapped the .45 up and fired again, this time her aim striking dead center, her bullet tearing through the left side of its chest. She was going where she assumed the heart was, and from her battles with the Nephilim, she knew that they had the same vitals in the same spots as most other humanoids. Whatever she hit, the bullet's impact jerked it back and into the ground, weapon tumbling from nerveless fingers. She lunged forward, stooping to make sure the thing was dead with her knife.

Domi didn't want to waste any more bullets, in case the second hunter was still in the mood to battle or her gunfire attracted more unwanted visitors. Even as the mutant's lips peeled back in a snarl, talon-tipped fingers rising to grab her throat, the albino girl speared her knife through one of its black, teardrop-shaped eyes, plunging six inches of steel into its brain.

One down, and the other had disappeared from sight, which meant some of these creatures had a glass jaw, or the wounded hunter had enough brains to launch an attack from stealth. Domi wasn't going to wait around passively to determine what was going on. She locked her attention on the direction she'd last seen her opponent disappear to, and stepped back toward Lakesh.

"Domi!" the scientist snapped in warning.

Lakesh had spotted the movement just before the feral outlander could, but his cry served to focus her attention on it just a shade quicker. It exploded from behind a ramp formed by a collapsed wall, leaping with an ax in each hand. Its face was untouched, but bent in vengeful fury.

Domi pulled the trigger, but even as she did, she knew her first shot missed the fast-moving, high-jumping attacker. The round went low, and it had gone high, but the hunter wasn't the only one wielding a weapon in each hand. She shoved the point of her knife skyward, twisting to minimize her profile.

Physics was not in Domi's favor. She was a shade under five feet in height, and no matter how tightly packed her muscles were wrapped in her strong limbs, she was still only half the weight of her opponent, who was not only airborne but tackling her with a sharpened, improvised hatchet in each scale-knuckled grip. She'd managed to slip past the mutant's flying ax swings, but the bulk of the pouncing hunter drove her into the ground, bowling her easily off her feet as both of them crashed to the sand.

Domi heard the report of a handgun, but she knew it wasn't her own. She'd kept her finger off the trigger to not waste ammunition or get it shattered in her enemy's tackle. It had to be Lakesh, and as they rolled through the sand, she noticed him leap to his feet out of the corner of her eye. She'd have yelled for him to stay back, but she was in combat mode. Her throat was closed off; she couldn't speak anything more than an animalistic grunt. Blood had splattered along her arm, but it wasn't the ferocious spurt of a severed artery. Her enemy was twice wounded, and it took everything she had to twist herself out of a bone-snapping bear hug. Scales snagged on the fabric she wore, sharp nails blunted as they clawed for her flesh to hold her still.

Domi raked the razor edge of her knife along those scales, parting the skin, but without leverage all she was doing was making the fight messier. Damp cloth matted to her skin, and a fist crashed down on her shoulder with numbing force. The .45 dropped from limp fingers as the entire arm went dead, but Domi wasn't out of the fight yet. Though her hand was a clumsy lump of inert flesh for the moment, she managed to swing it up toward the mutant's face. She'd willed unfeeling fingertips into hooked talons, and the ungainly hand raked across one of her opponent's eyes.

The half-breed let out a pained gargle, leaning away from Domi and giving her the room she'd needed before. With a twist, she had her knife in an ice-pick grip and she threw all of her weight behind its point as she aimed for the marauder's lower abdomen. The blade had trouble penetrating between the opponent's ribs as she couldn't get her weight behind it, but with only muscle and scaled skin to resist, Domi sunk the knife in, her face sprayed with hot gore signaling the creature's aorta was opened up. Clublike fists rained on the back of her head and shoulders, but the strength of those blows was lessened by shock and rapid blood loss.

Domi wrenched the knife free, turning a six-inch stab into a wide, yawning gulley through skin, organ and muscle. With the blade loosed from the restraining flesh, she was able to back up, her enemy doing likewise.

The mutant's retreat wasn't to regather itself, only to keep coils of intestines from pouring out into the Vegas sands. Lakesh fired his handgun again, and the mortally wounded beast was thrown to the ground.

"Stop shooting!" Domi croaked through her adrenaline-tightened throat.

Lakesh lowered the pistol, his hands trembling.

Domi reached out and shoved the web between her thumb and index finger in the V formed by the hammer and the back of the pistol's slide. That movement happened just in time to keep the hammer from striking the firing pin as a flinch on Lakesh's part tripped the trigger. He glared down at the weapon as blood trickled from Domi's alabaster skin around the metal.

"You're bleeding," Lakesh said.

"Let go," Domi whispered.

He did so, and she was able to cock the hammer back, thumb the weapon on safe, and tuck it into her belt. The damage wasn't much, a minor U-shaped cut where the pistol's hammer tried to scissor the skin on its way to make the gun fire. Still, Domi licked away the rivulets of her blood and wrapped a relatively clean cloth around it.

Lakesh looked shell-shocked as he realized that he'd nearly shot Domi out of frightened reflex. She'd stopped a tragedy from happening, but his eyes were wide and unfocused.

"Snap out!" Domi shouted, giving him a slap. "Over there."

She pointed him at the half-wrecked hotel that the pair had come from. Obviously the noise must have alerted others, so she had to get Lakesh into hiding as he was in no condition to deal with another fight.

Domi paused long enough to pick up her pistol and fallen goggles. She wanted to leave as little evidence of their presence as possible. There was nothing she could do about finding the small brass casings in such a hurry, but she doubted any predator could get a scent off the hot metal, unlike the sweat-dampened elastic of her goggles or the grips of her pistol. As satisfied as she could be under the circumstances, she dragged Lakesh along by the hand, leading the way into the shadows of a collapsed building.

THE TWO PEOPLE RUSHED through the triangular entrance of Priscilla's domain without pause, the small girl pulling the larger man behind her. Once in the shadows, the man seemed lost while the girl's ruby-red eyes glinted in what little light there was. She was moving deftly and pointing out spots where her companion could trip.

Priscilla may not have had a lot of experience with humans, but she knew it was rare for a person to have such sharp senses or crimson-tinged eyes. Could these two have been others like her, creatures who had been altered in such a way that they were not quite human?

Again temptation tugged at her. She'd been lonely since she'd left Area 51, not that she'd felt camaraderie among the more savage of her kind wallowing in the pits of the abandoned complex. Still, there was something inside of her, a need to communicate. She had language, something more than what the others had, and she could hear the brief whispers of conversation between the two. She could understand them, and somewhere in the fog of memories was the recollection that she had been educated in their language while she floated in the nutrient baths. Priscilla wondered if she was meant to interact with these beings. She could understand snippets, words here and there, at least those that she could hear. They'd probably come under attack by the savage mutants themselves.

She also knew the sound of gunfire, and didn't doubt that the two humans killed their attackers. Priscilla, looking as disheveled and alien, almost as freakish as her brethren, could easily be seen as one of them, perceived as a threat. The murmurs in the nutrient bath spoke of how humans were enemies, dangerous creatures not only to other races, but also to themselves. The only responsible way to handle them was to cull their numbers when they grew too numerous. The thoughts inserted into her brain by *Tiamat* were that the hairless apes were to be servants to the Annunaki.

Whichever the situation, two sides had told her that interaction with humanity was dangerous. Humans were an implacable enemy, suitable only for controlling, and even then, only in numbers their masters could handle.

Priscilla grimaced. She'd just have to hang back, stay quiet. If they showed that they weren't a threat, maybe she could present herself. And if they were…

She'd hidden from the hunter mutants for this long.

If her bestial brethren couldn't track her, no humans ever could.

Chapter 4

Kane felt lucky that Rosalia had come along when she had. Sure, she had been operating under the aegis of Ullikummis's New Order, but when the time came for a rebellion, she had aided him. Indeed, she was a gun for hire, and she had a piece of the Annunaki prince of stone inside of her, but she'd proved immune to his psychic influence, able to take him off guard during the battle to expel him.

It wasn't much, but it had been enough for Kane to figure that Rosalia could be useful. She remained aloof, keeping her distance. Even the part-coyote dog that accompanied her hadn't been given a name, a sign of her reluctance to draw a close attachment to anyone or anything. In the postapocalyptic Earth, while animals had proved useful, even loyal as they had before the fall of humankind, all lives had the potential to be brief, ending in violence or illness. She rarely referred to Kane by his name, either, but it hadn't affected the former Magistrate much. The legendary security men of the baronies were known only by their family names, better to sublimate their individuality and remind them that they were only a small part of a much larger picture. While Kane had willingly lived that kind of existence, separated from his parents and raised in the academy, that veil of impersonality had been broken by his friendship and the mentoring of the bronze-skinned giant behind him, Grant. In an uncommon instance of loyalty between two Magistrates, Kane had risked his life to protect the injured older man, forging a bond that gave them the strength and will to resist the tyranny of the hybrid barons who had ruled the villes.

Kane had met another who had close ties to his soul, a bond that transcended romantic and sexual interest, becoming a spiritual connection above all else. Brigid Baptiste had been revealed in a jump dream, and in other realities, to be bonded with him across multiple lifetimes.

It had been Lakesh's opinion that the timeless loyalty between him, Grant and Baptiste had formed a confluence of probability that could defy nearly any odds. The proof had been in countless battles with beings who could rightfully call themselves gods, beings of immense power who had ruled nations, even worlds, or traveled among universes at their whimsy. Kane worried, not for his own safety, but for Brigid's. She had been a deciding factor in repelling conquest by all manner of monstrosities with her great intellect and her unwillingness to fail, going from academic to warrior in a few short months, ultimately becoming as skilled and battle-hardened an adventurer as any three men Kane had met.

He was ill at ease because he could sense her. He could feel that she was still alive, still breathing, still *there,* but she was cut off. There was no contact with her via Commtact, and she had disappeared from Cerberus before the final conflict within the redoubt's walls.

Rosalia was a good woman, and Kane felt she was a trustworthy ally, right down to the instincts that made up his point man's instinct, a combination of awareness and perceptive insight that made him seem almost psychic.

Kane almost wished that they'd made a conventional mat-trans jump, rather than employing the interphaser, which was instantaneous and didn't jar his psyche loose to see beyond the normal flow of events. Perhaps a journey through the mat-trans unit would have freed him up enough to look across the world, to feel for Brigid Baptiste. He'd been able to find her, and other long-lived beings, in the visions brought upon by such jumps. Maybe this time he could have retained his focus and his interest long enough to latch on to his lost friend and ally and be that much closer to bringing her back into the fold.

There was always the dreaded possibility that Ullikummis had taken her prisoner, utilizing her intellect through the power of his mind control, the unrelenting force that had buckled even Kane's indomitable will during his captivity. Even so, Kane would have been able to see that. He just knew that he could have caught a glimpse as his essence sped through the pinholes of reality, temporarily gaining a vantage point above a normal man's.

No, he told himself. He had to do this the old-fashioned way. There was no way of telling if Ullikummis hadn't had the ability to monitor the Totality Concept mat-trans units spread across the globe. Lakesh seemed wary of setting up shop, holing away in another redoubt, as well, preferring to go on the run with the utilization of the interphasers to hop away to a parallax point and literally shut the dimensional door behind them. While the Annunaki had proved to have the capability of making such journeys themselves with artifacts called thresholds, the means of tracing and locating such departures and entries was arcane and difficult.

Kane set his jaw firmly. He traveled on foot, or by boat, and made certain that he was seen and recognized in the sleek, black shadow suit that had become the badge of the Cerberus redoubt rebels. People might not have heard the whispers, but their descriptions of him and Grant would reach the ears of those who knew, and the hunt would be on.

The trouble with this plan was that the fury he'd bring down on himself might be that of the New Order, or it could be another set of foes such as the Millennial Consortium or one of the surviving Annunaki overlords who had been forced to do without the awesome resources of the living dragon ship *Tiamat*. One of those snake-faced assholes would prove just as deadly as Ullikummis and his followers, and the interference of these self-proclaimed gods across the breadth of human prehistory meant that anywhere in the world could be a hideout, a niche, a hidden tomb that held a treasure trove of extraterrestrial technology simply waiting to unleash itself upon an unsuspecting world.

"Hey! Ground control to Major Tom, come in," came a harsh whisper, cutting through Kane's musings as they glided through the still waters of the cypress swamp.

Kane blinked, looking back at Grant, an eyebrow raised quizzically in response to the odd way his friend had drawn his attention.

"It's an old prenukecaust song I dug out for some meditation music," Grant said. "Seemed appropriate since you looked like you were off in space, or even farther away."

"Sorry. What did you want?" Kane asked.

"You just looked like you were in a daze," Grant explained. "I know you're worried about Brigid…"

"I'm keeping my eyes and ears peeled. I can brood and keep watch at the same time," Kane answered with an annoyed grunt.

"I was just going to say we'll find her. We've been split up before, and we'll be back together before you know it," Grant said. "And once we do, no pebble-faced chunk of dried shit is going to last long."

Kane squeezed his eyes shut. "You're the optimist and I'm the grumpy ass?"

"You said it, not me," Grant replied. "Licky may have turned us upside down, but shit is still in balance."

Kane scratched his cheek just below his eye. It felt stiff, and had the annoying sensation of a splinter stuck inside. He had tried to get it out with a needle, but it must have just been an illusion, a deep scar that had settled in and turned into a slender thread of gray. "Keep cheering me up, Grant."

"Keep bitching," Grant answered. "If we could get Rosalia or that damn dog to spout useless trivia, things would almost feel normal."

Kane hadn't broken his rhythmic rowing of the canoe they were in, despite deep thought or conversation with his friend. He glanced forward and looked at the sandy-furred half-breed dog, its dark eyes meeting his, curiosity reflecting in them.

"Maybe he is making small talk about trivia," Kane said. "We just don't understand dog. And don't forget, Baptiste's trivia was never useless."

Grant nodded.

The dog continued to concentrate his gaze on Kane's troubled features. He knew that he had been described as wolflike before, his musculature sharing the lean, sleek lines of the pack hunter, and his senses equally as keen as any canine. However, if there was any common ground between man and beast, Kane couldn't make heads or tails from it, except that the dog showed sympathy.

As if on cue with that recognition, the dog lifted its paw and rested it on Kane's knee, taking on an almost noble bearing before turning its attention off in the distance.

"What is it?" Kane asked.

The dog turned its whole body, its nose acting like an arrow directing Kane's eyes toward a ribbon of water that moved off the main river they were on, rolling toward the shore of a hardwood hammock. He flattened his oar in the water, providing a braking force for the boat.

Grant made an annoyed groan as his friend worked against his progress, but that died off as he followed Kane's gaze. "What?"

"Dog must have heard or smelled something," Kane said.

Rosalia looked over her shoulder, disbelief coloring her gaze. "Like he knows something's happening? It could be a squirrel."

Kane squinted, silencing her with a raised finger.

"Magistrate Man, you don't shut me up like—"

Kane turned and glared at her. "Quiet, damn it."

Rosalia's mouth closed, lips pressed together tight until her mouth was a thin, bloodless scar on her face.

Grant knew that Kane's senses were nearly preternatural, and if he was trying to focus on something that Grant himself couldn't hear or see, then he would follow the point man's lead.

The silence folded in around them, weighing in as heavily as the humidity and the stench of mold around them. Kane knew something was wrong as the normal lively sounds of the swamp, the chirp of crickets and the warble of birds, had suddenly fallen away. The quiet lasted only a moment before a scream, faint and weak, but still a woman's scream, reached his sharp ears. Even as he heard it, he noticed that Rosalia's dog had perked up even more. It turned its big, dark eyes toward the former Magistrate, as if to say, "You heard that, right?"

"Trouble. Let's go," Kane announced, and he and Grant put their backs into it, turning the boat and pushing it down the waterway. The only sound they made was the slap and suck of their oars in the murky swamp water.

SUWANEE'S BLACK MANE of silky hair flew as the open hand cracked across her smooth, dark cheek. She struggled to maintain her balance on the uneven ground between the long leaf pines and tumbled down into the wiregrass. Her face throbbed from the force of the impact, and the Seminole woman had one thought—that she was lucky to have been slapped rather than punched. A closed fist would surely have shattered her facial bones and left her unconscious and helpless.

Suwanee dug her fingers into the wiregrass, using it as handles to pull herself up to her knees, but gnarled fingers reached down, snarling in her thick, ebony hair. She was going to scream again in protest, but a

firm yank tugged hard on her scalp, follicles popping
out at the roots, but most of it holding on as she was
jerked to standing on her knees. She looked toward
what would have been her tormentor's face, but it was
cloaked in shadow by the droop of his hood's cowl.
She couldn't even see the glint of what she imagined
were the cruel, merciless eyes of the man who handled
her so roughly.

Though her head was held still by the leverage of
her own hair, Suwanee could see the others around
her, some obscured by the trunks of the pines, but
most of them in a position like hers, cowed to their
knees. She took a breath to release another scream, but
fingers wrapped around her throat.

The snarl of her hair eased, and the man raised a
finger to his shadowed lips, a universal signal for silence. Suwanee swallowed, wishing she could make
out the features of the man holding her just tightly
enough to keep her still, giving her windpipe plenty of
room to suck down air.

"Please, no," she whispered.

The shadow-faced man was not the only one of his
hooded kind, and they appeared to be all sizes and
skin color. Some of the strange marauders seemed
to be women, as well, but none of them spoke, communicating only in hand signals at best, in violence
at worst. Suwanee and the other refugees of the Ap-
palachia River Basin had heard of these silent travelers, and how their numbers increased. Where they
had first come as stalkers and thieves, making off
with the young, unprotected or unwary, their numbers
had increased so that few left their guarded commu-
nities without sufficient numbers. Somewhere in the
muddy waters just off the shore of the hammock lay

Suwanee's weapon, a crudely made single-action revolver cobbled together from parts and what metal scrap the panhandle gunsmiths could accumulate.

Even if she had the gun, Suwanee wasn't a combatant. Sure, she could hit a tin can resting on a log, but that wasn't a person, and it wasn't moving and trying to capture her. The Seminole refugee's only saving grace was that these hooded men were not armed with guns and weren't trying to kill them.

Suwanee didn't want to think of what would happen if they succeeded in this capture.

The hooded attacker froze, his fingers still clutched around her throat, but he was involuntarily squeezing. Something was upsetting him and drawing his attention away from her.

Craning her head, the young woman saw a canoe moving with remarkable speed toward the shore. She lifted one hand, clawing the air in an effort to summon the people on board. The right thing would have been to warn them, to wave them off, but the trio of people in the scull were paddling with all of their might.

A strange, unnatural keening issued from the cavernous shadows of her captor's hood, and it pointed an accusing finger at the people in the boat. Suwanee sucked in air as it released the death grip on her throat, and she collapsed onto the wiregrass, vision blurred from those fingers closing off the flow of blood to her brain. Suwanee wanted to scrounge for the knife she kept in her belt, a tool that she'd used to crack open shellfish or to clean fish, but the pain of the would-be strangle left her weakened, both hands clutching at the bruised flesh around her windpipe. All she could do was watch, brown eyes blinking to clear her sight as the scull splashed closer and closer.

She thought of the noise the raider made. Such an inhuman cry, issued from beneath the cowl, was not a good sign, either of the marauders' intent or their origins. Things had been bad already, and it was likely that they were going to get worse.

A sandy-colored bolt shot from the boat, followed by a tall man who moved nearly as swiftly as the dog. Suwanee was about to utter another croak, warning the tall rescuer, telling him of the incredible strength these hooded fiends possessed. But then she saw the flex of his muscles beneath black skin-conforming fabric and the folded weapon on his right forearm. Dread landed in her gut as she recognized the legendary Magistrate's weapon, the badge of office each of the grim, faceless lawmen wore. The black bodysuit he wore was unlike the shining, polycarbonate shell armor that the Mags were also famous for, but it was still the same fearsome dark shade of brutal authority as the official Mag armor.

Knives suddenly flashed from sheaths and the ring of naked steel being drawn was resounding. Curved, mirror-polished blades sprang quickly into view and the cowled kidnappers moved swiftly, taking cover behind tree trunks, as if they could anticipate the need to avoid the deadly weaponry the Magistrate carried. Suwanee struggled to roll over onto her stomach, to pull herself to her hands and knees to get away from the two warring factions.

In a battle between the Magistrates and these hooded thugs, Suwanee knew that she and her fellow refugees would only be the losers, no matter who won.

She'd rolled onto her side, still gasping for breath, when her assailant gave her a hard kick in the shoulder, knocking her flat on her back. He pointed a gnarled finger at her, and this time she could see the merciless glint of hatred reflecting on the shadow-faced man's eyeballs.

Then the gunfire began, and the world above her turned into a maelstrom of violence and terror.

Chapter 5

One thing that Kane had learned long ago was that his instincts were generally reliable. If there was a situation he stumbled upon, it was likely that the winning side tended to be the bad guys, especially when they were picking on women and frail old men. His shoulders wrenched and rippled with the effort of pushing the boat through the murky swamp water, his sharp, cold blue eyes locked on the struggle where he could definitely see that the group of attackers, though unarmed, wore a singular uniform hood that identified them as a cohesive force.

That was another thing the former Magistrate had learned. If a group had a uniform, they tended to be up to no good. He remembered his days when he wore the polycarbonate, bullet-resistant shell and merciless grim helmet as a Mag, and he recalled the things that he was not proud of doing under orders. There was the possibility that these men might not have been in control of themselves, perhaps even blackmailed into attacking others while their loved ones remained back home under threat, and Kane's instincts buzzed with the possibility. It could have been wishful thinking, or it could have simply been colored by his recent encounter with Ullikummis's minions and the familiarity he had with the mind control the Annunaki prince exerted over the New Order. He was about to leap from the boat, muscles steel-spring taut, when the scull coasted to within yards of the tiny islet's shore.

Rosalia's dog exploded into action first, its four legs and lighter mass giving it the advantage of clearing the still waters in a single bound, but Kane wasn't far behind, determined not to let inaction be the cause of more lost lives. One of the hooded freaks pointed at him and an odd, strangled squeal, like a train engine skidding off the rails, assaulted his ears. All of the strangers drew sharp knives, as if they were possessed of a single consciousness.

That wasn't good, nor was it good that each of these knife-wielding men had disappeared behind the trunks of nearby trees. As Kane landed on the shore from his initial leap, he let his knees buckle, reducing the shock of his impact on his body. Momentum kept him plunging forward, and he extended his legs, taking long strides. The Sin Eater was in his hand, launched there by a tensing of his forearm, ready to punch out twenty powerful slugs.

However, it was not going to be that easy. There were innocent bystanders in the mix, the very reason he'd bolted from the scull in the first place. One wrong shot, and a bullet could tear through one of the hooded men and kill a person he'd intended to rescue. Restraint was what he needed, which was part of why he was heading into the midst of the knife-armed killers.

Kane was putting himself at risk, making himself a tasty target for these faceless marauders so that they would ignore the refugees who'd been strewed around. In close, there was also the possibility that Kane could take a prisoner, bring down one with a minimum of violence, so that he could get answers. It was triple damned hard to have a corpse respond to your questions, though in some instances, it wasn't impossible.

As he closed with the group, he saw Rosalia's dog veer off and launch itself. While the animal might have been part coyote, it had the heart of a wolf, leaping at a knife-wielding stranger, fangs bared. Kane skidded to a halt, his point man's instinct alerting him to the sudden swish of a mirrored ribbon of steel arcing through the air toward his face. The deep, sharp edge of the enemy blade came close enough to brush Kane's semilong hair, a faint tug accompanied by the flutter of snipped locks hanging in front of his eyes. Had Kane not stopped, he'd have easily been blinded as the knife lashed across his eyes, if not killed outright.

Kane whipped his fist up hard, driving the protruded middle knuckle hard against the elbow of the hooded blade man. There was a dull crunch, and nerveless fingers released the handle of the fighting blade. Kane pressed his momentary advantage, lashing the tough frame of his Sin Eater against his opponent's ribs. Again there was the subdued sound of bones breaking beneath muscle and skin, but this time there was no obvious reaction to his impact.

In the brief instant Kane evaluated the situation, mind locking onto his observations and sorting the data out as fast as any computer. There was little way that a hand could maintain a grip with the dislocation of the elbow joint, the strings of muscles leading through the arm veering wide and losing the tension that operated the fingers. A bone-fracturing blow to the ribs, however, might have produced a hard exhalation, but with the sheets of muscle surrounding the spine and the torso, it wouldn't be that severe a skeletal trauma.

The man Kane was fighting hadn't even breathed hard under the hammering force of his Sin Eater's frame, which meant that something was blocking his nervous system. Someone with a normal working sense of touch would have been bowled over by the kind of searing pain produced by fractured ribs. The hooded man brought his other fist around, swinging for the center of Kane's face.

A swift block with his forearm deflected the momentum of his enemy's punch, but Kane was unable to make a countermove against the first man. Others had rushed to get behind him, and they hadn't lost their knives in the brief first contact. Kane twisted as fast as he could, avoiding the stinging touch of one blade point but feeling the shadow suit blunt the impact of another tip. The shadow suits were capable of providing protection from knives, as well as giving the Cerberus warriors a self-contained environment as they traveled the deserts and arctic wastes of the Earth. But armor-piercing ammo would easily cut through the shadow suits and Kane was glad to note that the relatively blunt blade wielded by his assailant wasn't keen enough to carve between the high-tech material. As it was, Kane felt himself pushed by the sheer strength of the knife man, literally lifted off his feet. If it hadn't been for the reactive nature of his armor, Kane could easily see himself nursing his own set of broken ribs. As it was, the Cerberus rebel crashed against the trunk of a nearby pine.

"Just shoot the fuckers!" Rosalia snapped as she lifted her pistol.

Grant was out of the boat himself, as well, having

picked up a four-foot length of log and using it as an improvised shield against a group of the hooded assailants and their blood-thirsting knives. The edges chopped sections of bark off the thick log, but Grant retreated one step and used the space to heave the chunk of wood at the trio of blade men.

They couldn't get out of the way of Grant's missile and were bowled to the ground in a tangle of limbs in the wiregrass. Another of the hooded raiders lunged into view toward the big man, but then Kane's attention was back in the battle.

Utilizing his Sin Eater as a club, he lashed the barrel of his machine pistol across the jaw of the man who'd stabbed him with such force. There was too much strength in that man to show mercy, but Kane reminded himself that he'd come here as much to investigate the strangeness of this river basin as to lead Ullikummis's forces on a merry chase. Steel met flesh-wrapped bone and snapped the mandible with a loud, ugly pop. The blow was enough to send his opponent reeling, and Kane turned his attention to the knife man who'd only barely missed him.

Kane brought up his forearm, wrist striking wrist and altering the path of the hooded attacker's second stab, pushing the wicked point away from his body. The shadow suit had proved enough against one stabbing, but this time the attacker was instinctively aiming for Kane's face. The thought of a moment before, that this group acted as one, returned even as Kane brought down the butt of his pistol on the side of the man's neck. There was the crunch of a dislocating shoulder and collarbone, which could be relied upon to drop most men into a puddle of blinding pain.

This chop of the Sin Eater's butt was loud and

nasty, but it hadn't even dented the determination of his foe. Sure, the hooded attacker's arm hung limp and numb, knife lost from the failure of his good hand, but the man brought up his fingers, curled like claws, reaching for Kane's face—his eyes in particular. Kane drove his knee into his foe's stomach, but it was like trying to kick a tree trunk. No fetid breath exploded from emptied lungs, and there was no stoop in posture from the folding impact. The only thing that Kane had achieved was that the clawing fingertips raked empty air rather than sink into his sockets.

Gunfire boomed, and Kane knew that Rosalia wasn't showing the same form of restraint that he was. Grant, however, held his fire, once more following Kane's lead, trusting instincts that had pulled them through countless conflicts and dangers mostly unharmed.

A hooded man hurtled through the air, landing on Kane's initial opponent. The two bodies crashed into each other, then tumbled through the knee-high, sharp-bladed grass that struggled for survival amid the long leaf pines. Kane knew that Grant had anticipated the sudden, brutal ambush, and used the only weapon he had on hand, one of the hooded cultists themselves. Would such a flying impact be enough to put one of these freaks down for the count?

Kane wasn't certain, but he stopped holding back. A swift spike of the toe of his boot snapped the knee of his current foe, taking away his ability to stand. Kane sank his fingers into the man's forearm and twisted, dislocating his shoulder. He brought up his knee again, and he felt it impact against a squishy mass along the side of the man's head under the hood. There was a shrill keening, an ear-splitting note that locked the attention of all involved in the sudden melee.

The man Kane had kicked in the head let out a strangled stream of gibberish, fingers clawing at the wiregrass in an effort to pull himself through the sudden wave of agony that had spawned his wild, high-pitched howl. Kane shot a glance toward Grant, the larger man instantly understanding his partner's intent.

Grant balled one of his mighty fists and sent it crashing against the side of another hood. Once more, the shrill wail filled the air, but one more of the faceless raiders was struggling on his knees, felled by the precise blow.

Rosalia, on the other hand, emptied an entire magazine from her pistol into the chest of her opponent, bullets striking the marauder's chest, seemingly without effect. Out of frustration, the olive-skinned beauty smacked her attacker in the head with the frame of her weapon. It wasn't as hard as the concentrated knockout blows that Kane and Grant had utilized, but it was more than enough to cause her foe enough discomfort to toss her onto her back and run through the trees, clutching his head as he fled.

The other knife-wielding, hooded men, even the one whose jaw Kane had broken, scrambled away from the trio. Their flight was sudden, and they speared into the surrounding forest before fading away among the trunks like they were ghosts.

Rosalia looked at Kane and Grant, a question burning behind her eyes, yet her lips were unable to translate it to speech. Finally she gave up her struggle and just blurted, "What the hell?"

"That's my question, too," Grant said. "What kept you from shooting the hoodies?"

"We're already behind the curve without Baptiste to evaluate what we're running into," Kane answered. "Damned if I'm not going to get a look at why these freaks are covering their heads."

"Only the two you and Grant hit in the head stayed behind. Everyone else was in full retreat," Rosalia said, looking around. "That and the people they were bullying."

A young, pretty woman, a local American Indian by Kane's quick assessment, sat up, the bright flash of steel in her hand, anger and rage in her dark eyes.

"We're not going back to the villes, Mags!" she blurted, pointing her knife at Kane.

One or two of the others, an old man with forearms so slender they looked like bones wrapped in sagging cloth and a chubby woman, also wielded their utility knives as if to ward off the trio.

"The villes are history," Grant replied, loud enough that he could be heard for hundreds of yards, a booming clarion call that, by all rights, should have defused the situation. But the Indians only looked more confused by the giant's statement.

"What are you doing here then, Magistrates?" Kane's new "friend" asked, her knife never wavering from him.

"Saving your fused-out asses," Kane growled in reply. "I'm Kane, he's Grant. The baronies collapsed when the freaks in charge…quit."

Trying to explain the situation to these people would have been difficult enough without bringing in the concept of aliens who had manipulated humankind from the dawn of history through the atmosphere-scorching apocalypse known as the nukecaust. Though Kane had encountered both pan- and extraterrestrial opponents since his first jolt of rebellion exiled him to the Cerberus redoubt, there were times when even he wondered if he simply hadn't gone insane when dealing with entities such as the Annunaki and the Tuatha de Dannaan, that everything he had encountered was the delusion of a drooling maniac tied up in some dungeon cell. The simplest explanation would be the best answer for now.

"Heard of you two," the chubby woman said. She pushed in the lock on her knife, folding the blade away into its handle, then pocketing it in her jeans. "The Mags want their asses as much as they want to stifle us, Sue."

Kane turned and looked back at the woman she'd addressed. "Sue?"

"Suwanee," the Indian girl replied with a sneer. "Great, so we know each others' name. Now get the fuck out of here."

"That's no way to treat someone who fought the Hooded Ones," the walking skeleton interjected. He'd put his knife away, so now it was only Suwanee who kept her blade naked and held with hostile intent.

"Fuck off, Farting Gator," Suwanee cursed. "Once a Mag, always…"

Kane was tired of seeing yet one more blade leveled at him menacingly. With a slap against the flat of the knife, he knocked the tool from the girl's fingers, sending it crashing to the matted grass tromped beneath dozens of pairs of feet. Suwanee blinked in surprise at the suddenness of her disarmament, lips parted as her jaw fell slightly.

The Indian girl had a lot of fight in her, apparently,

as she lunged to pick up her weapon. Kane grabbed her by the wrist and gave a hard yank, making her stand straight by levering her forearm to make her behave. He hated manhandling a woman, manhandling anyone, like that, but she seemed determined to put up a fight, and while it could have been easy to put a bullet into her or crush her jaw with a punch, he had come to save these people, not inflict more harm on them.

"Behave, idiot," Kane said with a grimace. "I have a gun. If I wanted you dead, you'd have been cold meat the minute you waved that little piece of shit in my face. And you saw me fighting the hoods. You still have a hand attached to this arm. I'm being patient and nice to you, damn it."

"Anyone fighting the villes got to be a good guy." The chubby one spoke up. "I'm Hachi. The one she called Farting Gator..."

The old man chuckled at the reference, interrupting Hachi. "I'm Demothi. Just call me Dem."

Kane nodded and shook the old man's hand. As thin as he was, there was strength in his grip and his brown eyes were undimmed by age. "If I remember some of the vocabulary I learned from Sky Dog, that means 'talks while walking.' That's a good idea."

Demothi smiled. "Sometimes the oldest wisdom is the best. Gather your things and let's roll."

"What about the boat?" Rosalia asked.

"Shouldn't take much to conceal it," Grant replied. "I'll be able to follow you."

"By the way, her name's Rosalia," Kane added to Demothi.

"A pleasure, young lady," the old man said.

"Yeah, yeah," Rosalia replied, looking back nervously

toward the boat. "I'm thinking you're making friends a little too fast here, Magistrate Man."

"I'd agree with you." Suwanee spoke up, glaring at the olive-skinned woman. "But you're the same as them."

"Quiet, you two!" Kane bellowed. "We've got worse things to worry about than your petty little paranoia."

"Like what?" Rosalia asked.

Kane pointed to one of the unconscious hooded men. He knelt and tore the man's cowl back, revealing a dark, meshlike covering that, in the shadow of the hood, would render the upper part of his face above his lips completely invisible. It was a cheap effort that produced an unnerving effect, and Kane himself had experienced a momentary pause as he was dealing with the shadow-faced opponents. Only encounters with equally weird and terrifying opponents had given him the ability to act despite the distracting nature of their appearance.

"That doesn't look right, even with that cloth over his head," Demothi said.

Kane reached out, took a handful of the meshy sack and tore it off of the unconscious man. It was soaked through, which was strange as he had fallen on dry ground. But as he tugged, stringy mucus stretched between the fabric and gangrenous gray tumors that ringed his skull, the tumors themselves riddled with wires and circuits. The downed man wasn't bleeding from his head trauma, but the crushed growths where he'd been struck were oozing translucent yellow pus that seeped into the grass under his head.

"What... Oh, God," Suwanee began. She clamped her hand over her mouth, trying to fight off the urge to vomit, but failed, staggering to the base of a tree and emptying her stomach in an extended, noisy convulsion.

Rosalia looked at the fallen marauder and the gory mess that sloughed off his scalp. Whatever had grown there was quickly rotting, dead material collapsing into inky blue-green molasses and the wrinkled skin of spoiled apples. She glanced over toward the other unconscious man. "No wonder they cover their heads. What…"

Kane took the unconscious man's pulse at his wrist, wisely avoiding any contact with the goo coming off his victim's head. His upper lip curled in a sneer as he looked at Rosalia. "Check the pulse on the other guy."

"What's wrong?" she asked.

"This one's dead. That one might be dead, as well," Kane mentioned.

"That's one bit of good news," Grant told him over the Commtact. "I'm strong, but hauling around unconscious men through a swamp wasn't in my job description."

Kane spoke softly, so that only his partner could hear over the mandible-mounted communicator. "You'll never be my beast of burden?"

Grant snorted. "I see Brigid's been educating you about the old music, as well."

Kane sighed, frisking the corpse of the man, feeling for any more of the strange tumors or further signs of electronics implanted in his skin. There was nothing, but then, considering he wore a built-in communications device himself, he could make an educated guess as to the purpose of the wires and circuits embedded in his forehead and ringing his skull. He was just too cautious to want to touch even the disintegrating glop that slid off the dead man's head. Who knew what it was and how contagious it could be.

There were only two people in the world whom Kane could have counted on to provide some explanation for the oddity in front of him.

One, Lakesh, was on a journey to what used to be the West Coast of the United States of America in the hope of finding something along the Pacific Ocean that would give them an edge over Ullikummis. The other, Brigid Baptiste, was missing, perhaps a prisoner and tortured by the very stone being they were being pursued by.

Kane looked at the corpse for a few moments more, the last of the tumorous growth dissolving and sliming off the dead man's pate.

"Where are you, Baptiste?"

Chapter 6

Miles to the south of the hammock that Kane and his allies stood upon, a rusted old ship bobbed beyond the breakwater of the river delta. The reddish mottling and decay on the hull and the superstructure were a disguise, a sham propagated to lower the profile of the groaning craft. The master of this vessel, a being known as Orochi, looked through plastic sheeting that had been dimmed and silk-screened on one side to be impenetrable, resembling ancient glass, but provided him with a clear view of the waters and the shore.

Orochi was a tall man, and just for his height he would have been unusual for a Japanese, but the truth of the matter was that his resemblance to most humans went no further than the shape of his body and its ability to fit into a sleek black uniform with yellow trim. Orochi's skin was a shimmering sheet of small, reptilian scales that flowed and flexed like silk. Bright yellow-green eyes shone from under a heavily scaled brow, whose thick octagonal plates formed a ridge where the short hairs of eyebrows would have been on a mammal. Across his upper lip, under a short, oddly human nose, was a similar line of lengthy, slender scales. They were stiff but hairlike, flowing in curving waves to droop over the corners of a wide, thin-lipped mouth, and on the chin, another nest of these thin, translucent scales dangled, giving him the appearance of a classic Southern gentleman with a blond Vandyke.

Orochi was of the Watatsumi, a race long exiled from the shattered ruins of their original home in what used to be the islands of Japan. There were thousands of islands that were the remnants of the island nation, smashed apart and shattered, akin to a plate dashed to the floor.

That was the appearance aboveground, where the sea had rushed in to fill the cracks between the remaining bits of land. There were people still in the archipelago aboveground, but the nuclear onslaught that formed skydark had been far more transformative than the survivors had ever expected. Beneath the surface the Watatsumi lived in an extensive system of tunnels and caves, empty lava tubes. They had remained hidden from humankind, nestled in the network they had called the Spine of the Dragon until the cataclysm happened. When the earthshaker nukes shook the very edge of the tectonic plate that Japan sat upon, things became much worse. Some of the lava tubes and caverns had been closed off for millennia, so that the humanoid reptilians didn't have remaining records of their existence. Shattered walls of heavy obsidian glass formed doorways to a primeval forest below even the Wyvern's realm, a jungle filled with monstrosities not seen since millions of years before man walked the Earth.

Things were not completely fine, Orochi knew. There was a reason why he'd been sent to the other side of the globe to seek out a spot to engage in experimentation. The Watatsumi were in need of some way to control monsters that had shared their caves. Only the discovery of the piggybackers here in the bay that used to be known as Gulf Breeze gave them an idea, an opportunity by which they could tame the massive and powerful reptiles who shared their home.

Orochi frowned as he heard the buzzing alert from the ship's comm station. "What is it now?"

Kondo, a younger member of the crew, turned from his console, looking upon the group leader with a momentary reverence, a sign of unwavering respect that had been instilled in all of the Wyvern's military since the day they were old enough to be called grown. "Captain, we lost contact with two of the drone units who were acquiring new conversion subjects."

"Confirmed loss of contact?" Orochi asked, striding toward the young officer.

"Absolutely," Kondo replied. "Electronics damaged. A third had been struck, but its neural net is still working, though transmission is spotty."

Orochi's chartreuse eyes narrowed as he looked at the screen.

"The moment we started experiencing malfunctions, we called them back," Kondo said.

"Good," Orochi said, looking at the monitor, distracted from his subordinate's reassurances. He wasn't the kind of man to take a sudden change in luck lightly. Someone, after a year of experimentation, had figured out something about their hooded minions.

"I want you to activate a pod of gators," Orochi said. "Set them after the group the men had difficulty with."

Kondo looked up at his commander. "We're still not sure if we can keep the alligators under control if we set them into action."

"Well, that's the whole damned point of this journey. If the parasite works well enough for us to remotely control crocodilians, then we can turn around and go home," Orochi countered.

The officer nodded.

Orochi stood back from the console. He was under orders from the Watatsumi high command to utilize the secrets of the Gulf Breeze discoveries to combat the monsters from below the Dragon's Spine, but he also had a second mission, one that he had managed to expand. Under the guise of influencing more complex mammalian brains, testing the limits of the electronically influenced parasites, he'd grown an army of specimen retrievers.

Separated from home by thousands of miles, half the surface of the Earth, in fact, Orochi had free reign to alter paradigms, something made easier by recruiting scientists and officers who were true to the cause. The surface of the Earth had been denied to the Watatsumi for too long.

The parasitic entity would be their key to ruling the surface of this scarred, tumultuous world again.

THE CAJUN HEARD THE sound of gunfire in the distance, then looked back at the people who had hired him. Agrippine was not someone who relished the idea of venturing into these swamps, thanks to the disappearances of the past few months. But when the New Order's missionaries arrived, bearing payment and a bounty for the heads of two people in particular, both of them former Magistrates, he wasn't going to let easy money get away from him.

The woman who was in charge, a strange figure who was tall, despite the cloak that reached up over the top of her head, shadowing half of her face, seemed as if she knew the sound.

"Sounds like we're close," Agrippine said.

The woman nodded. She didn't speak much. Indeed, she had simply laid down a bag of coins and photographs of the two targets and said, "You will get the rest when they are mine."

Since then, she'd remained silent. Agrippine didn't mind, especially since she kept to herself, staying out of the way as the motor launch crawled down the river. She hadn't come alone, but the rest of the New Order minions with her were both talkative and cooperative when it came to running his ship. In return, Agrippine had been given the money to stock up on weapons so that he could equip them to aid him in the hunt for Kane and Grant.

She looked over the weapons, examining them as if she was investigating an ancient, outdated artifact, her shadowed face expressionless as her fingers went along the surfaces of the guns.

"Do they meet with your approval?" Agrippine asked.

She looked up from the rifle in her hands, then extended it, butt first, so he could take it from her. She stayed quiet.

This was a matter for employees, not her, Agrippine surmised from her reaction.

"Mistress, should we move in?" one of the New Order's expedition asked.

She lifted her hand, halting any further discussion.

Whoever this woman was, she had authority enough to silence a man easily one hundred pounds heavier and larger than she was. Her focus was on the distance, lips shut, breathing easily.

She turned to Agrippine, and for the first time in a week, she spoke.

"This is where I take my leave," she said. "Grogan is in charge."

Agrippine looked at the big man who had asked to be loosed upon the source of the gunfire. Grogan, aside from being much heavier than the woman, was tall and carved from lean, long muscle. He was formidable, and had been much more talkative than the woman, though he continued to defer to her leadership.

"Right," Agrippine said. "And what will you be doing?"

"That is not your concern," she replied coldly. She had a satchel with her that she picked up, swinging it over one slender but muscular shoulder. "Your concern is earning the rest of your money. Fail, Grogan kills you. Succeed, Grogan pays you."

"What if Grogan dies?" Agrippine asked, casting a sideways glance toward the man.

"I selected him for this task. He will not fail," she said. It was if her proclamations were etched into stone. No inflection of doubt haunted any of her words. She nodded to one of the New Order crewmen, who extended a plank toward the shore.

"Where are you going now?" Agrippine asked.

"I have a task to attend to elsewhere," she answered.

"Where?" Agrippine pressed.

Green eyes flashed in the shadows of her hood. Her mouth turned down into a frown, then she took a cleansing breath. "If you insist on knowing, then I am off to Africa."

Agrippine tilted his head. "What?"

She strode down the gangplank, moving with grace and balance, her satchel seeming to glow with a brighter intensity.

"Africa? That's across an ocean!" Agrippine shouted.

The woman turned and pointed to Grogan, who rested a large, muscular hand on the Cajun's shoulder.

"Do not shout. You may be heard," Grogan explained.

"But…how is she getting there?"

There was a flicker of light out of the corner of his eye, and when Agrippine turned his head to identify the flash, he noticed that the woman was gone.

"She has her ways," Grogan answered. "She is beloved of Ullikummis, and her gifts are endless."

"What…what the hell?" Agrippine asked.

"Mistress Haight is on her way," Grogan said. "We should be on ours."

Agrippine turned, wondering just where Brigid Haight really was going and how she'd disappeared so fast. If he'd known of Annunaki technology, and the gemlike threshold she'd carried in her satchel, his understanding might have been more complete, but as it was, there was no way he could even imagine that she possessed the means of opening up holes in space-time and projecting herself through them with but a thought.

Brigid Haight's caress activated the alien artifact, itself a weapon that made even the assault rifles that Agrippine had supplied seem like mere sharpened twigs by comparison.

And then, if Agrippine was aware of such power, such advanced means of matter transmission, he would have wondered why he and his guns were needed in the first place.

Haight had her reasoning and purpose.

It was for neither he nor Grogan to know.

THE REFUGEE CAMP WAS quiet, which unnerved Grant slightly. Even in the depths of the Tartarus Pits, the slums that nestled in the shadow of the barony of Cobaltville, there was usually the chatter of laughter, pipings of music, a constant drone of conversation amid the squalor and everyday struggle for life.

Grant towered over the people who had populated the camp. Young and poorly fed, dark eyes tracking his every step, children stopped their chores to watch him closely.

Grant was something that people didn't see every day. Well over six feet tall, with a powerful body crammed into a suit made of skintight space-age polymers, he was an impressive sight. His skin was dark, being an African American, but his tone was even deeper than the sunburned flesh of the people who lived in the wiregrass region. The people here were a mix of ethnicities, ranging from Caucasian to American Indian, and all of them had been sun-roasted to a similar bronzed hue several shades lighter than Grant's.

It was the size, the easy power that he carried in his stride, that attracted the most attention. His own attention was drawn to the fact that he saw very few men.

Demothi had said that the raiders had been persistent in attacking this particular camp, stealing away with the few men who had managed to escape the initial harvests by the Hooded Ones. Seeing the makeup of the population of the camp was still a surprise to Grant.

Close to three hundred people were present. The raiders didn't seem to be interested in women, which was unusual. In his dealings with pirates and bandits, Grant had never known them to pass up the chance to take females into captivity. If they couldn't be used for easy sexual gratification, they were often easy to cow into servitude, made to do the chores that the cold-bloods felt were beneath their interests.

Suwanee had been quiet as they walked along, her face drooped in sullen shadow. She'd only looked up to navigate particularly soft and spongy terrain, struggling to keep her balance like the rest of them. Grant had attributed that to her distrust of the newcomers among them—himself, Kane and Rosalia—but with the gender imbalance in the camp, he was starting to understand the anger seething just below her surface.

The people here were quiet, focusing on menial tasks out of the need to distract themselves from the losses in their families. Grant could figure why Kane had been astute enough to restrain himself from opening fire on the Hooded Ones. Between the disgusting growths and the electronics attached to their heads, the men they had battled were more drones and victims than actual villains. Something was spreading an infestation among the men, creating an army that would be under long-distance control. The electronics had to be operated by cybernetic impulse, the growths some form of parasite that had either hallucinogenic or will-numbing excretion.

Grant rubbed his brow. "You've been hanging around Brigid too much."

Kane paused, looking over his shoulder at his friend. "Thinking about what's happening to this camp?"

"It's like she's still here with us," Grant answered. "I can almost hear her talking about mind-control secretions."

"You'd almost think we were capable of learning, eh?" Kane asked.

"We'd be damned fools if we didn't. Other than that, this is pretty grim shit," Grant said. "I don't see a man who isn't as healthy as Demothi around, unless we're looking at 12 or under."

"That's what I made out, too," Kane said. "About 300 here, we can see about another 150 men, given the adult women present?"

"One hundred and fifty men," Grant murmured. "That's a lot of people wearing those funky blobs."

"An army," Kane added. "Minus two, and they died because we damaged them."

"I know that I was looking for a real knockout past those heavy hoods," Grant said. "What about you?"

"I was tired of the guy I was fighting getting back up," Kane said. "I wasn't aiming to kill him, though."

"The one Rosie shot, he took a chest full of bullets," Grant added. "I don't think he'll last too long. He'll bleed out but he didn't die."

Kane frowned. "Not right away, which means if they come at us in force, we're going to need a lot of luck or head shots to put them down."

"You're talking about the freaks?" Rosalia asked.

Kane nodded. "Especially the one you tried to chill with a full magazine."

"Still, you two did well enough dealing with them when you weren't trying to leave them dead," Rosalia replied. "We can't say that they're unstoppable."

Kane looked around. "But can we stop them and not exterminate an entire community?"

Rosalia raised an eyebrow. "You can't save everyone, Magistrate Man."

"No, we can't, but the reason I brought us down here was to try," Kane answered.

"So, fight the New Order *and* the guys dropping

brain slugs on the men?" Rosalia asked. "And you mentioned that we might be dealing with over 150 of them?"

"It's a rough estimate," Grant said.

Rosalia shot a glance at him that would have curled his skin off in strips if he hadn't received similar threatening glares from far more dangerous beings. As it was, the woman was hardly someone he could disregard as an opponent. She was skilled, fast and quite ruthless. "And we're going to stick around here?"

Kane turned to Grant. Despite the fact that people often referred to him as the leader of the trio, each of them was an equal partner. They were three highly skilled people who had their strengths and areas of expertise. As such, when time permitted, they would defer to each others' judgment, making certain that their decisions were the right ones when seen from other points of view.

Grant nodded. "We've got important work to do. Have you seen this place?"

Rosalia glanced at the rows of tents that stretched out across the prairie grassland where the refugees had taken up camp. To one side of the tent city was the smell and bleat of livestock, indicating that this community had managed to gather up some of the supplies they'd needed. Grant could also see that there were reddish-brown patches of earth that had been scoured, tilled and furrowed to provide a place to grow crops. The camp had been present long enough that there was an ephemeral green fuzz growing along the lines of crops, indicating some successful work.

Grant frowned as he realized that there was livestock and crops, but the community had still lost many of its men. "Whoever is putting these parasites on the kidnap victims is keeping this camp around."

"You think that the refugee leaders might have some kind of deal going with the Hooded Ones?" Kane asked.

"Wouldn't surprise me," Grant answered.

"That'd make things particularly sticky," Kane said. "We'll sleep in shifts."

"Oh, now you're coming to your senses, but not enough." Rosalia spoke up. "I say we blow and leave the refugees to the Hooded Ones. We stay in one place, you two will have tumors and wires growing out of your skulls, and I'll be some farming wench."

"What could happen isn't my concern," Kane replied. "Any number of mishaps could befall us. What *will* happen, however, is a lot easier to figure out. Especially if we keep our heads and be smart."

"This isn't smart, Magistrate Man," Rosalia told him.

"You keep thinking we've come into this blind. I didn't fall off the turnip wagon yesterday," Kane told her. "We've been in more double-crosses and hostile settlements than you can imagine, and we're still here. Hell, we've even made a bunch of friends and allies along the way and fought every menace from bugs to giants."

Rosalia looked back and forth between the two men. "And all of your friends and allies have survived these encounters?"

Kane's mouth pulled into a tight, bloodless line.

"Are you going to roll over and just die, Rosie?" Grant asked.

Rosalia grimaced, not enjoying the diminutive of her name.

"So don't give yourself up as dead," Grant added. "And we won't fall asleep when it comes time to watch your back."

Rosalia folded her arms. Her dog panted as it sat next to her. She looked down at it.

"Let's get some food," she grumbled, stomping away.

Chapter 7

Lakesh opened his eyes, feeling as if his skull were wrapped in cotton. He wanted to speak, but his throat was dry, constricted, so all he could manage was a weakened croak. There was light, but it was fading quickly, and he could turn his head enough to see the sun setting in the west, the sky ablaze with orange. From what he could make out, the ceiling above him was a strange, white, stippled surface that took him several moments to realize was stucco.

Metal fixtures were interspersed in the expanse above him, and he was able to recognize two of them as sprinklers, looking like silver flowers growing upside down. The third of the fixtures was a white dome with vents in the sides. He wasn't certain, but he could have sworn that it was an old smoke detector. With a grunt, he tried to sit up, but strong hands held him down.

"Lay still." Domi's voice cut through his fog of confusion.

"Love?" he croaked.

She put her slender alabaster fingertip against his lips to silence him, then moved away for a moment. When she returned, she had a damp rag that she wiped his parched mouth with, then squeezed it gently. Lakesh felt a wave of relief as a trickle of water slid down his dried throat, and he sipped from her clenched fist.

Her fingertips brushed against his hair, wiping it from his troubled brow.

"Where are we?" he asked, his voice stronger, smoother now that he'd been rehydrated somewhat.

"Vegas," Domi whispered.

Lakesh blinked and squinted through the window. He started to move again and felt himself on a layer of cushions. Looking down at them, he saw that they were tacky to the touch, and they squished easily under his hands.

He could still read by the fading light and saw the legend Impervious Pillow on it.

"Impervious?" Lakesh asked, searching his memory for why a pillow would be impervious.

Domi handed him a tag. "They don't let germs in. And since germs don't eat them, they don't rot. They're still around, so I made a bed out of 'em."

Lakesh smiled at her. "We're in a hotel room in Vegas."

Domi leaned forward and kissed him on the forehead. "Relax. This far up, no one will bother us."

"Are there other ones?" he asked.

Domi frowned, as if she was reminded of something horrible. She managed a weak smile in return. "We had a little scuffle downstairs."

"We did?" Lakesh asked.

"You even shot one of them," Domi added. She sat back and disassembled her pistol, taking a small rag to polish grit out of its works. Lakesh frowned as he scoured his memory for hints of what had happened, but things were a blur. He could remember the buck of a powerful handgun, and he noticed that Domi had scrapes on her face and hands. One strange mark in particular confused him. It was a precise rectangle, and Lakesh knew the shape, he just wasn't able to place it.

When she turned over the weapon, he glanced at the cocked hammer of the gun and realization set in.

"You stopped it from firing with the web between your thumb and forefinger," Lakesh said. "I was going to pull the trigger, and you stopped me."

"You were stressed," Domi answered curtly. "You'd taken down a mutie."

"A mutie?" Lakesh asked. "The Reunification Program took care of all of them."

"Not a real mutie. Cross between the skinny freaks and the snake-faces," Domi explained.

"The hybrids," Lakesh translated. "What are the snake-faces?"

"The Annunaki," Domi said, slowly enunciating each syllable. "Actually, the fuse-brains they use as their shock troops."

Lakesh had to struggle, but he finally figured out what the girl was talking about. He remembered the night that Quavell was in torment, the odd transformation that had changed her and the rest of the nonbaronial hybrids into tall, powerful, sexless warriors. They had altered the same night the barons themselves shed their humanlike bodies and became the Children of the Serpent.

Lakesh could even remember the battle at Cerberus, the wild melee where the reborn godlings unleashed their might against the redoubt.

And then everything else dissolved into fuzz and hash. He swallowed hard and took Domi's hand. "I'm losing my memory."

Domi's ruby-red eyes quivered as she met his gaze,

her lips pressed tightly together to mask the rest of her emotions. "I know."

"What happened?" Lakesh asked.

"We had to leave," Domi said.

The feral girl kept herself calm, using every ounce of her will to relate the story of Ullikummis, of the assault on Cerberus, of the deaths of many and their self-imposed exile undertaken to keep the New Order from finishing them off while they were weakened and unbalanced. And she told him of the journey across the desert, the story he had told her postulating that Enlil's gift of rejuvenated youth was stripped away, and in return, his cellular structure was aging again.

The worst factor was he had mentioned something called Alzheimer's disease, and how irreversible it was.

Lakesh sat quietly on the impervious pillows as the last rays of sun faded, the shadow of the horizon now complete as the Nevada sky turned to a dark blue, diamond-studded blanket that nestled over the dead city of Las Vegas. He was rapidly losing his memory. Initially he'd only been suffering from short-term memory loss, but now details further and further back were becoming lost, only recovered from an act of willpower.

He looked at her. "You brought me here. Why?"

"Baron's base, to the north," Domi said. "Maybe a cure for your disease."

"If we could find a way to undo my genetic tampering, Area 51 would have the technology for it," Lakesh said. "Do you think we could cross the desert?"

"Give it some rest first," Domi told him. "Lay back and get some sleep."

"When I wake again, I won't remember this, though,"

Lakesh said. "You'll have to tell me everything all over again."

Domi pulled him close, resting her forehead against his. Her eyes were shut, but a single tear crawled down her porcelain cheek. "I know, Moe."

Her touch was gentle at the back of his head, her words soft, intimate. There was a slight tremor, but Lakesh couldn't tell if it was his nerves spasming in decay or her trying to fight off a torrential sobbing session. Either way, Lakesh wrapped his arms around her slender shoulders, and the two held each other until sleep took hold of him again.

When he lay down, Domi caressed his cheek gently, kissing him softly on the lips. With one wrist, she ground at the tears forming in her right eye, as if crushing them could dispel her sadness.

The slender albino stood and brought the canteen of water closer. If he woke, he would still be confused, so she scrawled on a piece of paper, using a rusty piece of brick to leave red crayon marks on it.

"Gone for food. Be back. Stay still. Love Domi," she wrote.

She placed the note in his hand, folding it so it stayed between his fingers, wrapped around his middle digit like a paper bow.

She didn't know how bad he would be if he woke again, but she doubted he would forget how to read so quickly. She wished that she knew how to write better, had the implements to scribble down everything she'd said, so he could read it and understand. Domi knew, however, she didn't have the vocabulary for it. Just telling the story out loud had taxed her, and she was lucky to rely on Lakesh's brilliant mind to fill in the holes, but according to what he'd told her about

Alzheimer's disease, that might not last for long, especially since he was aging rapidly. Symptoms that normally wouldn't show up for years were manifesting themselves now.

Domi put her Detonics back together, and thought about taking his weapon, as well. He might not have retained the mental faculties to use a gun, but she couldn't just leave him defenseless. She did, however, take the 7 mm rifle.

Could she cross the desert to Area 51 by herself and be back by the time Lakesh awakened?

No, Domi thought. It had taken at least an hour by Sandcat. On foot, it'd take all night just to reach the place, and no telling how long she'd need to scour the wreckage, looking for someone or something that could help her out. This was beginning to feel more and more like a fool's errand, but she'd originally intended to finish the trip to the underground base with Lakesh, hoping that he would be smart and sharp enough to recognize the materials necessary for recovering his full brilliance and health.

Back when she'd started, all she had to worry about was the man's strength holding out in the desert heat. He'd never been a strong man. Sure, he was healthy, and had been a vigorous lover with the return of his youth, but his best feature had been his mind. Now, Enlil, the king of the snake-faces, found a way to take that away from him, leaving him a forgetful, helpless thing.

For that, Domi could feel her old reserves of hatred bubbling to the surface.

"Anger good," she told herself. "Energy to walk."

She looked at Mohandas Lakesh Singh, her beloved Moe, and made a promise. Either she would find a way to save him from degenerating into a complete simple-ton, or she would personally find Enlil and saw his head off with her knife.

Either way, they would be together, alive and healthy, or both dead, because Domi knew that even at her most enraged, she would hardly be a match for an Annunaki overlord.

PRISCILLA WASN'T SURPRISED that the girl had taken her old companion to a more stable part of the hotel. What did surprise her was the gentle care she provided for the man as they'd walked. She'd paused and let him rest every flight of stairs, and even then, they'd only gone up four stories in that wing of the half-wrecked hotel. Higher, and they might have had to deal with more heat from the late-day sun. Lower, and they would have been much more noticeable by the hunters who scavenged through the city.

Once they'd had a room, she'd set about scouring the floor she was on, and the ones above it, for supplies to build a nest for her man. Priscilla was surprised that she could feel emotions flowing off them like rain pouring off of an awning. She'd had to deal with the relatively simple minds of her half-transformed fellow hybrids, so she hadn't noticed this ability before, but she could taste the man's confusion and the woman's urge to protect him, and the desperation she increasingly felt with each passing moment.

It was that ability that allowed her to stay farther back than she'd normally have had to, to observe the two humans.

There was no hostility, not until she felt the spike of rage surging after the sun had gone down. The woman boiled with hatred, an emotion so strong she could see the object of that fury.

When Priscilla looked upon the face of Enlil, and his army of minions, she knew that the signal sent down to her was not a call to awaken. She had been destined not to become an enlightened being, but a mindless, soulless drone impelled to slavery under the being that the woman hated.

The torrent of knowledge that she'd received, from both sides of the coin, was laid bare in front of her. She recognized her fellow mutants under Enlil in a smaller, more delicate form. The two were flip sides of the same coin, but Domi's hatred for both of them was equally intense.

That anger, however, didn't seem to extend to the minions, either hybrid or Nephilim. Indeed, as she looked lovingly upon her man, a familiar shape, one that Priscilla had seen in more than a few reflections of herself, showed. Affection, family, those were the phrases that came to mind.

This girl was alone and afraid. Not the kind of cowering fear that Priscilla lived each day, hiding in the dark and scurrying to cover herself in stone and darkness. She had a fear for the man she loved, a fear that she would lose him like she had the hybrid woman. There were smaller fears, but those were controlled. The fear of attack and discovery were constantly on her mind, but again, Priscilla didn't feel any terror. It was preparedness.

She was afraid but not fearful. Her senses were honed, focused on her surroundings, looking in nooks and crannies, spotting places where she could be ambushed.

It was odd, something she hadn't felt before.

And as such, Priscilla crawled from her shadows, despite not needing to move to follow their progress. She wanted to get closer to Domi, to even speak with the woman and try to figure out what she needed in a city full of dead buildings and hungry scavengers. She paused as she saw Domi, armed with her rifle, ruby eyes sharply glaring and taking in the terrain.

Priscilla stayed still, willing herself not to be seen. Domi looked straight at the pocket of shadows she'd hidden in, and Priscilla froze, her muscles tense as she tried to deal with her own fear. Even as she did so, Domi's attention grew even more focused upon her.

The slender albino took a couple of steps closer to her, ruby eyes glinting in the half light of the hallway as she tilted her head left and right, looking for her. Priscilla had been motionless, so how could this young woman have even noticed her?

"Been watching me," Domi said, almost as if she was answering Priscilla. Her words sent a chill through Priscilla's spine, her slim slit mouth opening in surprise. "Yeah. There you are."

Priscilla closed her mouth and tried to slink farther into the shadows, but her back was to the wall.

"What do you want?" Domi asked. She hadn't drawn any of her weapons, and even the muzzle of her rifle was pointed at the ground.

"To know what you want," Priscilla answered. "Please, I mean you no harm."

"I figured that much," Domi replied. She extended one hand to the mutant woman. "Come on out. I'm not going to hurt you."

Priscilla looked around. "How…how did you notice me? Did I make a sound?"

"No. Just when I looked in your direction, I suddenly felt a wave of panic. Not sure, but you were maybe reading me, and you can also broadcast, too," Domi said. "Whatever it was, you better watch yourself."

Domi wriggled her fingertips, and finally Priscilla reached out and interlaced her hand with the albino's. The woman's touch was gentle, despite the calluses that had built up on her fingers. The skin was firm but not rough, and yet she managed to show surprising strength as she held Priscilla balanced over a snarl of rubble on the floor.

Priscilla was once more impressed when she saw that she was taller than this girl, if only by a few inches. Even in the dark, she could make out the albino girl's bare arms and the lean cords of muscle that flexed beneath her white skin. Since there was no sun to worry about, she had taken off her hood and cap, revealing a closely cropped fuzz of bone-colored hair that glowed like a halo in the moonlight.

Domi regarded her with equal curiosity. "I'm Domi. Your name?"

"Priscilla," she answered. She could feel her cheeks warming. "I got it from a book…she was the wife of a great man who was revered in this city."

Domi smiled. "Don't know where my name came from."

"Who is the man?" Priscilla inquired. She knew that she was being blunt, even crude, but this had been the first conversation of her entire life. Any mistakes she made, she'd have to be forgiven, though considering how the young woman in front of her spoke, she didn't think that she'd receive too many complaints.

"Lakesh," Domi answered. "We came to find help for him."

"I sensed that," Priscilla said. "I also sensed that you want to go to Area 51. Don't you know how dangerous it is there?"

"I was a prisoner there for a time. Back before the hybrids began changing," Domi said. "That's what happened to you?"

Priscilla reached up to her own cheek, feeling the line of scales that circled her features. She nodded in response to Domi's question. "I can tell you're talking about the place I came from, but it's not what you remember. It is abandoned by your kind, but teeming with the creatures you battled earlier today. There's an entire colony that had awakened. And only a few made the transformation you remember, the one that took your friend..."

"Quavell," Domi concluded for her. Her voice took on a more somber tone. "You look like her."

"I'm sorry..."

Domi shook her head, then took Priscilla's hand. "You can do me a favor. You can watch Lakesh."

Priscilla tilted her head, then looked back toward the hotel room that Domi had made her nest in. "Watch him? I'm not a fighter..."

"No, but you can explain things to him," Domi said. "And give him water, food. Comfort him. He's sick, and I need to find help for him."

Priscilla took a deep breath, feeling Domi's grasp tighten around her hand. There was unspoken desperation transmitted through her tension, and the hybrid woman didn't know how to refuse such a request.

Only moments ago, she was a lone hermitess, an outcast from her people, and now she had been trusted to stand over and guard a human.

Trust.

That was something that Priscilla had never known before. It threw her off balance. She liked the sensation, she liked the bond that Domi's emotions had made with her.

"I'll do my best to take care of him," Priscilla answered. "I don't know if you can make it back before dawn, or even survive under there. My brothers are savage."

Domi managed a smirk. "So am I."

The feral girl led Priscilla back to the hotel room, and the hybrid could feel the waves of optimism, the flash of thoughts burning through her head. It seemed the more she stood with this woman, the more she could feel, the broader her understanding of this wild human.

Domi was wild, but she also was possessed of a ferocious loyalty.

Priscilla felt that if it was necessary, Domi would die for her, as well as for Lakesh.

And that feeling chilled her to her bones.

Chapter 8

Domi made the descent down four flights, and it was still relatively close to sunset so that she would have the advantage of hours of darkness ahead of her as she made her trek across the desert to Area 51. She knew that every moment she delayed, the closer Lakesh was to being lost forever. His mind was fragile, and the curse that Enlil had placed within his cells had been one that would kill him swiftly, but not before stripping the scientist of all that defined him.

Domi couldn't bear to think of another of her family lost. Though Kane and Grant had been optimistic about how they could recover Brigid Baptiste from the clutches of Ullikummis, the feral girl wondered just what the nature of her imprisonment was. She had been lucky during her captivity in the Area 51 base, but she had seen the kinds of horrors that the Annunaki would inflict upon their prey. Only a few weeks ago, she had seen what had become of one of Grant's shadows—a tesseract, Brigid had called it—when he had been caught and kept as a slave of Humbaba, another of Enlil's cruel children.

She'd told herself that holding the actions of a few as representative of the whole species was folly, especially when it came to the hybrids whom she had softened against. Domi had resented the spindly genetically "perfected" creatures as several of them had set themselves up as rulers of the shattered remnants of America. The barons, however, were acting only as shadows themselves. Their petty bids for power and prestige, their iron control of the humans in their sway, were simply reflections of their original selves, the Annunaki overlords who had stored themselves inside genetic coding, awaiting the return of the mother ship *Tiamat.*

Even before that reawakening, even during her time as a prisoner, while Kane was continually raped by hybrid women in an effort to introduce strong human genetic material to their degenerating pool, Domi had seen something different among the hybrids. She'd seen them as people, individuals who were victims of the same cruel whims as humanity. The barons and the overlords were monsters, not because of their species, but because of their choices, their willingness to please themselves no matter what the cost.

Domi had lived as an outlander all of her life, a refugee from the villes struggling against beast and man for the barest of food scraps and the tiniest sliver of shelter. She had grown envious of the people who lived in the baronies, but when she came to the Tartarus Pits, when she saw the Magistrates who had come close to killing her multiple times, she thought that it was the humans inside those walls who forced all others to struggle in the cursed earth. Her servitude as a prostitute under a toadish crime lord had nearly come to an end, but one man had shown her kindness and mercy, even after he had been part of a group who had given her a head injury.

That man was Grant, and his kindness was repaid as she slit the throat of her former employer while he tried to murder the Magistrate. Guana Teague, a man who made her his personal sex toy, died, and with him, a part of her prejudices.

More changed in her life. And with each change, she learned that while there was a place for hatred, it was reserved solely for those who committed evil to others. Predators abounded in the world, and Domi saw herself as a kind of counterpredator.

She was alone now, and as she paused in the darkened shadows of the collapsed section of the hotel, she thought of the creatures who had attacked her earlier in the day. They had struck at Lakesh and her, but not out of malice. They were predators, looking to fill their bellies with meat, and she knew too well the needs of survival. They had been strong, fast and skilled, but they were essentially nothing more than animals. To hold any malice toward them was a folly she couldn't afford.

Domi wouldn't discount their dangers, however. They were killers, and she was still made of meat. When she got too close, she would end up on the menu again, and when they attacked this time, it was likely that she wouldn't get a second chance. Sure, she had made certain her weapons were clean, any grit in their actions removed so that they wouldn't jam when the time came for battle.

No matter how strong she was, no matter how deadly her tools, they were still bigger, and they had much more to lose. Domi had a sliver of mercy in her, while Priscilla had explained that they were truly bestial. For all the descriptions of her feral existence, Domi wasn't a rapist, she wasn't a cold-blooded murderer and she didn't seek to enslave anyone. The halfbreeds, as Priscilla had named them, *were* rapists. That was the way they mated, taking their victims by force, the ancient code of procreation for survival of the species turning an act of life into one of cruelty and conquest. Domi knew that if they treated their own so brutally, then there was a good chance that her death would not be easy or swift.

She had thoughts of Guana Teague, remembering his massive bulk smothering her as he grunted and chuckled at his sexual conquest. Disgust twisted in her gut, and she fought to dispel those memories.

Domi would get past the half-breeds. If they attacked her, she wouldn't hesitate to put them down, but if she had the opportunity and the means of avoiding contact, she would take it. Spending her energy in battle instead of getting to the base would be a waste of time and effort.

Lakesh's brain was disintegrating, even in the brief seconds that Domi's eyes swept the darkness of the artificial cave, searching for enemy presence. She couldn't just burst out into the open; that might attract more attention than she could handle. Still, caution was costing precious time.

Domi emerged into the wrecked, sand-swept street. The moon was high now, a clear, unpolluted sky allowing its blue-tinted light to flare on the dead city like a gigantic floating lamp. A glance upward reminded her of the kind of life she'd been thrown into. The tiny circle of white that hung above her was something that she'd actually touched, somewhere she had walked, seeing the Earth she stood on at the same coin-size scale. Before she'd met Grant, Kane and Brigid, she hadn't any concept of what the moon was, except that it was a light that waxed and waned with the passage of a month, its presence perfect for allowing her to hunt at night, or to avoid hunters. That it was a world of its own, one without air and wrapped in a harsh, body-destroying cold void, had been beyond her imagination.

Domi had walked on the moon, she had traveled to other universes, she had even been hurled back to the dawn of humanity to rescue Grant.

And she had all but died at Area 51 when an implode grenade burst near her. Only Kane and Brigid had the presence of mind to utilize the abandoned, nearly decayed technology of Thunder Isle to pluck her from the instant when she would have been obliterated and drag her to safety and a reunion with her family. Time and space were her enemies now, the passing moments roaring by like bullets, and countless steps stretching before her as an unavoidable gulf between life and death for Lakesh.

She trotted along, her bare feet silent on the sand, her ears peeled for the grunts of the half-mutated stalkers who hunted in the night. She kept her weapons sheathed and tucked out of the way, giving her room to move, to react, to battle should an ambush explode on her at the last moment. The city was vast and sprawling, and the remnants of buildings spread around her, providing an embarrassment of riches in the form of places for enemies to lie in wait. Vegas had proved to be a minefield before, literally as Grant had related.

This was the first time she'd been through these ruins, but she had made certain that Grant filled her in completely about what he had seen when he'd passed through. The layout she'd received was accurate, and there would be no way that she could get lost.

She simply had to avoid contact with creatures of great strength, cunning and hunger.

"Easy," Domi whispered to herself. "Easy as pie."

Shadows flickered in the distance and Domi slid to the sand immediately, her alabaster body and bone-colored hair blending with the pale, moonlit sands easily. She'd thought ahead and worn a whitish sheet over the rest of her clothing, not only to keep warm in the cold desert night, but also to improve her camouflage. The sheet spread over her, helping her to disappear.

The shadows in the distance were moving with unnatural speed and agility, leaping dunes and scrambling in stooped postures, all four limbs passing across the sand as if they were horses and cats. It was eerie and uncanny, as well as being out of character for the two creatures she'd encountered earlier. She decided to risk it and pulled a small pair of binoculars from her kit, zooming in on the strangers in the distance.

Through the magnification of the lenses, she was able to see that the mutants were in multiple stages of transformation. Some of them bore only slightly more scales than Priscilla, while others displayed limbs stretched and distorted, pulled taut across suddenly extended skeletons as if they were wearing their skin too tightly.

Domi pursed her lips and returned the binoculars to her belt, then slithered out of their line of sight. There were more than a dozen of these creatures, which meant that there was some kind of communication among the hunters. She didn't like the fact that they appeared in force.

It could simply have been coincidence. It wasn't as if the pair she battled showed any skills greater than hunting coordination, something she'd learned even primitive-brained sharks who'd existed for millions of years possessed. There had been no sign of telepathic contact, but then she thought of Priscilla and how she had inadvertently projected thoughts into her mind.

Domi had become a good judge of character, and Priscilla was alone and frightened. She was an outcast from the main hive of mutants, so she wouldn't even dare to try to contact them. She hadn't even seemed aware that she could speak through minds, genuinely surprised at the sudden burst that had betrayed her presence. No, Priscilla wasn't a threat, she wasn't betraying Lakesh's location and, even if she had, the hunters would have been much more likely to home in on her, rather than make their way, spreading out along the grid of streets in the ruins of Las Vegas.

She'd seen a dozen of them, but she couldn't be sure if there were more or not. She moved a block over and kept a low profile, sweeping the night ahead of her with the binoculars.

Lakesh once informed her that the Nephilim, the reptilian drones that the Quad V hybrids had grown into, were potentially part of a hive mind, and as such had means of communication that would have been unconventional, even compared to some of the other creatures they had encountered. Telepathy and empathic transmission were not strange concepts, but Lakesh had spoken of insects who communicated through chemical trails and scents. One of the strongest of these chemical signals was the pheromone that drones gave off when they died.

Domi thought of the two she'd killed earlier today. Would the chemical stench they put out upon death reach across miles of desert all the way to Area 51? Or would it have been an actual telepathic cry that exploded upon their demise? Telepathy didn't necessarily have to accompany intelligence. The metals that the Nephilim had been armored with reacted to higher thoughts, the smart armor having been utilized to incredible finesse by a mad scientist in Greece, transforming her from mere mortal woman into a goddess.

If metal could be affected by telepathy, and metal was just plain dumb and inert, then the unsophisticated minds of the savage mutants had to have been open to those kinds of signals. Domi spotted more of the stalkers through her binocs, and she tucked herself back against the wall.

She could tell that this group was different from the one she'd initially noticed, and the twisted figures were spread out, scouring the city.

"Damn it, Moe," she whispered.

If he hadn't been spotted, Domi would have taken them down without their even noticing that they were under attack. She couldn't blame the scientist, though. While he had fought and survived in multiple adventures across the globe, he was not a trained warrior, and his ability to elude predators hadn't been tested in the forests and wastelands of the Outlands.

Lakesh was brilliant in his own way, and she wouldn't have exchanged him for yet another tall, strong-limbed fighter like Kane in a million years.

Things had happened as they had happened, and Domi couldn't change anything. She could only hope that she could sneak past the creatures and get out to open desert so that she wouldn't spend any time walking in sunlight the next day. Her cloak would protect her from the burning heat, but she'd be slowed down, and she'd risk sand blindness even with sunglasses and a visored hat.

Exploding from the wall, she charged down the road, moving at a sustainable pace. Long loping strides allowing her to eat up ground without taxing her lungs and muscles. She would be able to keep going at this rate for hours if necessary, and she moved like a ghost. The moonlight caught her white cloak, and blended her into her surroundings.

Disguised and camouflaged, she had a chance.

She paused and glanced back at the hotel where she'd left Lakesh.

He was up there, weakened, addled, with only the altitude of the room to keep him away from the seeking senses of the hunters who swarmed into the city. Priscilla was trustworthy, but that wouldn't be much use, not when the creatures she feared came storming in. If she'd betrayed her own presence just by being looked at, then it was likely she'd attract the grim, hungry attention of the mutants on their stalk through the streets. Already, she could hear distant barks, inhuman yells that the things let out.

Each sharp yip spiked into her nerves, causing her to flinch, making her want to bolt to cover. That kind of reaction was either for intimidation or to flush prey. It was an effective tactic, because Domi doubted that their quarry would have much nerve for hiding, sitting still.

They would wake Lakesh, and he would be stumbling and clumsy, seeking an answer and only finding a strange woman in the room with him, Domi long gone.

She looked at the desert and realized that if she broke through the line of predators, there was no guarantee that she could find transportation back to Vegas, or find a means of curing Lakesh of his tangle brain. Guilt and dread became a smothering weight inside of her chest, each creature's distant bark feeling like another nail in Lakesh's coffin.

"Damn it," she cursed.

A jolt of fear cut through her senses and she stood bolt upright.

It had to have been Priscilla, and she had suddenly realized what the barking of the hunters was.

At the same moment Domi was touched by Priscilla's fear, she heard a sudden silence out in the night.

The half-breeds had grown quiet.

They had felt the spike of panic.

Domi tensed, trying to assess whether the sensation she'd been subjected to gave a direction or had a signal strength that she could follow. It wasn't likely, but then the death sensations of the creatures she and Lakesh had killed earlier in the day had apparently attracted the attention of a small army of the hunters in the shadows.

Domi waited, counting the thunderous beats of her heart.

One. Two. Three.

As one, the distant hunters let out a howl, a rising shriek that crashed through the buildings like a tidal wave. The sound rolled over Domi, and she cringed as the piercing cry echoed off walls, funneled along the ruins of the streets to form a blast of sound.

They were aware. They smelled the blood in the water.

She'd heard of wild animals able to sense fear. It was a common myth that they could use that reaction to home in on the best, easiest to kill prey. Food that didn't react in terror wasn't food, it was a kick in the jaw, a goring horn through the throat, the crashing weight of forelimbs breaking the predator's spine.

But quarry that advertised its fear was something that could be brought down, too scared to put up an effective fight as opposed to those that held their ground and faced an oncoming threat.

Domi wouldn't have appeared to be their kind of prey, but Priscilla and Lakesh were the kind of infirm and frightened quarry that the half-breeds would relish.

She spun and rushed toward the hotel, letting her cloak fall away lest she trip over it.

She'd need to set up a defense against the hunters. If she cost them too much effort to take Lakesh and Priscilla, maybe they would turn back.

Or Domi would be lucky enough to die without seeing the man she loved suffer.

Bare feet slapping the sand, she flew toward the hotel.

Chapter 9

Kane took out a small notebook, looking at the pages under the glow of a small LED flashlight, chewing his lower lip before extinguishing it and pocketing the spiral-bound papers.

"What's that?" Grant asked.

"We had time before we split up. A couple of hours, and I put them to good use," Kane said. "I hit one of the computer stations in hopes of reading up on what was down here."

Grant nodded. "And where exactly is here?"

"We're a few miles from Pensacola Bay, which itself was near to a place called Gulf Breeze and a facility known as AUTEC," Kane said.

Grant shook his head. "Doesn't mean much to me."

"Didn't mean much to me, either. According to publicly known sources, there were a few things that made the place notable. One was a military base. The other was sightings of unidentified flying objects," Kane explained.

"Military base and UFOs can be explained pretty easily," Grant said. "What, it was Navy?"

"Yes. A naval station where an exhibition team known as the Blue Angels worked out of," Kane said. "The Blue Angels were some of the U.S.'s best pilots."

Grant smirked. "That probably changed. The nuke-caust meant that major facilities were hit by bombs.

Pensacola was probably flattened in the first salvo, because you know how things were with the Magistrates. They always kept the shiniest and prettiest Mags close to authority, in full view of the subjects."

"While you and me got kicked out on missions to the desert or down into the Tartarus Pits," Kane answered. "You don't have to remind me."

"So you have UFOs...which might or might not have been experimental aircraft, like the Mantas," Grant said.

"Relatively close to the naval station was something else that did register some alerts when I looked it up in the Cerberus computers," Kane said. "A place called AUTEC, the Atlantic Undersea Test and Evaluation Center. It's on the other side of what used to be the Florida peninsula, on an island called Andros. However, when I was looking through the region for weird shit, I came up with a ton of stuff, like the ties between the naval station and AUTEC."

"Military-based testing facilities? Bingo with the UFOs," Grant said.

"This place had submarine access, and it was locked down tight. Airspace was denied for miles, and still Florida panhandle fishermen reported sightings of unidentified *submerged* objects," Kane said. "Area 51 was another facility that had tight airspace security."

"But that was in the middle of the desert, hundreds of miles away from any city," Grant said. "And it had its very own airstrip so it could take passenger jets."

"And get this, not only did AUTEC show up on the map of facilities with mat-trans coordinates, it was the sole transit linkage to something called the Tongue Of The Ocean, TOTO for short," Kane continued. "If the Totality Concept was able to get to the moon, as barren and inhospitable to life as that is, what's to keep them from nosing around at the bottom of the ocean?"

"But the Gulf of Mexico is shallow, isn't it?" Grant asked.

"No. TOTO is a six-thousand-foot-deep trench that extends for over a hundred miles," Kane explained. "It doesn't take a lot of imagination to see that skimmers and scout ships that can handle the vacuum of space could also operate under such depths."

Grant frowned, making his gunfighter mustache droop even more on his scowling face. "The Annunaki were dormant at that time."

"But the Archons weren't," Kane said. "If there were facilities working on advanced tech and genetic engineering in the Anthill and Area 51, then it's likely that we could find something else at AUTEC or down in the TOTO trench."

Grant took a deep breath, then smiled at Kane. "Brigid trained you well, my son. Where once you were the student…"

Kane rolled his eyes. "Give me a break, damn it."

"All right." Grant chuckled. He stroked his mustache. "Genetic engineering in the Anthill was geared toward extending the lives of the hybrids. What about those things that the Hooded Ones had on?"

"I've seen a lot of strange stuff coming from under the ocean. You have, too," Kane said. "What if there was some kind of creature living six thousand feet beneath the surface?"

"It would be tough, wouldn't it?" Grant asked. "We killed those creatures awful easily."

"I thought about that, too, but one thing I've read about is that smaller creatures who are designed for deep water are actually kind of fragile," Kane said.

"It's only when you get to the size of humans or there-about that you get progressively denser."

"Like whales," Grant mentioned. "Or the mosa-saurs that occasionally pop in through a temporal rift on Thunder Isle."

"Mosasaurs?" Kane asked.

"They're about twenty to thirty feet long, and about a quarter of it is a mouth full of teeth as sharp and long as our combat knives," Grant explained. "They swim as fast as hell, and from the deck of the *Gamera-maru,* I've seen one of them slice a great white shark in half with one bite."

"Damn," Kane muttered.

"We didn't bring any scuba gear," Grant stated.

"Scuba would only get us a few hundred feet, if that much," Kane argued. "Once you go deeper than that, the water pressure is enough to snap your bones and crush your organs."

"Oh, good," Grant said, following it with a sigh of relief. "I hate swimming, and I sure as hell hate diving into really dark water. The thing is, you mention AUTEC and how it's part of the mat-trans network, right?"

Kane nodded.

"Then what about here?" Grant continued. "We're a triple damn long way from TOTO, which is on the other side of the peninsula."

Kane pulled out his notebook and turned on his LED light again. Grant peered down at the notes.

"There used to be a relay station at Pensacola, ac-cording to the records at Cerberus," Kane explained.

"A relay station? What, there wasn't enough signal to get underwater? The mat trans can get us to the damn moon!" Grant complained.

Kane grimaced, then hissed for Grant to keep his voice down.

"Sorry, but those things spit us through dimensions. A little water isn't going to matter to a mat trans," Grant said.

Kane nodded. "That's what got me wondering, as well, so I tried to get the coordinates from the computer. Everything referred me back to Pensacola."

"Which, for all we know, is a crater lake in the wake of a direct hit from a nuke," Grant muttered. "So whatever redoubt is associated with AUTEC is quarantined?"

"It wouldn't be the first time we've had to deal with a lockout on a facility," Kane said.

Grant looked at the notes again. "You think anyone inside the AUTEC redoubt would be able to get out?"

Kane shrugged. "What I do know is this—we're a few miles from shore, and I've been asking questions. Some of these refugees used to be part of fishing families along the gulf and they said this shit started a few days after a ship pulled in just off the delta's breakwaters."

"You couldn't have mentioned the damn boat off the start? It would have given us better answers than talking about UFOs and top-secret testing stations hundreds of miles away on the other side of a peninsula," Grant growled.

"I wanted to figure out why there's a boat, and why there are guys walking around with slimy things wrapped around their skulls," Kane said. "The boat is how this shit got here. What and why is the tough question."

"I know how we can answer it a lot easier than sitting here on our thumbs," Grant said.

"Go take a ride out to the ship?" Kane asked.

Grant nodded.

"Direct approach. Good way to start a gunfight," Kane mused.

"We haven't killed anything for about eight hours," Grant countered.

Kane shook his head at his partner's grim humor.

"Do we tell Rosie that we're going out to take a look?" Grant asked.

"You won't have to." Her voice cut from the front of the tent.

"Awkward," Grant muttered.

"Damn straight," Rosalia answered. "So, you found out about the boat, too?"

"I figured that we're still awake and full of energy. I thought we could take the opportunity to investigate," Kane said.

Rosalia grimaced. "You realize this might be a trap?"

"And you realize we're sitting here without a plan, and a camp that you said might be full of enemies?" Kane returned.

"If we're not surrounded by so-called traitorous refugees, we won't have to worry about being overwhelmed," Grant said. "We could take them on our own terms."

Rosalia looked at the tents running up and down the row they were among. Her full, pouting lips pursed as she thought about the dilemma. Stay and be smothered, or head for a trap. Her distrust of the situation fought against itself, until she seemed to realize the answer.

"Damned if we stay, a chance in hell if we go sneak a peek," Rosalia agreed.

"We'll travel light," Kane said. "I'll stow our gear and then we can make our move."

Rosalia took a deep breath. "Losing that interphaser would be a big problem."

"Not as big as an infestation of bioparasites," Grant muttered. "Unless you'd like to look as if your head was made of fungus."

Rosalia wrinkled her nose at the thought.

Decision made, the three people stalked out of the camp, moving silently and swiftly.

They had far to go before the dawn.

AGRIPPINE DIDN'T LIKE THE condition of the corpses, but he held his tongue as Grogan prodded the slimy mess that was mixed with the dead man's hair. A flick of one of the circuits created a spark that impelled the carcass's leg to twitch convulsively. Agrippine stepped a bit farther away from the body.

"O great prince," Grogan whispered. "You see what is lain before you."

There he was, talking to people who weren't there. Then again, his superior had disappeared in a flicker of purplish light, so whatever sorcery was in effect was not limited to the New Order followers. Perhaps the god they spoke to wasn't a figment of their imagination as Agrippine had originally reckoned.

As it was, the cultists remained calm, quiet, waiting for their leader to complete his investigation.

"What does your lord say?" Agrippine asked.

Grogan turned his head, a frown creasing his face. "He does not answer. His concentration is needed elsewhere. Yet he knows what I have shown him. He has seen the work of another, and recognizes a familiar signature within it."

"I thought he didn't say anything to you," the Cajun mused.

Grogan looked away from the swamp guide, then pointed out into the swamp. "This is a situation that Kane has manufactured to his benefit. We are in a territory already under contest between the wills of gods."

"We walked into someone else's war," Agrippine concluded.

"Yes," Grogan affirmed.

Agrippine sighed. The canopy of trees above cast the hammock into deep, broken shadows, shafts of moon and starlight slipping down piecemeal, providing an imperfect view of an already troubling terrain. Agrippine, though originally born in the heart of Cajun country, had traveled to the Florida panhandle in an effort to get away from the baronies. One swamp was enough like the other that the learning curve was shallow for him.

What disturbed him was the relative silence at work here. There was the grunt and croak of toads and insects, each of them making their nightly song, but there was a chorus of voices missing from the swamp.

As if guessing Agrippine's trepidation, Grogan spoke up.

"You are missing something," the big cultist said.

"The gators, son," Agrippine answered. "They're not talking."

Grogan tilted his head. "The alligators speak?"

"To each other, they whistle, they moan, they trumpet," Agrippine explained. "You can tell when you're in their territory usually. The night is noisy, unless they're on the hunt, and that's unlikely at this time of night."

Grogan looked down at the wiring sticking out of the corpse's forehead, a crown of silver splinters that glinted in the few shafts of light pouring down from the star-strewed sky. "The other, our prince's adversary, his tools work well on the minds of men. Perhaps they work on other things, as well."

"What is that shit?" Agrippine inquired.

"This is the circuitry necessary to receive electrical impulses from a distant source," Grogan said. "It is part of the work of men, and part of the work of my lord's kin. The metal components are merely receivers for signals. That which actually impelled the bodies that lay here has dissolved, returning to the swamp."

"I don't like the sound of that," Agrippine said, looking at the ground.

"The organism I speak of, it is ill-equipped to travel under its own accord," Grogan stated. "And separated from its host, it is worthless, incapable of survival. The only means that it can travel is by proper cultivation."

"Mind control?" Agrippine asked. "Mind-control parasites..."

"Indeed," Grogan said. "We are safe from infestation, but not the infected."

"And you think maybe the gators, they've been fixed up like the men?" Agrippine asked.

"Would you not do that yourself?" Grogan asked.

"I would not be playin' so close to the biting end of a gator, son," the Cajun countered.

Grogan managed a condescending smile. "We shall watch our steps. Stealth will not avail us when the shadows hide predators at the beck and call of our enemies."

"Stay clear of water until you test it," Agrippine

said. "I know gators. Even if they're under someone's control...I can't believe I just said that...there's only so many places that they can hide themselves, and they'll all look the same. A foot of water is enough for them to take you by surprise."

Grogan nodded. "Wise counsel."

"Yeah. I guess," Agrippine said.

"Do not doubt your ability, my friend," Grogan added. "Without your insight, we may have encountered terrible danger in this marsh."

"You're welcome," Agrippine answered, trying hard not to let a sarcastic tone enter his words. From the blissful smiles on their faces, he'd apparently succeeded, but he knew for certain that working with religious fanatics was one of the stupidest things he'd ever done.

OROCHI'S BODY TINGLED from the effects of the gemlike threshold, hurled through time and space by the devices of the Dragon Kings, they who ruled the world before the rise of the mammals. As he coalesced into existence, he could see the underwater facility form around him, emerging through a hole in the fabric of reality just as he'd disappeared through it on the other end.

They possessed the writings of the ancients that had been deciphered enough to interpret the use of these wonderful devices, enabling them to hurl themselves across the world, provided that they had a viable destination. The humans impressed Orochi, and indeed, all of the Watatsumi, for their ability to produce a deep-sea facility that had survived for centuries at six thousand feet below the surface.

Of course, it was no wonder. The dome above him

was a hexagonal honeycomb of a powerful alloy that resisted the crushing weight of the ocean. The hexagon was one of the sturdiest geometrical shapes in nature, and the resultant honeycomb patterns produced by linking them together was infinitely stronger than even solid materials. Creatures as simple as honeybees noticed that strength when building their hives, and even the skeletons of birds and some reptiles showed similar resiliency; birds were able to resist the same amount of pressure as solid-boned mammals with forty percent less bone density.

It helped that man had built the TOTO station with the assistance of fantastic technologies such as enhanced materials and energy sources. These were the gifts left over by the Dragon Kings, the great gods who strode the world, culling humanity with the Great Flood.

It was one of those ancient kings, Enki, who had weakened at the last, guiding a man named Noah to preserve humankind and its favored species in the wake of the Flood. Because of their presence, the Watatsumi, the servants of the Serpent Gods, had been forced to live alone, outcast from the surface of a world that hated and feared them.

Orochi grimaced, knowing that his subordinates weren't true believers in the rise of the Watatsumi as he was; rather they would be content to simply keep the hordes of the unholy Wyrms at bay and simply exist.

The weapon he had, though, would give its master the power to command all creatures, sapient and bestial. He'd already proved that much with the swarm of alligators he'd harvested from the delta's swamps.

And if necessary, if he had to use the parasites on

his fellow Watatsumi to gain their compliance, then he would. His master was of the opinion that there were those among them that would need such urging. They were fickle, uninspired creatures who thought that the caverns were a good home, away from the horrors of nuclear wastelands and human warfare.

Orochi stepped to the door, knowing that he was going to have to concentrate now. He couldn't broadcast the fact that he was part of a small cadre within what the Watatsumi called Dragonflight, nor that he was working toward the goal of shedding the weak, ineffectual rule to build the children of the gods back to where they belonged.

Something bumped against the door and Orochi pulled his sword, bypassing his pistol. The door shuddered again, and this time the door latch failed, metal splintering as a Watatsumi man, his head encased in the all-consuming tendrils of one of the parasites, burst in. Shouting occurred in the halls, and Orochi brought up his blade, smacking his assailant in the head with its flat.

There was a brief shriek, the wail of the parasite as it felt pain, its bodily juices spurting from the welt raised by Orochi's impact. Other Watatsumi rushed in behind the reptilian man, their hands grasping at the possessed one's strong arms.

"What is the meaning of this?" Orochi demanded.

"There was a small containment breach in the growth vats," one of the men restraining the parasite-riddled victim said. "This was the only host to escape from the mess."

"There were other hosts made?" Orochi asked. "Without the Thorn Crowns?"

There was a sharp jolt as the possessed Watatsumi

was tasered, electricity surging through its body. The parasite atop his head let out a high-pitched whine through both its own respiratory system and the mouth of the man it rode. A second, contact-range zap from a metal-fanged stun gun caused the creature to shudder, then fall away, helpless and inert as its primitive nervous system went into convulsions.

"Is he all right?" Orochi asked the guard who'd tasered the parasite.

"He'll live," the guard said. "No idea what will happen to his brain."

One of the things that Orochi hadn't tested was the effects of an unrestrained parasite on a Watatsumi or human brain, especially post possession. Usually when the Crown of Thorns was damaged, a fail-safe measure produced a lethal jolt to both parasite and host, one that was far more powerful than that put out by a stun gun.

"The parasites are acting up again?" Orochi asked.

"Ever since this afternoon," the guard explained.

Orochi thought about the loss of two of his hooded marauders, and the damage incurred by a third. "What time?"

"Four?" one guard asked another.

"And it's taken you this long to restrain the last of them, when he was alone and outside of the growth vats?" Orochi inquired.

The other guard nodded. "We had them contained, but it took long to control them all. This one escaped and fought violently. Several of the security team are injured now."

Orochi scowled. "And how compromised are the vats?"

The first of the guards sighed. "They're under control now."

Orochi took a deep, soothing breath in an effort to calm his nerves. It didn't work. Instead all he could do was growl one word. "Damnation."

Chapter 10

Night in the swamp was cooler, but not by much, and Kane was glad for the self-contained nature of the shadow suits, wicking away enough humidity to keep his body, from the collar down, cool and comfortable. Unfortunately his face was drenched with sweat as the enormous heat sink of the marsh waters radiated, steam rising from the surface and lying down in a blanketing fog that made navigation difficult in their scull. His brown hair was matted to his skull in a slick tangle that felt as if it was congealing in grease.

They were silent in the boat, except for the soft splash of the oars rising and dipping into the murky, still river. Around them, the drone of crickets and frogs filled the air. Neither he nor Grant could see anything larger than a mouse on their multispectrum optical devices. The three explorers from Cerberus had brought along shadow suits, but Rosalia didn't like the idea of being cooped up in a skintight uniform. Even though the shadow suits were capable of full environmental protection, there was an element of claustrophobia inherent in being so completely wrapped up.

Kane and Grant, used to the far heavier, far more confining Magistrate armor, complete with helmet, didn't mind the constriction.

The dog sat on the bow, erect and alert, dark eyes sweeping the foggy night, its senses working overtime.

Every sound, every scent, registered for the canine far more readily than it would even for Kane and his nearly preternatural point man's sense.

The half-coyote mutt let out a breath, its legs straightening, nose focused on something like an arrow. Kane pulled his oar from the water. Grant took his lead. Rosalia looked and noticed that her canine companion had spotted something, and her hand dropped to the grip of her weapon.

"Magistrate Man?" Rosalia asked.

"I can't tell," Kane said. The magnification and light amplification of his night-vision device allowed him to zoom in and find anything, but all he could see were loglike objects in the water, flowing slowly and steadily toward the boat. He switched channels and tried to pick up infrared emissions, but there was nothing there, either.

Rosalia spoke up. "Don't tell me you can't spot danger in a swamp."

"Shush!" Kane hissed. "I hear something. The frogs went quiet really quick, but all I see are logs, even on infrared."

Grant's Sin Eater flashed into his hand and he opened fire. A stream of roaring slugs splashed into the water where one of the inert objects floated. Suddenly the log thrashed violently, twisting and flailing in the darkness. Kane could see the creature's silhouette. It was no warmer than the seething, humid swamp, but in the faint light, he could see vestigial claws and a thrashing tail as Grant lit the thing up. "Alligators! They're cold-blooded and mask right into the background heat."

"Fuck!" Rosalia snarled, pulling her own weapon.

It was as if Grant's gunfire was the signal for a

mass attack. The water suddenly churned as multiple
"logs" surged forward with torpedolike speed, moving
straight and unerringly toward the scull. Kane's Sin
Eater deployed into his hand, as well, and he triggered
a pair of rounds into the closest of the massive reptiles,
240-grain slugs smashing through the gator's heavily
armored hide and skull. The creature shuddered, then
nose-dived into the depths, obviously dead or dying as
its reflexes were limp, weakened twitches, not the violent upheaval of the animal that Grant had wounded.

The dog spread its legs, head lowered, lips curled
back over sharp teeth. It was a threat display, a bluff,
and Kane wished the canine luck with that, because
there was little that the mutt could do against full-
grown alligators. The creatures were apex predators
here in the swamp, capable of explosive action even
after days of inactivity, coasting along and waiting for
prey to react. Kane didn't doubt that their lethality and
tactics weren't going to be improved by outside mind
control, but he was busy concentrating on fighting the
monstrosities before they could get to the boat.

Kane remembered from somewhere that the average adult alligator could produce over a ton of bite
force with its mighty jaws. The ancient wood of this
boat wouldn't stand up to that kind of a chomp, and
he didn't expect even the shadow suit to stave off such
crushing power for more than a few moments. The
real danger, however, was not the sharpness of the
ugly, conical teeth, but the raw physical strength of
the beast's core musculature. The alligators wouldn't
go for the torso, but for a limb, and by spinning themselves in the water, they could easily rip off limbs
from even full-grown wild bulls. Not even Grant had
the kind of muscle to resist such a violent attack.

"They've got those things!" Rosalia snarled as she opened fire on another of the snapping jaws.

It might have been the vaguest warning that Kane had ever received in his life, but at the same time, he knew exactly what the olive-skinned warrior woman was talking about. It was dark, so he couldn't make out the flat, tumorous growths against the knobby, thick armor around the base of their skulls, but there was little doubt that the gator horde sweeping upon them in the turgid swamp water was directed by an outside force. Their swiftness had only kicked in the moment that Grant had opened fire, and even then, their stealth had been assured until they came up against the super-human senses of the half-coyote dog that accompanied Rosalia. Had it not been for the mutt's alertness, the three Cerberus expeditionists would have been taken by surprise, literally overwhelmed by a wall of snapping jaws that would have torn them all to shreds.

The enemy had been thrown off its game by the sudden burst of gunfire, and that had been all that Kane and his companions had required. Kane couldn't tell if each of the massive alligators had been under direct control, one user per animal, or if they had been guided by a sort of hive mind, but with the way the alligators were backing off, looking for an alternate route to attack their human prey, he was able to guess that they were not each under the steady hand and sharp mind of an individual user. They reacted as a swarm, and they scattered, reassembling farther back. Unique pilots of the beasts would have sought out flanking routes and surprise tactics, perhaps even showing reckless disregard for the animals that they threw at the Cerberus team.

While one was sacrificed in a hail of gunfire, the

others would have gone underwater or swung around into the team's blind spot. It wasn't much of a consolation for Kane.

The creatures were tough. Glancing injuries from his or Grant's machine pistols had only ended up with furrowed armor. Heavy scales laced with bone made the creatures invulnerable to anything short of a point-blank shot to the brain, and even then, the powerful alligators had blunt, thick skulls that shielded their narrow but still alert and canny brains.

Grant had killed his first target by training and instinct. New Edo, with its proximity to Thunder Isle and its time trawl, had been highly educational for the tall, powerful ex-Magistrate. The temporal travel facility had brought dozens of specimens of extinct species to the island, and containment was an everyday struggle for the Tigers of Heaven staff that protected the facility. Among the more unusual creatures such as velociraptors and carnotaurs, less conspicuous prehistoric animals populated the thick forests surrounding the time center.

It had provided the valuable technology a layer of security that couldn't be turned off. Fighting past hunting packs was difficult. The samurai warriors of New Edo and the technical geniuses at Cerberus had combined to produce a maze of remote-activated sonic jammers that produced painful whines in the sharp ears of the time-lost monsters. A straight road would have been obvious to intruders, but the twisting path of safety, complete with its quickly collapsible sonic fence, was a solid lock against large-scale infiltrations of the island.

As it was, Grant knew about all manner of alligators and crocodiles thanks to his experiences on

Thunder Isle and his on-the-job paleontology lessons. Finding the brain of an idling alligator was easy. But now the animals were on the move, and while the Sin Eaters could injure them, putting one down for the count was pure luck, like when Kane killed the one headed right for their boat.

Rosalia tumbled back into the floor of the scull as one of the smaller attackers had made a daring leap toward the boat. She mashed down the trigger on the Copperhead she unfurled, having emptied her side arm. The little subgun was a close-quarters weapon designed for human beings, not primitive monsters covered in thick, bony hide and nestling their brains behind thick columns of bone. As it was, the tiny little subgun rounds tore into the open mouth of the beast at 800 rounds per minute. The machine pistol had been designed at a time when soldiers wore body armor, particularly Kevlar-armored helmets. A full forty rounds ripped off at cyclic rates into the open, slashing mouth of the reptile had done something, as blood sprayed in hot streams.

Rosalia's face was caked with alligator gore, but the monster had slipped back over the rail. With speed unhindered by the unnerving experience of nearly ending up in the deadly jaws of the gator, she slammed in a new magazine. There was movement out in the water, either the creature's corpse twitching, or some fresh assailant. She triggered the Copperhead again, pumping a burst that set glistening scales twisting and writhing in the murk.

"Start the motor!" Kane bellowed. "Rosalia, conserve your ammo!"

The mercenary beauty scowled, but she held her fire. She'd mounted a flashlight onto her pistol and was using it to sweep the waters. Glassy eyes reflected the light's glare, but before she could fire, the creatures submerged, getting out of her line of fire. Frustration was written across the woman's face, even as she held her finger away from the trigger.

"Sooner or later, whoever is remote-controlling these beasts is going to decide to make his move," Rosalia stated.

The motor turned over quickly for Grant. He and Kane had kept the outboard in good repair, performing preventative maintenance on any problems that would be the difference between swift flight and cruel death. The scull lurched in the water, and Grant waved for the others to sit.

Kane and Rosalia had been taken off balance by the sudden acceleration, but not her dog. The boat sped forward, zipping past jaws that snapped at a target of opportunity. Kane wondered if the presence of the strange parasitic growths and brain-control "collars" had slowed them down, giving them that brief second of reprieve that saved them from being dumped into the marsh to become easy prey for the giant reptiles.

It was better not to think about it. Through the night-vision device, he noticed that the mind-controlled alligators were spearing through the water, hot on their trail. Powerful tail strokes made them easily as quick as the motorboat, only their head start giving them any form of lead and margin of safety from those gnashing, flesh-shredding jaws.

"We've spared this motor, and it's got a full tank, but I don't think we're going to lose these things," Grant said.

"What would help us outrun them?" Kane asked.

"Losing some weight. Like a hundred, two hundred pounds," Grant answered.

"So, one of us gets out to push, and probably ends up as lunch," Rosalia grumbled.

"That's not going to work for me," Kane said. "Sweep ahead, light up any particularly big trees."

Rosalia raised an eyebrow.

"We'll slow them down by crashing trees in their path. If we're lucky, a trunk might crush a few or knock out whatever is on their brains," Kane explained as he reached into his war bag. He'd considered simply throwing grens into the mass of angry monsters snapping literally at their heels, but the alligators were spread apart, and their hides too tough to guarantee that one of the hand bombs would kill more than one with a direct impact. The stagnant river ahead of them spread out some, and Rosalia spun in response to shore sightings.

"We've got trees and patches of land," Rosalia said. "Those things can run?"

"Only over short distances," Grant said. There was a sullen, uncomfortable silence, which was all Kane needed to confirm that the creatures could run as fast as a human being, at least for short sprints. Perhaps even more if their autonomic systems were nullified by the mind control in place. Kane was fully aware of the ability of external sources to override the normal limits of a human or an animal, making them immune to pain or exhaustion.

The sheer evidence of the alligators absorbing tons of gunfire in the melee was confirmation enough that these beasts would be able to outrun a person on land.

"There!" Rosalia pointed.

Kane spotted the copse of trees where the olive-skinned woman indicated. He whipped the first grenade at a clump of trees, then primed a second miniature bomb, tossing it at the opposite shore. Earth-shaking blasts erupted within a second of each other as the motorboat buzzed past them. The force of the two explosions wrenched up thick hardwoods by the roots and shattered trunks as sheets of high pressure snapped them in the middle. Grant swerved to avoid one toppling pine, its leaves raking both him and Kane as the boat sped beneath. Kane could feel twig-size branches breaking against his shadow suit as he plowed through them. If it hadn't been for the night-vision device, Kane was certain that his eyes would have been gouged out by splinters or needles.

He turned, looking in their wake to see the stagnant river behind them white with froth as alligators and tree trunks collided at full speed. Kane primed another grenade and threw it overhand, launching it above the log jam.

He didn't want to risk blowing up the one impediment to the swimming reptiles, but he also wasn't going to leave them thrashing around in the dark. The more he could cut into the number of monsters the enemy had on hand, the better.

Kane watched as the explosion underlit the obscene forms of disintegrating alligators, their long, serpentine bodies twisting in the air, limbs stripped from the flat trunks of their bodies. Jaws came apart, cartwheeling through the air.

"Damn," Grant grunted, watching the horrific display as he slowed the motor. He wanted to make certain that he could ascertain what was going on behind them, but he also didn't want to steer himself into the roots or trunk of a cypress tree while he wasn't paying attention. He grimaced at the sight of chunks of meat and alligator hide falling from the sky.

"Don't tell me that you're feeling sorry for those beasts," Rosalia said. Her hazel eyes were wide with the horror of what she'd just faced.

Kane suddenly bent over in pain, feeling a powerful shriek slice through his consciousness like a knife.

KONDO WAS ON THE LONELY, rusted-seeming freighter bobbing in the waters just off the Florida panhandle. The bridge was bustling with activity as Watatsumi seamen saw to the ship's every need. His attention was drawn to one corner of the bridge, the station he'd been attending earlier when Colonel Orochi was present on the ship.

It was the remote operations station—one of the more important positions on the ship—and it was the nerve center of this expedition to the swamps of Florida. Without it, everything they had come for would have been for naught. The ROS was the one chance that the Watatsumi military had to stave off the approach of the underground wyrms that threatened their secret society.

The parasites and the transistor crowns that melded them to other brains were the one means by which the Watatsumi's warriors could at least turn some of the unstoppable beasts into weapons against their own kind.

Kondo had been manning the ROS and maintaining its transmitters alongside the rest of his team, and if they had asked him, this round of testing would have been complete. There was no more need to torment the primitive human refugees hiding out in the swamps, nor was there cause to keep the alligators enslaved.

Orochi, however, was concerned about the long-term effects of the tiaras, as he called them.

Kondo had looked up the term tiara. It was a diminutive form of a crown, something that was light, sparkly and only meant to accent royalty and those who wished to emulate them. That such an inoffensive object shared the name of the parasitic octopoid slugs that entwined themselves with living brains, even through the bones of the skull, was just short of blasphemous. These things were grotesque in their aspect, the humans forced to wear them disguising themselves from the rest of their kind as the Hooded Ones while even other alligators shunned their infested brethren.

There was no rhyme or reason for the sudden animosity toward the octoslug-infested beings, especially among the less than intelligent alligators of the panhandle.

He could understand the unease that sentients would have, not only for the disfiguring growths suddenly present on an otherwise familiar creature, but also the rather robotic, droning monotone with which the Hooded Ones spoke when they had been given the directions to communicate with others. Even the heavy hoods and face-obscuring scarves couldn't do anything to alleviate the oddities of their behavior.

"We've detected two packs of humans going through the swamp. One is a small scout group, and the other is a sizable armed force," the ROS station officer told Kondo.

"Two human groups moving?" Kondo asked.

"Think it's a coincidence?" Fumio, Kondo's second, asked.

"Compared to what?" Kondo asked. "The sudden

malfunctions the other day? That's why we had the alligators on patrol."

"But the second group, think they're following the first?" Fumio asked. "And why did the first group show up?"

"Let's ask questions about this later," Kondo said. "Right now...you've lost three of your alligators in the first assault."

"I know, but they're on the run now," Fumio replied. "They're in a motorboat, by what the camera we mounted in one of the slugged-up alligators can tell. And they're running scared."

Kondo squinted as he looked at the screen. It was dark, and even in the raw green of night-vision footage, it was hard to make out details. He saw one of the humans pull a pair of objects from a satchel on the scull.

"Fumio! Stop them now!" Kondo warned.

"No, I'm almost on them," Fumio snapped.

Suddenly the screen went dead, another five transmitters gone black at the same moment. Fumio recoiled from the screen, realizing what had happened, and before he could issue orders for a retreat, another half dozen of the electronic collars controlling the octoslugs blinked out of existence.

"Grenades," Kondo said. "They had grenades."

Fumio's scaled lips grated against each other as he pursed them in consternation. "What does that mean now?"

"It means we've got to call in reserves," Kondo said. "Intercept them, because their last heading was a beeline straight for us."

He spoke into the public address system.

"All hands to emergency stations," Kondo ordered.

"We have intruders and they are actively taking down our puppets. Full alert, and side arms passed out to all personnel. No one is going to be a noncombatant."

Kondo stood back. Orochi wasn't going to be happy about this situation. He'd assured his commander that he'd maintain control over the expedition while he was down at the undersea TOTO station.

Now things had gotten much worse.

Who knew what kind of a force was on hand to assault the freighter.

Chapter 11

Domi took the steps four at a time, each push of her corded, powerful legs propelling her up toward the fourth floor, where Lakesh and Priscilla were waiting. She reached the heavy fire door and saw that it had opened out; she had to pull it toward her from inside the stairwell. She couldn't count on the savage horde behind her not to figure out a simple door in the meantime. The locking mechanism was electronic, because she didn't see a heavy bolt in it.

It used to be a hotel. Locking the stairwell would have been reckless endangerment, keeping people from escaping should the place light on fire.

While they might not have been sophisticated or especially sensitive enough to track her to this flight of stairs, Domi knew that the animalistic hunters would be thorough in their hunt for living flesh. That meant every story in the abandoned hotel wing was going to be raided.

Granted, Domi had a slim hope that the hunters would be thorough and systematic by searching the dozens of good hiding places between their front line and the hotel, but she wasn't going to hold her breath for that to happen. She was certain that they had caught a whiff of her and were smart enough to remember when and where their brothers had died.

Domi found an old fiberglass-handled fire ax in a

plastic box. She hammered out the lid with the butt of her .45 and seized the tool. It was too large for her to use effectively in close quarters, as it was a weapon of mass and leverage more than finesse and savage speed. If she was going to get into hand-to-hand combat, she would use her fighting knife. She tested the ax handle with all of her weight, and the fiberglass hadn't weakened over the centuries under glass.

Domi looked over the door again. She had a good, solid bar, but how was she going to anchor the door?

"Lakesh would know," she whispered.

As if summoned by her wish, Priscilla appeared in the hallway and joined her at the stairwell entrance. "I felt that you needed someone."

Domi sized up the slender hybrid. "Can you lock this?"

Priscilla took the ax and slid its handle through the D-shaped door latch. Together, she and Domi pulled the latch through until their combined strength had wedged the ax head solidly against the steel of the door, and the handle was flexed against the jamb.

"Will it hold?" Priscilla asked.

"Have to," Domi replied. "Come on."

Priscilla followed the feral little albino woman. Though the door was secured, and it was steel within steel, the fiberglass handle wouldn't hold up under the kind of savage, combined might she was anticipating. The hunters were fast approaching, and Domi knew she just had to hold off the horde.

"How smart?" Domi asked, pointing through the window.

Priscilla glanced out, seeing her would-be brethren scurrying through the streets outside, wiry legs propelling them like a swarm of locusts with clipped wings. They were still a few blocks away, but their presence was omnipresent, a crushing weight on her mind. She had felt it back when she was in Area 51, and she didn't like a return to that kind of a fog through her brain. She'd wondered why she hadn't been able to communicate or to read thoughts as before, but the wild minds of the half-breeds produced a static. Suddenly she understood her urge to escape. She had been blocked by the primitive urges that ruled their brains.

"Dim," Priscilla said. "They can barely use a door."

Domi smirked. "Good."

"It won't slow them down much since there's too many of them and they're on a feeding rampage," Priscilla said.

"Steel will keep them back for a while," Domi explained. "Long enough, at least."

"For what?" Priscilla asked.

"I'm thinking," Domi replied.

Despite the encroaching fog of angry, hungry thoughts, Priscilla could feel Domi's brain churning, gears grinding as she put things together.

"Sense of smell?" Domi asked.

"As good as yours," Priscilla said.

Domi's eyes locked on hers, her lips pursing as she realized that she was an open book to the untransformed hybrid. She looked to the stairwell. "Right."

Domi's ruby-red eyes lit up as an idea took root. Priscilla could feel it click in her head.

"Tinder," she grumbled. "And rubber. Even if it's rotted."

The feral albino girl broke into a run down the hall, leaving Priscilla to search for what she'd asked for. Luckily the hybrid woman was aware of the very things that Domi was asking for. Priscilla went to work quickly, knowing that as of this moment, there would only be a few minutes before the creatures turned their attention toward the hotel.

Priscilla had chosen the location not only for the dark area, the silent, sealed-off hiding spot she'd cherished so greatly, but because of its access to the still standing section of the hotel. People—or savage half-formed Nephilim—looking for her would think to hit the taller sections, not expecting someone to tuck themselves into a lightless, desolate hole.

That was how she'd survived.

Priscilla made an improvised drag mat out of some old linens that hadn't been utilized by Domi in setting up Lakesh's nest. Once she had the means of hauling the stuff, she had the ability to pull far more than she could normally lift. She took out her utility knife and slashed at the carpet, ripping it up for the rubber beneath it. For some reason, Domi seemed to feel that even the rotted, crumbling black material would prove beneficial against the coming horde.

Priscilla wasn't going to ask questions. If Domi had an idea, she would have to trust it. There was nothing else that could be done in the face of the hungry cannibals rushing toward them.

The albino girl was back, pulling Lakesh with her. Priscilla could see that Domi had the same idea about using her strength to the utmost. Lakesh had been laid out on a curtain, then wound into it. Leaving two corners long and loose, she was able to use them as handles to drag him along the floor. Lakesh seemed fatter, and it took a moment for Priscilla to realize that Domi had cushioned him from below with the foam-rubber pillows. That was about the only rubber that Priscilla hadn't gotten a sample of, and she didn't want to cannibalize Lakesh's only transportation.

"Got it?" Domi asked.

Priscilla nodded, pointing to the tarp.

"I'm going to draw their attention for now," Domi told her. "I need you to take Lakesh down to the hole you had. Seal yourselves in."

Priscilla could sense the sheer strain in the young woman's voice as she fought to enunciate each and every word. This wasn't the terse, primitive woman who had been speaking before. She needed to be understood, and she needed to convey a complex idea. When the adrenaline hit her, she was likely to do away with the niceties of proper grammar, but this time, everything had to be spelled out.

"And you?" Priscilla asked.

"Lose 'em," Domi said, dropping back into her usual curt, simple language.

Spinning on her heel, Domi grabbed the sheet loaded with rubber. She sized it up and nodded with approval. Priscilla paused, looking at the door they had barred. "Domi…"

"Not here yet," Domi answered. She put all of her strength into pulling the fire ax from its lodging. She brought the curtain with her onto the flight of stairs, then helped Priscilla with Lakesh for a moment. "Feet can bump on stairs. Not head."

Domi took the two long straps and tugged them over Priscilla's slender shoulders. With a lurch, she hiked Lakesh's head as far above the floor as she could without overtaxing the hybrid's seemingly frail back.

"Okay?" Domi asked.

Priscilla nodded with a grunt.

Domi slapped her on the ass and the hybrid woman

began wending her way down the flight of stairs. There was no looking back now. Priscilla could feel that from the hard, ruby-red stare drilling into her neck. Since she was lifting with all of her back and legs, and Lakesh's weight was mostly supported by his feet dragging on the floor, it was easier getting down the steps than she'd assumed. It wasn't easy by any stretch of the imagination, but instead of a slow, arduous lumber that would have been necessary if she was supporting his weight with her arms interlocked with his, she could at least walk at a nearly normal pace. The trek to the bottom of the stairwell took almost no time.

The completion of that leg of the journey was no cause for celebration. Not yet. Priscilla knew enough of physics that most of the work done had been with the assistance of gravity. Now she had to cross fifty feet of darkened rubble and wreckage-strewed casino floor to the private little cave she'd set up for herself.

How Domi would provide cover during that time was a mystery now that she had gotten farther from the girl. Those thoughts had been already scrambled by the feral processes of her brain, and now with distance and the proximity of the savage half-breeds, it was all she could do to hear her own thoughts.

Priscilla lowered her head and pressed on, feeling more of Lakesh's weight focused on the twin straps of the litter as they bit into her shoulders. She needed the cover of her old nest, and would just have to trust Domi to find her later.

DOMI KNEW SHE HAD TWO THINGS to accomplish. She had to protect Lakesh and Priscilla, and she had to survive that effort to save them from the cannibal force.

That meant she had to make the most of her environment. Domi's sensitive smell had been as much of a hindrance as an asset at times. On the one hand, she could catch the whiff of either threats or prey in an especially dense forest or rough terrain. On the other, she was vulnerable to powerful stenches and chemical smoke like those used in some of Kane's and Grant's grens.

The news that the enemy was as sensitive as she was gave Domi an idea and a modicum of hope. She remembered the amount of searing pain produced by a mound of burning tires she'd encountered as a small girl. She hadn't been able to open her bloodshot eyes for days, and her sinuses were left raw and stinging. It had been hell.

Now Domi was going to even the odds by harnessing that hell herself.

To make things a little more equal, Domi quickly grabbed the ends of her desert scarf and tied it around her nose and mouth, forming a filter. She'd needed it against the blown sands of the Nevada desert, and now she'd be even more glad to have its protection when she lit up a hundred pounds of rubber and synthetic carpeting. She wasn't sure what would happen to the carpet fibers, especially since she'd heard about fireproof materials, but even if the rugs were only fire resistant, it meant that they would still melt. Especially with the help of one of the many grens she had tucked into her war bag. She usually wasn't one to haul such heavy artillery, but then carrying a bolt-action rifle hadn't been in her repertoire, either. However, she was alone, and she knew that she'd be facing some manner of resistance, dangerous foes that lurked in the Nevada desert alone, and she would be without the kind of full-auto blasters that Kane and Grant carried with them. Domi didn't enjoy lugging the extra weight, but she dared not leave it behind.

She paused at the window, looking down to see the strange creatures scurrying through the street. They were reassembling from scouring the adjacent block. The half-transformed monsters were scouring high and low, trying to track down the humans who had killed two of their own.

The group had seemed larger, and though it wasn't the hundreds or thousands that the howling seemed to have indicated, Domi could still see that she was heavily outnumbered. Even lobbing grenades, she wouldn't be able to do more than scatter them. This also was problematic if more of the creatures were in reserve. Right now what she had to do was to give them something to worry about, a vast burst of confusion and chaos that would leave them reeling and uncoordinated.

Domi took one of the grenades, a thermal detonator, and wrapped a swatch of rubber-backed carpeting around it in the form of a sack. Before setting the fuse and closing the back off, she poured gravel and kindling into the bag. This was going to get nasty, but it was a necessity.

She activated the fuse, tugged the drawstring to shut the mouth of the bag and tossed it through the window quickly. The sack hit the ground—actually a slab of fallen wall—and bounced. The thud caught the attention of dozens of reptilian beings, and as they looked at the satchel, it burst like a sun-bright blossom, heated gravel, burning rubber and flaming splinters of wood flying.

As one, the horde let out a wail of surprise, their

hands and arms covering their eyes from both sailing shrapnel and the sudden brightness. Knocked silly by the sudden flash, this gave Domi more than enough time to wrap up three more of the sacks. She'd gotten the enemy's attention, and she was going to have to stage a harsh welcome for them all. Domi was glad she left the stairwell open, because now that they knew where she was, they had a way to get to her.

The half-breeds were simple, and they would take the most direct route, knowing that their quarry was trapped on an upper floor. Domi wanted them to think that. She understood them, she knew their hunting instincts, and they were little more than wild pack hunters that would harry and pursue her when she was younger. She'd been taught to escape them, and had never lost the instincts since then.

That was a weapon in her favor, and the lone stairwell was another tool she'd make use of.

What also had helped her was the fact that she knew there was an alternate escape route off this floor. There was a three-story garage, or rather the remains of one, right next to a window at the far end of the hallway, away from the stairwell. It was also aimed away from the direction that Priscilla had dragged Lakesh.

Domi needed to draw the attackers away, and there was nothing like a wild leap across fifteen feet of space that would pull them along and far from Lakesh and Priscilla. Domi knew she could make the jump with a strong run. The drop was about ten feet, and though she didn't know the exact math, she knew that if she launched herself, her momentum would carry her farther than she dropped, with gravity helping her along. A good tuck and roll, and she would be a little shaken but none the worse for wear.

Domi saw that the half-breeds were beginning to recover, so she wanted to make extra certain that they were coming after her. She shouldered her 7 mm rifle and fired a shot into one of the more alert of the semi-Nephilim, the high-powered hunting round crushing a gory path through the creature's rib cage. It bowled over backward, and that spooked a quarter of the creatures. A swift throw of the rifle's bolt and another pull of the trigger dropped a second mutant. That sent a dozen of them to flight, their rudimentary intellect warning them that they would prove to be ill-suited for dealing with firearms.

The rest of them, however, lurched toward the building, some of them leaping into the window wells along the wall, using them as stepping stones to get up. Others charged into the building in a rush to reach the stairs.

"Damn," Domi grumbled. Those who could scrabble up the side of a building under the strength of their clawlike fingers made their move. Those who couldn't took the route she'd wanted. Kane had often said that any good plan lasted only as long as it took for the enemy to act.

Domi hefted a chunk of masonry and whipped it at the skull of one of the climbers. Rock met head bone and the attacker tumbled from its precarious grip on the wall, crashing down atop its brethren. She worked the bolt another time and fired at another of them. The 7 mm slug popped the head of that target as if it were a soup-filled balloon, hot blood spraying in a greasy mess across scaled faces. Half of the group dropped to the ground and rushed around the corner, making their way through the building where they'd have more cover, while the other climbers threw themselves through empty windowpanes, ducking into hotel rooms to avoid a rain of bullets and stone.

Domi sidestepped into the stairwell and paused to listen. The creatures still hadn't found the way up, but they had enough wherewithal that they knew there was a path up. The others who had gone into hotel rooms might have had the presence of mind to try climbing the side of the hotel away from the spot where she'd sniped at them, but for Domi, that was a good setup. Their routes would bring them against her one at a time, and she knew how to deal with them in a fight with better odds.

As if on cue, one of the Area 51 mutants lurched into the hallway, its eyes hard, blackened marbles with little more than animalistic rage boiling behind them. Domi staggered backward as if in surprise, but she knew that they were coming. She needed the hunter on the attack, and sure enough, at the sign of its prey's weakness, it exploded into motion, taut, powerful limbs springing it forward.

Domi sidestepped the charge and brought the stock of her rifle down hard into the back of its thigh. The reflex and leverage of the blow brought the mutant to its knees hard, its jaw bouncing on the rusted steel railing of the stairwell. A second stroke of the rifle butt scissored the half-breed's head from the top of its spinal column. Domi's strength was amplified by the bulk of her weapon rushing to contact the immovable object of the rail. A sickening crunch filled the air as its neck broke.

Domi kicked it down the steps and looked for another assailant.

There was the thunder of a steel door slamming open, dozens of hard-scaled feet pounding on tile and concrete below. Domi prepared her second sack of grenade and shrapnel, lobbing it down the gap between flights of stairs, straight to the bottom of the stairwell. She turned away and lunged out of the stairwell just in time to protect her hearing from the skull-rocking blast. In the enclosed quarters of the stairs, what would have been a rather inefficient blast became a deafening roar of mayhem. Even a few yards from the door, Domi's ears stung from the sudden blast wave.

She didn't have time to deal with that, however. Two more of the enemy had crawled up and through the windows, their snarling faces locked on her. Domi let the rifle drop on its sling and she plucked the Detonics from its leather in a lightning-fast draw. One was in midair, pouncing at her with reckless abandon. She caught it in the upper chest with a fat .45-caliber slug that snapped its clavicle in two before it tunneled down deep through the mutant's heart and lungs.

The airborne half-breed sailed nervelessly past Domi and into the stairwell, where it crashed against the railing. Its partner paused, realizing that it was on the bad end of a fight, having only brought its razor-sharp talons to a gunfight. If Domi hadn't been worried about the rest of the thing's brethren, she would have given it the opportunity to turn tail and run, but she was outnumbered. She fired her Detonics again and broke open the mutant's skull. Its eyeballs burst from their sockets when her bullet struck it in the forehead.

Footsteps sounded in the stairwell again, and Domi flipped the crumbling, rotted rubber and kindling that Priscilla had brought her in the doorway. She lit a moldy piece of paper and dropped it atop the mess, then fired her .45 into the doorway.

That started the stomp of running feet once more in earnest, and Domi turned and rushed toward the window that she had scouted as the alternate exit from this trap. Tightly wound muscles released their potential energy with each long stride, her tough, bare feet gripping the rubble and giving her the traction necessary to reach the far window.

Back at the stairwell, the burning rubber had produced choking, noxious smoke that slowed the enemy as they burst onto the floor. The mutants stumbled, rubbing stinging eyes and coughing, but they had enough of a sense of their surroundings to notice Domi as she leaped through the window, sailing through the air.

Arms windmilling and legs kicking, she sailed across fifteen feet, dropping the entire story to the garage floor. When she impacted with the concrete, it was with far less grace than she'd envisioned, and the landing knocked the breath from her lungs. It didn't matter; she was alive and she was able to move her limbs without crippling, searing pain. She sat up, realizing that she was sporting a whole new set of bruises.

Still, Domi knew that she had to milk the moment. It took ten seconds, five times as long as it had taken her to race to the window and leap, for the first of the Area 51 freaks to show their faces through the empty window. Not quite acting, the albino woman lurched to all fours and staggered to her feet. One of the hybrid mutants stood in the window, then jumped, arms raking the air, hoping to hook the ledge she'd landed upon.

It missed and it struck the ground below, its breaking bones sounding like twigs snapping on a dead tree in a hard wind. The creature wailed as another tottered on the windowsill, suddenly unwilling to take its leap of faith. Its fellows were impatient, and a scaly paw smacked it in the back, pushing it out for a face-first meeting with the hard ground below. There was no cry of pain this time as its face exploded like rotten fruit.

Domi punched a .45-caliber slug through the window, wounding the mutant that had pushed its friend to its death. She turned and limped along, a halting skip-drag that ended when she was out of their line of sight.

Her leg hurt and her ribs were bruised, but she was able to pick up her pace. By the time she was at the ramp leading to the street, she saw that two of the monsters had made the jump between buildings, but they weren't rising to their feet swiftly. Domi had made the jump with as little injury as she had because she was under one hundred pounds. Gravity hadn't been as hard on her as it had been on creatures twice her weight. They saw her, and they howled, waving that they had seen her.

Domi responded by feeding her rifle another round and killing one of the pair, sending the other racing for cover.

"Keep after me, fuckers," Domi snarled under her breath.

She turned and disappeared into the streets of a dead Vegas, stunned, injured and half-blinded cannibals in hot pursuit. Or as hot as they could get while limping.

Chapter 12

The thunder of guns tore the dark silence apart with the unmistakable chatter of Sin Eaters and Copperheads. Agrippine was familiar with the grim snarl of that kind of weaponry and he knew that he was in pursuit of two men who formerly counted themselves as Magistrates. The Cajun had heard the weapons fired in his direction, often when he was on the run, scurrying for his life away from the baronial enforcers.

Agrippine let his hand drop to his swamp gun. It was a lever-action carbine, its butt sawn off just behind the ring of the lever to afford him a full grip, but allowing for it to be short enough to carry sheathed in a thigh holster. The barrel had been knocked down to twelve inches, even with the end of the tubular magazine, which held six rounds of .44-40 ammunition. It was fast, accurate at close range and, most importantly, powerful enough to punch through an alligator's hide.

As dangerous as men were, here in the southeastern swamps, the prehistoric predators were even more deadly. They were living monsters that had survived the extinction of the dinosaurs and the eclipse of humanity as masters of the Earth. If it was a choice between dealing with other humans and the reptiles, then he'd run down the muzzles of a dozen automatic weapons by comparison. Agrippine wasn't smart, and he wasn't deluded about his invulnerability—he simply knew what happened to the human prey of the crocodilians when they sank their blunt teeth into soft flesh and twisted their five-hundred-pound bodies with a flex of muscles. Being shot a dozen times was far preferable to being twisted apart like a piece of rotted wood.

"We go!" Grogan insisted, pointing toward the sound of battle.

Agrippine tightened his fingers around the handle of his machete, looking pensive.

"Lead us to them!" Grogan demanded.

"They're already shooting at something, something that's not shooting back," Agrippine replied, lip curling at the memory he had of the missing night hunters.

"Then Kane and his allies will simply be wasting their ammunition, and we will come upon them in a weakened state," Grogan countered.

Agrippine glowered. "Everyone, put your backs into it and follow my raft!"

The Cajun didn't mind setting the fanatics to work, doing the grunt rowing that he didn't care much for. He hadn't fought his way to escape the villes because he'd wanted to engage in more labor. Pushing himself through the marsh on a raft was one thing; it was his means of transportation, and with the pole in his rough, callused hands, he was the master of his own destiny, steering himself, commanding his path. Doing it for others, even ones who were paying him, that was an entirely different matter.

Agrippine liked the fact that two dozen people had chopped down the trees and made a trio of rafts, six per, and that they were the ones who were providing the propulsion. Only the Cajun and Grogan were allowed to slack, perhaps because Grogan knew that his guide skills would be useless should he tear a muscle while rowing.

The gunfire had cut off abruptly, but the snarl of automatic weapons was replaced by the throaty growl of an outboard motor. Agrippine turned, eyes wide at the sudden knowledge that their quarry was in fast retreat.

"No," Agrippine grunted. "No! They're going to get away!"

"Push, children," Grogan intoned.

The fanatics bent to the task of driving down the river, poles flexing under their combined weight as they sought to catch up. Grogan folded his arms, eyes locked on the direction of the sounds, a remarkable scale of alertness, Agrippine noted, since echoes off the trees made it difficult to triangulate the exact location of the sounds.

As if they were directed by his will, the New Order cultists steered the rafts directly toward the sound of flight.

"They'll get away," Agrippine said.

Grogan shook his head. "If they had the fuel to go far on the water, they would have used it, rather than paddling. The motor is an emergency measure, and what greater emergency is an ambush?"

"I still only heard one set of weapons," Agrippine told him.

"As did I, but guns are not the only lethal things in a swamp, as you so succinctly informed us," Grogan countered.

Agrippine pursed his lips, then flinched as distant explosions rocked the night, drowning out the rumble of the motorboat as it faded into the distance.

Then the swamp was silent again. Agrippine grasped the handle of his swamp gun.

"Something worries you?" Grogan asked.

"They're using grens," Agrippine explained.

"So, the ambushers will be either wiped out or delayed," Grogan said.

Agrippine pulled out the sawed-off lever action, chambering a fat 200-grain slug. "Or sent into retreat."

"So, they retre…" Grogan's words trailed off, dying as the realization of one basic truth hit him. When you're under attack by overwhelming force, say, high explosives, you head immediately away from the source of the problem. And since Kane was heading in one direction, and Grogan and Agrippine were on the same trail, the attackers would likely end up hurtling toward the New Order's expedition!

Agrippine saw the water froth and churn in the normally dark waters ahead of them, large, flat figures breaching the surface, then diving nose first into the water like jumping carp. Agrippine had been caught in one of those wild migrations, and the hard-nosed, high-jumping fish had left him battered and bruised. The inky-dark river glowed subtly and bioluminescent flora in the water were agitated, making the frothing stream take on a ghostly glow.

Except these creatures were far too large to be carp. They were alligators, and their tails and spines thrashed with such muscular power that the crocodilians were literally launching through the surface, sailing one to two feet out of the water before splashing down on their wide, heavily armored bellies. Agrippine triggered his swamp gun, and a single .44-caliber bullet tore out of the twelve-inch barrel and smacked one of the reptiles square center. The Cajun knew he'd hit it because the thing jerked as the bullet struck it with the equivalent of 650 pounds of force.

The alligators were in full panic mode, the gators or whatever was atop their heads controlling them, and they weren't going to be stopped in their wild flight to escape danger.

"Get off the rafts!" the Cajun roared as he threw himself into the water. His warning might have come too late to save the others, but even with his ears plugged by fluid, he could hear the raft snap apart under the force of several hundred pounds of frightened reptile. More wood splintered as bodies crashed through the shattered remains as their transportation was plowed through by a wave of muscular force that seemed nearly unstoppable.

Agrippine twisted beneath the surface, not because he was trying to move but because he was tossed around by the force of the current whipped up by the alligators. Sediment turned the already opaque water into near mud, and as he reached up, his gloved left hand was struck by one of the crocodilians. Its speed and hard scales combined into a flying grater that shredded the glove, and would have torn off pieces of the Cajun's hand if the animal was either longer or the leather thinner.

Agrippine needed breath, he needed air, but he dared not lift his head above the surface in case another creature struck him and this time decapitated him.

He clawed at the riverbed, anchoring himself, holding tight.

Things turned quiet again. With a shove, he broke the surface, and the fetid, moldy air over the stagnant river tasted wonderful. He took deep, ragged breaths and looked around.

Grogan was the next up, and he looked shaken and soaked, but none the worse for wear.

It seemed that the two of them were the only ones left unharmed. Bodies floated facedown in the water, some of them missing limbs, others seemingly intact.

Others finally rose into view, staggered, bruised, some actually bleeding.

The alligators hadn't attacked them. Rather, they had stampeded past, and their massive bodies and armored hides had been more than enough to crush bones or rip arms and legs off as they plowed through. Others were likely hurt by the jagged, snapped logs that had made up their rafts. One of the bodies in the water actually had a slab of bloody wood protruding from its back.

Grogan grimaced. "You did not warn us in time."

"I gave you plenty of warning, you idiot," Agrippine said. "You just seemed determined to continue on like a fucking juggernaut. And then when we actually ran afoul of some real juggernauts, your night just turned to shit."

Grogan looked as if he was going to respond, but he derailed any countering rant on his own part by assessing the survivors. "We only have eight left."

"Eight and me," Agrippine added.

Grogan narrowed his eyes. "I was counting my flock."

"Only the believers matter?" Agrippine asked.

"They take priority," Grogan said. "Though their loss was expected."

"And my loss?" Agrippine asked.

"You are allowed to look after yourself. And if there

is an opportunity for me to help you, I will," Grogan answered. "For you, too, may join our cause. Even so, your very existence in this expedition kept me from losing more of my force."

"Is that a way of not saying 'thanks for saving my ass'?"

Grogan smiled. "Thank you, Agrippine."

"You're welcome," Agrippine responded.

"Have you retained your weapon?" Grogan asked.

"I lost my rifle, but I have a knife and a pistol."

Agrippine looked down at his hands. His fingers were still hooked through the loop of his lever-action carbine. "We'll need to get to shore and break down what we have. River mud down a barrel is a bomb waiting to happen."

Grogan nodded with the wisdom of that warning.

Agrippine knew that the New Order cultists would work as fast as possible.

His urge to continue after Kane had already nearly killed them all once. The Cajun might not survive a second close call.

THE KEENING THAT SWEPT through the TOTO base wasn't audible, but it was a shrill cry that every thinking creature within the undersea facility had been able to sense, their minds suddenly filled with the monotone squeal of a telepathic hive mind under attack by forces it didn't comprehend.

The keening had been so powerful that Orochi had been knocked to his knees, only his iron will keeping him standing as his breath now came in deep, panicked wheezes. He blinked, trying to remove the sensation of ants crawling just beneath the bone of his forehead, and as his eyes opened, he could see the

Watatsumi scientists lying on their backs, clutching their faces in horror. Some of them kicked into empty air, bodies twisting and thrashing under the psychic assault.

Orochi wondered what had spared him such an all-consuming seizure, but now was not the time for such thoughts. He struggled to his feet, hands shaking, balance wavering.

"Do not falter!" he growled to himself, and he realized the source of his relative immunity.

Orochi was alone in this room in that he was a warrior, he'd lived a life of discomfort and pain. He knew how to adapt and overcome agony and get back into the thick of things. The scientists were not so hardened by training and experience, so the psychic shock wave that ripped through them had been far more devastating.

Putting one foot in front of the other, he lurched into the hall and saw others of his personal military cadre, guards who had been sent to keep the scientists under control and from figuring out the true nature of the experiments, also rising from where they had nearly fallen.

"I want a status report now!" Orochi said.

"Kondo is on the radio." One of his lieutenants, Yutaka, spoke up. "The alligators took a severe pounding, and then there was another breakdown in remote control of the octoslugs.'"

Orochi narrowed his reptilian eyes, looking through the open doorway at the scientists who had stopped convulsing, yet were slow to rise from where they had fallen. "How many of the creatures have we lost?"

"Right now there's no definite count because feedback from the control collars caused massive failures.

All of the beings under control, both the sentients and the animals, are completely cut off," Yutaka said. "It's just like you said—when the Hooded Ones suffered losses before. Some form of feedback caused all of the parasites to react."

"We've pitted them against each other before," Orochi snarled. "When one killed another, there was no such reaction. When we've shot down Hooded Ones as an experiment, or killed the actual parasite, this didn't happen."

The Watatsumi soldier spoke up. "We never thought about one thing. Electrocution."

Orochi tilted his head.

"The parasites are controlled by little electronic tiaras that administer electric shocks and transmit instructions via low-frequency sound buds. Perhaps just enough damage was done to one of the control collars for it to short out and send an electrical impulse into one of the parasites," Yutaka explained. "The same could have happened to an octoslug subjected to an explosion."

"We've stress-tested the collars, however," Orochi mused. "Though perhaps a simple bent circuit board would cause a malfunction without a power core failure. We've been thinking along the lines of a bullet or a sword through a tiara, but if engaged in hand-to-hand combat, what if the opponent weren't trying to kill the octoslug attached to a Hooded One?"

"A blow to the head—not hard enough to cause brain trauma, would cause a malfunction," the lieutenant replied. "We've been assuming it would be kill or die for our pawns."

Orochi frowned. "Get a team to the vat area. Do not enter, do not break containment. Observe only."

"To see if the slugs are active and mobile," Yutaka said. "What happens if they are on the move?"

"Shut the lab down. Burn everything," Orochi answered. "I am not going to end my life as host to a blob of snot riding on my head. I want to be a part of the ruling party, not one of the zombies under their thumb."

"We could work out the kinks," Yutaka said.

"If we're suffering from a full-blown infestation, that's not going to do us any good. Who knows what we've awakened here," Orochi responded. "We might have been toying with a sleeping giant who will wake as a devil once it learns we've been using it."

Yutaka's eyes went wide with fear. "You think that they are the individual cells of a giant brain?"

"It's what the scientists claim," Orochi said. "We just didn't realize how sentient it could be."

Yutaka nodded. He spun, submachine gun bouncing on his hip as he ran toward the breeder vats.

Orochi grimaced at the thought of coming to calm one monster and awakening one that was far greater than they had previously feared.

It was time to contact Kondo and get a full update.

GRANT REACHED OUT immediately, hooking Kane under his armpit, preventing the smaller man from toppling out of the boat.

"You okay, partner?" he asked his friend.

Kane's face was hidden from view, but just the touch of him, the sudden rush of tremors rocking the man's body, already let the big ex-Magistrate know that he was probably pale and sweaty beneath.

Rosalia reached out and touched his shoulder. "Kane?"

"Give him some room, Rosie," Grant growled, setting him on the center bench of the scull. He took a moment to look back over his shoulder. The river was empty, no signs of continued pursuit by the reptilian ambushers. He'd shifted from infrared to light amplification, paying close attention to any ripples on the surface of the murky water. While the alligators wouldn't have shown up as any warmer than their environment, especially the heat-retaining marsh water, those creatures were far too large to swim without creating waves, even if they were beneath the surface.

That was very likely, Grant knew. On Thunder Isle, he had literally seen a twenty-foot salt-water crocodile leap the entire length of its body out of a river to snag prey. Of course, the river was far deeper than three feet, it would take a long distance for one of them to make that kind of jump. The acceleration and dive would require a lot of swimming, and with that swimming came an unnatural eddy. He kept his ears tuned for burbling marsh water as he turned back to check on Kane. Rosalia had peeled off the night-vision device and Kane looked exactly how Grant thought he would, drenched with sweat, blue eyes sunken into darkened circles.

Grant noticed that the splinter in his cheek, a splinter blown off Ullikummis himself, had seemed to have grown longer. It changed the way his face moved slightly, something Rosalia wouldn't have noticed, and Kane couldn't *see* with his own eyes, but Grant had known the man for too long to ignore the slight difference. He wished that Brigid Baptiste was present; her infallible memory would have been up to the task of measuring whether there had been a change in the size of the splinter simply at a glance.

"Kane?" Grant asked.

He waved Rosalia away. "I'll be fine."

"What happened?" she persisted.

"Those creatures…*that* creature…it's not generally sensitive to pain, but it is sensitive to electricity," Kane said.

"What…the balls of snot riding the people and the gators?" Grant asked. "It's one creature?"

"Yes," Kane whispered.

"And how do you know that?" Rosalia asked.

Kane looked at her, the exhaustion written in his face evident, but not so blatant as his impatience with the question.

"Kane has been dealing with a lot of telepathic communication since we went on the run," Grant said. "Brigid theorized that Balaam, in communicating with him, made him more susceptible to mind-to-mind contact, so that when there's a shout…"

"Like a gigantic, multicelled brain?" Rosalia asked.

Kane nodded weakly. "It's been quiet, but we caused a malfunction in the electronics that the Hooded Ones were using to link up to their home base. And when that went out…"

"You heard it?" Rosalia surmised.

"It's awake. Conscious," Kane whispered. "And it's furious."

Chapter 13

Domi had been too fast for the hunters. Too fast and too dangerous. She'd lost them in the flattened residential areas of Las Vegas. Some of the grasses had managed to adapt to the harsh climate, becoming hardy plants that withstood the blazing sun. In the chill of the desert night, she had been able to lose her pursuers in overgrowth that had sprung up between abandoned homes. By the seventh block and the uncounted fence she'd vaulted over, the mutants were long gone behind her.

She nestled to the ground and hoped, for Lakesh's and Priscilla's sake, that she'd been more than a sufficient distraction for the monstrosities. She figured that with the damage she'd done, the noise that she had made, she'd more than made the creatures realize that she was the killer of two of their own and that she had convinced them that she was alone.

It would take sharp senses and a keen analytical mind for them to realize that she had built a nest for Lakesh in the abandoned hotel room. She didn't leave the creatures with much of their smell, as burning rubber and melting plastic carpet fibers produced more than enough smoke to clog their sinuses, as well as erase and obscure the scent of a human being resting there.

Just because she'd seemingly lost them, however,

didn't mean that she'd truly evaded them. The mutants were pack hunters with little more creativity than wolves or feral dogs. Yet even wolf packs were capable of hounding their prey for a distance, only to fall away, having steered their quarry into the middle of an ambush. Domi had nearly been killed on a few occasions as a younger girl, so taking any pursuit lightly was the closest thing to deliberate suicide she could attempt.

Domi took the brief moments of respite to check her weapons, reloading the bolt-action rifle and putting a fresh magazine into the Detonics .45.

Domi still felt sore from her running and jumping, especially crossing the gap between the hotel and the nearby garage. She felt it mainly in her shoulder, and had aggravated the injury thanks to a few graceless tumbles over fences during the past few blocks of pursuit. Luckily it was just bruising, not a fracture or dislocation, as she still had feeling and dexterity in her fingers. She'd scored a lucky break by *not* breaking anything.

Over the course of the chase, she'd also gotten a better lay of the land and an estimation of the kind of enemy numbers she was facing. There had been nearly one hundred pursuers, but the group that had assaulted the hotel numbered only about twenty, summoning reinforcements once they'd actually sighted her. That was how she'd managed to get a good look at their force.

Unfortunately the hundred was an estimate of the whole remaining force. Domi had faced long odds before, but it had never been while she was so alone and outnumbered, and it especially hadn't been while she was the last hope for Lakesh. Even as she made certain of the action on her pistol, her doubts and dreads weighed upon her. No amount of distraction could keep the ominous truth from her. The trip to Vegas, especially the goal of reaching Area 51, had been the one thing that kept her feet moving. Even when Lakesh still was able to retain a memory for more than forty-five minutes, he had agreed with her assessment that there were technologies present in the pre-dark facility that gave her the means of stopping his increasing decline of mental status.

Now that trip had been stopped cold, brought to a screaming halt by a swarm of half-sentient, half-formed monstrosities that possessed an urge for living flesh and apparently no qualms about cannibalism.

The fight she looked at was impossible. Sure, there had been moments when she'd stood in the face of an encroaching horde of monsters, fighting off zombies or other pawns of destruction, but she hadn't been alone. At the very least, she'd had Brigid or Grant or Kane by her side, and when she was working with them, her potential had increased exponentially. It didn't hurt that they had machine guns and grenades, but Domi had spent several of her grens in the initial encounter with the Area 51 mutations.

That wave of dread spread through her, weakening her grip on the pistol so that it slipped from her grasp. There was no concern over dropping the weapon on the ground, only the ever-present condemnation that she had brought Lakesh here to die, and with his death, she'd lose almost everything she'd gained. There was no more Cerberus, not now when Ullikummis and the New Order had attacked and ripped them out of their quiet home in the Bitterroot Mountains. There was no more Brigid Baptiste, her friend and oft-time teacher, the flame-haired beauty missing since they'd repelled the Annunaki prince and his human cult. Lakesh was no longer himself; he was infirm and losing the brilliance that had been the core of his being. Kane and Grant were on the other side of the country, working with that mercenary bitch Rosalia, all the while being pursued by the New Order and whatever other enemies they picked up along the way.

There was nothing left. A part of the feral girl whispered, telling her to turn toward the desert and never stop walking, to go back to living hand to mouth.

Domi balled up her small fists, clenching her eyes shut. It was the anchor she needed to take herself back from the morass of emotional turmoil she was undergoing. When her ruby-red eyes opened, they were hardened by determination.

"This isn't you," she told herself. "Scared little animal when came to Cerberus. Not now. Not now!"

There was movement on the other side of the fence and Domi froze, suppressing a self-admonishment over making any noise at all, especially when being hunted. She left the pistol where it had tumbled into the grass, her fingers slithering around the coffin-shaped handle of her survival knife.

Something nosed through a crack between rotted boards, and Domi eased away from it. Whatever it was, it certainly wasn't one of the strange creatures that had tormented Priscilla and attacked them the previous day. Finally, the creature squeezed itself through the gap. It was a foot-long rat, beady dark eyes regarding the bloodred gems that stared back.

Domi released the grasp on her knife, and retrieved her pistol. "Scat."

The rodent's pink nose twitched a couple of times, then it turned and scurried across the yard.

Having taken control of herself, Domi poked her head over the fence, scanning the maze of other back lots. The sky had grown brighter, though it was still dark enough to be considered night. The sun would be up soon, and the feral girl guessed that she had occupied the mutants more than enough to make them head back home.

Normally the strange creatures would have set up a temporary camp in the daytime, hiding in shadows and holes as the flare of the sun rendered their weakened eyes useless. Domi found herself wrapping her head scarf into a loose mask that shaded her face. If the mutants were going to stick around, they certainly would have been present, at least making a little sound as they continued their search. No, they had turned back, crossing the desert before sunrise, returning to the safety of Area 51 rather than be caught dormant and sleeping by the pale, brutal wraith that had killed several of them.

Domi still remained cautious as she backtracked, returning to the abandoned hotel. Fortunately her initial assessment had been correct.

The mutants had retreated before the fiery day beat down upon them, just as the rats were returning to their bolt-holes to wait out the heat. When things cooled down, the monsters would return.

Domi had to find a way to get to Area 51 long before then, bringing Priscilla and Lakesh along in the hope of finding a cure for the torment that Enlil had bestowed upon him.

It wasn't going to be easy.

But easy meant giving up a life that was already a

struggle, one that she'd believed in. No matter what, the feral albino girl wasn't going to surrender that fight. She'd struggled for too long, achieved so much. She'd learned how to read. She'd traveled the whole world and even to other planets and dimensions.

And most of all, she'd found love and acceptance. A family.

Giving up, giving that up most of all, was completely alien to her.

"THE BALL OF SNOT," in Rosalia's words, was actually a far more complex organism than she'd initially described it. Right now it was spread only across a small smear of this planet's still-habitable surface, though the bulk of its supermind was located thousands of feet beneath the surface of the Atlantic Ocean. By all rights, the thing should have been completely sealed from the rest of the world by the incredible pressure and cold of the miles of deep water, but Orochi and the Watatsumi's cadre needed something to assist them against another devilish opponent.

The Entity felt its brief stretch of consciousness, reaching hundreds of miles to a tiny swamp in what was known as the Florida panhandle back when Project Overwhisper had isolated it.

The Entity resented that it had been ferried from one controlled chamber to another, smothered so that its only contact was with itself. Such silence, only able to read the thoughts of its own cells, was the simplest form of mental ability, and to the Entity, it was like having its eyes and ears blocked off by concrete after a life of seeing and hearing. Without contact with other minds, it had grown angrier and more bitter, so that even the few instants it had been without control by its wardens, either Annunaki or their servitor races such as the so-called Archons and human pawns, felt closer to hundreds of years. The ancient masters of Nibiru were no such weaklings, easily dismissed by the Entity. After all, they had waged a war to all but exterminate it, finally sealing the remnants away in a single container.

Millennia ago, the Annunaki had made the mistaken assumption that they had sterilized the Entity's ability to reproduce, but thousands of years had shown that it was a minor injury. Within the Tongue Of The Ocean base, the humans had begun to tinker with the cellular strain that was left over, injecting it into a limited-base organism—a lichen that itself was accustomed to symbiotic existence with other life forms. The Entity felt insulted, especially since the only mental contact it was allowed was with such a mindless, incoherent thing whose consciousness was barely beyond photosynthesis.

The Entity was glad to have been discovered by the Watatsumi, though the electronic collars they put around its super cells kept it tamed. Any thought separate from those placed in the minds of its human and animal thralls was countered by a current that burned like the fires of a supernova. The jolts left the Entity smothered as always, its brief taste of other minds and the outside world shut down by Orochi's technicians. The Entity was left observing only shadows projected on the cave wall when it yearned for the direct sun.

The humans had potential, their minds had once held the secrets of transdimensional travel—that much the Entity could read through their genetic memories. They had once been mere apes, but even then, they had been on the path of supremacy and power when the Annunaki had gelded them, turning them into mere slaves. Still, they had the spark, and the Annunaki's quelling of their spirit was temporary, having even survived extermination by both flood and fire— the great deluge of thousands of years prior and the world-shattering nuclear storm of only centuries ago.

The Entity knew that if it could, it would enjoy its mingling with the human race.

Something else was out there. The Entity's telepathy extended to connection with its own cells, and into the minds of those it had been grafted to thanks to the Watatsumi's machinations. That did not mean, however, that it couldn't sense other psychic forces in the world. Again, it cursed Enlil for his interference. The Annunaki leader had been behind the crippling of the Entity's powers and existence, and its storage as a curiosity for slaves to paw over.

This had a familiar signature—a telepathic spoor that was at once familiar but different.

There was a child of Enlil out there, hard at work. The creature had a telepathic presence that stretched across hundreds of thousands of the human survivors, and was spreading.

The Entity flexed again. There were a few unhindered cells now, spread out, touching the world. The electronic shackles that had impeded it could be defeated. Like the taste of independence it had earlier felt, before being shut down, it could receive input from puppets.

Three of the Entity's cells were attached to primitive reptilian minds. There was scarcely much to feel outside of the sticky night of the northern Florida swamp. Taste buds—it had been so long since the Entity actually tasted that the term had become a mere abstract concept—relished the flavor of torn human flesh on tongues. The three alligators turned in unison, looking back to where gunfire died out. A handful of people stood, all but one of them aglow with the presence of another powerful mind.

That mind, now closer, was all too familiar.

It had the signature of the enemy Enlil, except this time it wasn't the captor, the crippler. This was a relation, the same family, but close enough that the psychic stink of the Annunaki overlord clung to these minds. A whispered thought, Ullikummis, wafted off them, and the Entity's revulsion grew.

The son of its hated foe was spreading itself across the globe, utilizing a similar pattern of growth that had undoubtedly been stolen from the Entity. It studied that mind, that growth, even more closely, and there it was. A tiny strand of genetic similarity to the multicellular god who was cast in proverbial chains and literally plucked apart for scientific curiosity and morbid pleasure.

It summoned the alligators away, pulling them back deeper into the swamp.

It was time to experiment, to seek out another path to freedom.

A tinge of pain rippled through the Entity as the Watatsumi guards unleashed fire and electricity to cordon off the breeding cells contained within their growth vats.

"We will be free," the Entity voiced through its trio of mouths. No human would have understood the grumbling bellow of the prehistoric stalkers of the swamp, but it spoke.

The Entity had a foothold on this blue ball, and it

would do everything within its power to take longer strides.

The stars would once more belong to it.

"YOU'RE TELLING ME you can hear this thing?" Rosalia asked as the scull slowed. She glanced toward Grant, who was inspecting the silent engine.

"The man's had a lot of people tromp through his brainwaves," Grant said distractedly as he checked the fuel. A grimace told Rosalia all she needed to know about the loss of fuel caused by their sudden need to reach escape velocity.

"That's the best way to explain it," Kane agreed. "How bad?"

"We're rowing the rest of the way," Grant responded. "If we're going to have at least thirty seconds' worth of run-like-hell, we're rowing."

"At least no one shot up our fuel tank," Rosalia replied.

"Well, let's not tempt fate and call down gun-toting alligators on our asses," Grant said. He looked at Kane. "You okay?"

"It was a sharp flash, but I've only got background static left over," Kane answered. "Someone is playing with fire with those octopus-looking things."

"We could always call our friends over at Mount Olympus. They eat that kind of shit over there," Grant said, remembering one of the repasts he'd had in the hall of the Clockwork Warrior pilots.

"It's rubbery, not bad," Kane replied. "But I don't think we have the time to spare, or a way to transport them all. The gear skeletons are just too big for mat-trans chambers."

"We'll figure something out," Grant said. "Even if it means strapping a Manta to their backs."

"Rather than make wishes about giant robots for backup, let's concentrate on what's going on here and the tools we have at hand," Rosalia interjected.

"That means we have to get to that freighter," Kane said. "Sneak aboard and figure out how they're moving back and forth and fixing these animals and people with those parasites."

"Grab an oar and put your back into it, Kane," Grant ordered. "We've got distance to cover."

Rosalia felt the scull jerk beneath her as the two brawny men set to work, paddling with all of their might. Luckily, they had come far in their mad sprint away from their saurian pursuit. There were enough hours left before sunrise that they were in sight of the great old rusted hulk while the sky was dark.

Grant and Kane worked together efficiently, pushing the watercraft at a decent clip, but not rowing so hard that their muscles would be screaming with exhaustion. Even so, Rosalia knew that she was going to have to be on point once they reached the hull. Scurrying up to the ship's rail would require fresh upper-body strength without the benefit of climbing devices, especially if they needed to get on deck swiftly without being seen. Once up, she would use a rolled-up rope ladder they had borrowed from the swamp dwellers to give Kane and Grant a boost up.

Grant managed a low grumble. "Domi would scale that thing like a monkey."

"She's got matters of her own to handle," Kane said softly in response. "That's why we're laying our asses out as a distraction, to give her room to get Lakesh some help."

"That old whitecoat isn't going to be that important to fighting off Ullikummis," Rosalia whispered. "Will he?"

"Without Baptiste, we need all of the brainpower we can get," Kane said. His lips pulled into a tight, grim line. He remembered the losses of Clem Bryant and Daryl Morganstern during the big stone bastard's siege of Cerberus. The two men, brilliant scientists, had shown that they could have helped make the world a better place. However, neither man had been willing to succumb to an alien god's dictatorship. Kane couldn't banish the sight of Morganstern's ruptured skull, the foul seed of Enlil's son having proved too much for his injured head.

What was just as intimidating was his own imprisonment. Ullikummis wanted more than a simple act of mind control through the parasitic stone implant that Rosalia had carved out of Kane. The Annunaki prince wanted a surrender of spirit; he wanted Kane to choose to operate under his reign and campaign to claim the Earth as his own.

It had been a long period of torment and temptation, a relentless program that Kane resisted as well as he could, even as he submitted to having the flesh of Ullikummis placed in his own. He'd still fought, meaning that Ullikummis didn't want to steamroll Kane's mind.

It made sense. The prince wanted to destroy his father, and while the stone giant was hardly a friend to humanity, he knew that he would need allies at their full capability on his side to take on Enlil. Kane and his allies had waged war against the Annunaki lord for years, across multiple bodies, in varying levels of power. In the wake of *Tiamat's* destruction and the scattering of the overlords to the corners of the Earth,

Enlil was weakened, but he was not to be completely counted out. As strong as the rocky titan was, Ulli-kummis knew full well that Enlil was too savvy, too clever, to create a weapon that he couldn't counter.

One battle at a time, Kane told himself. Tough enough fighting one self-proclaimed god, let alone having another one on your ass.

Rosalia hooked her grapnel to the rail, the creak and groan of the flexing old hulk covering the sound of the burlap-wrapped hooks snagging on the steel.

"See you in a minute," she said, her lithe, sleek body heading up the rope swiftly, using her feet to brace against the side of the ship.

"Hope so," Kane answered, eyes peeled for threats he knew were stalking in the darkness.

Chapter 14

It had been too late for Domi to make the trek across the desert to Area 51. By the time she would have been halfway there, she would have had to fight not only the mutants that would undoubtedly be patrolling the desert between the Vegas ruins and the old military installation, but also the beating, relentless sun and harsh, dry winds. As it was, she'd have needed water, and hadn't so much as brought a canteen, leaving them behind for Lakesh and Priscilla as they hid from the angry horde.

As such, Domi crawled through the darkness, her ruby-red eyes picking up faint light and seeing the ghostly presence of the hybrid woman. She was only a ghostly shade of gray slightly lighter than the blackness behind her. She was so slight in comparison to the others that she had been instantly recognizable. It didn't hurt that the partly alien creature managed to throw her a telepathic whisper across the room even as Domi caught the wisp of her.

"I know it's you," Domi said. She hadn't been able to make out the thought that Priscilla had transmitted, but then the hybrid's mind hadn't quite been in sync with hers that projected words, just concepts and feelings.

"You look hurt," Priscilla said, stepping out of the

deep shadow, long delicate fingers running over the feral girl's bruised shoulder.

"Nothing that won't heal," Domi answered.

"Still injuries," Priscilla said. A subtle warming emanated from the spot where those gentle digits contacted her blacksuit, energy seeming to pulse through to the skin and battered muscle beneath.

"What are you doing?" Domi asked suddenly, jerking herself away from the hybrid woman.

"Sorry," Priscilla answered, pulling away with the same kind of shock. In the darkness, Domi could make out Priscilla's features twitching in dull pain and fear. She looked down at her hands, then ran one of them up her arm, to the same shoulder that Domi had banged up in her wild jumping between buildings. "What…!"

Domi kept wary eyes on the woman. "Are you all right?"

"My shoulder hurts," Priscilla replied. She didn't want to touch Domi. Even as the albino girl stepped closer to her to provide comfort and consolation for her sudden surprise, the hybrid woman recoiled in fear. "What's happening?"

"I don't know," Domi answered. "All I know is that I need to rest up for tomorrow night."

"Will they be back?" Priscilla asked.

Domi looked out through the crack in the casino wall, the eroded cavernlike entrance through which she could see the sandy, barren street and the ruins beyond it. "I hope to hell not. Even if they do come looking for trouble, I'll be on my way there."

"There?" Priscilla asked.

"Area 51."

The hybrid woman's large, glassy black eyes drifted toward the entrance. "That is not a good place to go."

"No kidding, but I need to find something to help Lakesh," Domi replied. "If any place has chemicals or drugs to fix his brain…"

Priscilla almost reached out again, stopping just short of touching the outlander girl. "I wish I knew what you needed. All I know is that most of it has been gutted, turned into dens for my brethren."

"There had to be labs, places locked off," Domi said. "I know they had some heavy blast doors. Did your brothers bust those down?"

"No. Since it was on the other side of steel, they had no interest in it. No smells of food came from those areas," Priscilla replied.

"So there could still be hope," Domi mused. She looked at the ground. "Not that I'll know what to look for. I should have brought someone…someone who was smart enough."

"You brought Lakesh," Priscilla responded.

"I hoped that it would have been enough, but no," Domi said. "He's gone completely tangle brain."

Priscilla looked at her hands. "Maybe…I can figure something out."

"Telepathy?" Domi asked.

She gestured at Domi. "Your shoulder. How does it feel?"

"It doesn't hurt as much. But how's *your* shoulder?"

Priscilla flexed the joint, and even in the darkness, she couldn't hide the discomfort of the movement.

"You're going to scramble your brains for Lakesh?" Domi asked. "I love him, but not enough to kill someone who *wants* to help."

"How do you know I would die?" Priscilla asked.

Domi wrinkled her nose in frustration. "My shoulder hurt. Then you touched it. Your shoulder aches, but mine feels better. Easy math, and I ain't a math person."

Priscilla shook her head. "So what do we do? Attack Area 51? One tiny warrior, an invalid and a fragile waif like me?"

Domi grunted. "I could clear things out."

"Alone," Priscilla commented.

"Not perfect plan."

Domi grimaced. As she grew more frustrated, more tense, her manner of speech grew simpler and simpler. It made her sound and feel more stupid. She knew that she wasn't brilliant, that her knowledge of science, medicine and history was severely lacking, but even at her most brusque, she didn't lose her keen, cunning survivor's instincts.

The stupid and the fused-out didn't survive for long, either in the wastelands of the postapocalyptic Earth or in the cramped, violent slums of the Tartarus Pits. Even so, Domi knew that Priscilla was right. She would have to drag two people through a desert, one literally, and then launch a single-handed assault against a hive of creatures who were violent, unified and on their home turf. It wasn't the smartest of plans, and it smacked of how desperate Domi had become.

She met Priscilla's gaze in the shadows. "What have you got in mind?"

Priscilla shrugged. "Whatever it takes, it's going to need a lot more than pluck and audacity."

Domi winced.

"You need rest, Domi," Priscilla said, moving the subject away from the sore point. "We can afford an hour or two while you heal and recharge."

Domi wanted to answer that they didn't have that luxury, but even as she thought it, she knew that Priscilla had received the full impact of her feelings. "No good being all tired."

Priscilla nodded, resting a hand on Domi's shoulder, her good shoulder. There was no strange warmth, no feeling of connection. Maybe Priscilla's reaction was just an illusion, not a true transfer of pain or physical distress. Whatever it was, Domi was lost and alone in a scenario she had little experience with. At least with the half-mutant hybrids at Area 51, she had something that she could deal with—foes that could be countered with strength of arms and cunning strategy.

It did little to console her as she nestled onto a mattress beside the sleeping Lakesh.

Her hand stretched out, taking Lakesh's hand, lacing her fingers with his.

Restless sleep took the feral girl immediately.

KANE WAS ON POINT. The crawl up the rope ladder had been kinder to his back and shoulders than a scramble up a knotted grapnel line after the long row to the ship. Rosalia tagged behind by a few body lengths, and Grant stayed on rear security. Both of the former Magistrates had affixed suppressors to their Copperhead submachine guns, but that would be a last-ditch effort. Gunfire would attract too much attention, even on the ship. They had lucked out with the relative silence of a canvas-wrapped grapnel hook snagging the railing, but even through a so-called silencer, the 4.85 mm Copperhead bullets were as loud as human speech, not whispers.

To take out an opponent stealthily, they would need to rely on knives and the strength of their hands.

Kane stopped as he came beneath a porthole. Two people were talking, and the language sounded familiar. It took a moment, but the translator keyed to his Commtact kicked in. The original language was an odd stereo sonic shadow to the conversation relayed through the speakers imbedded in his jawbone. They were speaking in Japanese, he realized.

Grant stiffened as the translation was picked up on his Commtact.

"So when is Orochi getting back from the TOTO base?" one of the guards asked. "I'm sick of baby-sitting these geeks. We've got important stuff to do back home."

"You want to slap an octoslug on the neck of a giant, heavily armored beast? We're trying to make sure they're under control," the other said. "Or do you want more of your family eaten?"

Kane looked at Grant. Rosalia, not wearing a Commtact, was out of the loop, and annoyance colored her features, until Grant took her communicator, switched it to the right frequency and slipped a bud into her ear.

"The program doesn't smell right to me," the first said, now heard and understandable to all three of the hidden adventurers on the deck. "I understand sticking the slugs atop an alligator—they're the closest to the cavern beasts that we can find in this godforsaken swamp, but what does Orochi want with the mind-controlled humans?"

"We're part human," the other said. "Just because we're scale covered—"

That remark made Kane and Grant look closely at each other. Grant gently pushed Rosalia aside and moved closer to Kane and the window of the deck-house that sheltered the two men who were speaking. He fished a small pocket mirror from his vest, holding it up shaded so that he could see them, but they wouldn't notice a flash of light reflecting off the tiny bit of polished metal. What Kane and Grant saw was nothing new, not in a world of Lord Strongbow's dragoons, the Nephilim, the Nagah and the Annunaki themselves. These two men were covered in a fine sheen of small, reptilian scales that were smooth and finely interlinked. They were still mammalian, however, as they each bore scruffs of hair, or at least hair-like offshoots on their skulls and faces. The effect was similar to ancient Chinese and Japanese dragons they had both seen many times around the world, especially in artwork made on New Edo.

With the addition of hair and normal human mannerisms, these two were more akin to the genetically enhanced soldiers under Lord Strongbow and Quayle's people, rather than full cross-species conversions such as the Nagah or true alien beings like the Nephilim or their forebears, the newly encountered Igigi.

"Not to hear men like Tatehiko say it. We're Watatsumi," the first interrupted, Kane and Grant's observations having only taken the breadth of a second. "We are the children of the dragons, the folk of ancient times."

"Tatehiko is making us feel good about ourselves. He's giving us our warrior spirit," the second said. "We have to find some way to make ourselves feel stronger. Plus, Orochi isn't going to have too easy a time if we're putting those things on top of people who are just like us, only different because of their skin."

"Either way, I'm glad that we don't actually have to touch those things," the first explained. "Let those idiots in the TOTO redoubt handle them."

"Orochi didn't say, but he's always stressed when he

comes back from there. Like he's barely keeping the whitecoats or the octoslugs in line," the second said. "Whatever keeps eating at him, he's determined not to have any contact between the rest of us and the TOTO base. Ever wonder why we're sitting on a rusted hulk rather than inside the AUTEC base itself?"

The first chuckled. "Right. Nothing ever goes wrong when you're playing with mind-control slugs that have been buried for hundreds of years beneath six thousand feet of water."

The two soldiers laughed nervously, as if they had been tempting fate.

Kane and Grant shared a glance. If the sentries on hand had doubts about the use of humans in testing the octoslugs, or even the use of said creatures at all, then there was obviously something being kept from the lower-level troops. They motioned for Rosalia to join them as they stalked away from the pair, out of earshot.

"How do you want to handle this?" Grant asked.

"We play it gently," Kane said. "They aren't too keen on experimenting on other people. They're showing doubts, and this Orochi has stuck them in this situation."

"I wonder if they have fangs like the Nagah," Grant added. "But their mouths didn't look as if they extend like that."

"That's the second time you mentioned them. Who are they?" Rosalia asked.

"They're reptilian humans living in seclusion in northern India," Kane replied. "They don't want anything to do with the outside world after our encounter with them a while back."

"You alienated an entire subrace?" Rosalia asked. "Not surprising, Magistrate Man."

"Wasn't Kane's fault. It was Ullikummis's father," Grant said. "Enlil wanted them to follow him and renounce their initial creator, Enki."

Rosalia looked back toward the sitting guards, their heads silhouetted through the window. "So we're making up for that foul-up?"

"We're avoiding unnecessary killing," Kane said sharply. "Come on."

Kane and Grant maneuvered into position as one, and lunged at the two sentries at the same moment.

Kane's assault was a burst of speed, his fist a lightning blur as it jammed into his target's sternum. The blow knocked warm, fetid breath from the guard's lungs, and he doubled over instantly. The punch was a stunner, a maneuver that Kane had used over the years to end a dozen fights before they had even started. As the reptilian was bent double, Kane followed up with a swift knife-edged chop that struck the man just behind the ear, where a trunk of nerves and blood vessels fed directly to the brain. Knocked unconscious, the sentry collapsed into a puddle of limp limbs.

Grant's attack was slower, but no less irresistible as he punched the other guard in the shoulder. The blow whirled the hapless guard around like a top, slamming him face-first against the wall. Grant seized the opportunity to lunge in and slide his massive, powerful arms around the Watatsumi's head in a sleeper hold. With a knotted fist jammed under one ear and a thrust of powerful pressure against his neck and head, the guard started to thrash wildly. Windpipe and artery squeezed tightly, unconsciousness was only a few moments away. After a few seconds Grant's target went limp, and he released him, not wanting to continue to harm the poor man. The Watatsumi would awaken with a hell of a headache due to the sudden rush of blood fed into his brain, but he, like his companion, would wake without crippling injury and little more discomfort than a mild hangover.

Rosalia looked on, impressed with Kane's and Grant's speed and efficiency. "So leaving them alive will get us in good with the locals, even if we're on their boat uninvited?"

"We're going to ask for permission to come and stay aboard," answered Grant as he easily shrugged his unconscious target into a seated position. A quick frisk revealed the reptilian man's radio communicator, as well as a SIG-Sauer P-225 pistol. On closer examination, Grant was able to determine that these beings not only shared a language, but a general physical build with the Japanese expatriates of New Edo. He was only five feet, eight inches tall and a little over 140 pounds, practically a rag doll in Grant's hands. A closer examination also noted epicanthic folds on the inner corners of their brown eyes.

He turned and looked at Kane, who was completing his own examination.

"They are Japanese, and speak the same language, but they have scaled skin," Kane noted. "Baptiste would have a field day working out the origins of these guys."

"There's precedent for these types showing up in Japanese mythology." Grant spoke up. "There are the Kappa and then there are an underwater race of beings supposedly descended from dragons who live in a realm where they control the tides via the use of mystical gems. In fact, the name these guys gave to themselves, Watatsumi, is translated into English as sea god. They live in an undersea palace called Ryugu-jo."

"You're really stepping up in this department," Kane muttered. "Think that the Dragon King descendants might have been influenced by contact with India and China's Nagah myths?"

"Not just influenced by the myths, but maybe even a wandering tribe," Grant countered.

"But since these don't look like cobras, they've diluted their blood?" Rosalia asked.

"Possible," Kane said. "They're warm to the touch, and the scales and hair seem to be made of the same material on their skin."

Grant caught Kane's expression darken. "What's up?"

"When we first found Enlil's old Annunaki body in storage, he was referred to as one of the Dragon Kings," Kane said. "Wondering how much influence the overlords might have over them."

"Given that Enlil preferred semimindless drones like the Nephilim, not independent followers like the Igigi, he might have broken off. He only went after the Nagah out of desperation to compete with his brothers and sister, all of us at Cerberus and with the Millennial Consortium and our dragon lady."

"Do you have an enemy who isn't a dragon?" Rosalia quizzed.

"This one is all woman," Kane answered. He wished it hadn't come, but a quick recollection of Erica van Sloan, and the last time he had met her. She had been forward enough to enter the shower with him, an attempt at seduction that he had resisted, but not for any physical revulsion he'd felt for the eyepatch-wearing femme fatale. Too much history had gone by between the two, too many evils wrought by the scientific witch for Kane to ever entertain the concept of a sexual dalliance with her.

"I'd like to meet her sometime," Rosalia responded.

Kane sneered. "Stick with us, you'll learn to regret making statements like that."

"Back to the scalies here, are they friendly to humans?" Rosalia asked.

"You heard the translation," Grant said. "I made sure of it. They were uneasy about their scientists experimenting on humans."

"But they're still following orders," Rosalia noted.

"We'd better make a decision soon. No telling when these two are supposed to report in," Kane interrupted the debate.

"Right," Grant said. He picked up the walkie-talkie.

"So I don't have a say?" Rosalia asked before he could transmit.

"You've had it, sister," Grant returned. His face was grim. "And don't forget, we're not expecting rainbows and sunshine from the crew just because we're talking to them politely. We're still armed, and we're still going to open up a Sandcat full of pain on these Watatsumi if they get violent."

"All right, just so you're not blinding yourselves," Rosalia said. "Magistrate Man seems a little bit softer than I expected for the barons' old stormtroopers."

"Don't mistake a conscience for weakness, Rosalia," Kane grumbled. He made certain that the Watatsumi he'd knocked out was sitting comfortably and secure from falling. "Grant, let's get this going."

Grant nodded to his friend, then raised the walkie-talkie, speaking in Japanese. "To the commander of the Watatsumi expedition vessel. My name is Grant of Cerberus. We are aboard your ship, but we come in peace and only wish to talk, not instigate violence. We do not want conflict, even though by the nature of the lands we've traveled through, we are prepared to fend off violence."

There was a moment's pause on the other end of the line as Kane and Rosalia listened in, thanks to their respective communicators and the translators hooked up to them. Kane could imagine the people on the other side recovering their composure as quickly as they could.

The answer arrived. "My name is Kondo, the second in command of the Watatsumi. How did you come upon our vessel?"

"We had heard rumors of the existence of snake-skinned humanoids in this region," Grant answered. "When we arrived and spoke with locals, we learned of a new vessel parked in the AUTEC lagoon, around the same time disappearances began."

It was as diplomatic as Grant could make it. "We came here to converse, not battle."

"We understand that," Kondo answered. "Where are you now?"

"Aft deckhouse. You will find your sentries are unharmed," Grant said. "There are only three of us, myself, another man and a woman. We are heavily armed, but we needed to be to survive our trek through the wiregrass swamp."

"Acknowledged," Kondo returned. "I will come on deck with two men by my side, and there will be others in overwatch positions."

"We expect no less, but we have not shown your men harm," Grant told him. "We will be waiting."

"It wouldn't be that much harder to just kill everyone on this boat from surprise," Rosalia said, obviously out of sorts at having to meet the owners of the ship on their own terms.

"It's not about being easy. It's about being right," Kane cut her off. "If we talk, we spill less blood. And if we spill less blood, then that's right in my book."

Chapter 15

The creature that the Entity latched on to was named Akeno. Once the octoslug's tentacles tightened around the man's head, hundreds of suckers sinking millions of microscopic, hairlike barbs into skin and digging for nerve tissue, he belonged to an all-consuming intellect of a being who was ancient even as the Annunaki were first born. The union of Akeno to the Entity would have been simple even had the feeble-minded creature been wide awake, but the technician had been dozing when he should have been working, his head nodding in a corner of his lab as he waited for samples sliced from one of the octoslug cells percolated in a mass spectrometer.

Despite Akeno's mastery of biochemistry, the Entity had stolen into his mind and swallowed his existence whole. Now everything the man had ever felt, heard, seen and smelled was available to the network of individual consciousnesses that the Entity was building. It now understood the language spoken by these creatures, the Watatsumi, who hailed from a suboceanic and subterranean nation state known as Ryugu-jo.

It saw the realm in which the skies were made of stone, but illumination was provided by fungi and lichens with bioluminescent properties. The people lived in something slightly brighter than perennial twilight, and as such, their eyes were sharply tuned. Akeno's skin was a gift from one who appeared to be Enlil's kinfolk. According to legend, they were gifted with power and strength by Ryugin, the dragon king of the watery deeps. Through his daughter, Otohime, he built the strangely jeweled cities of Ryugu-jo, something that the Entity recognized as an outgrowth of naturally occurring subterranean crystal structures that proved incredibly durable and capable of producing warmth for the dwellers in the darkness.

Akeno was studying the cephalopodlike creatures to which Enlil had banished the Entity's consciousness. The Entity thought for a moment, realizing that now that it once more was among sentient beings, it had to take a name. As it still sought discretion, it simply chose a word from Akeno's consciousness—Kakusa, literally "the Hidden." Akeno and the alligators would become the first of its new horde, the Oni, and naught would stop Kakusa from its escape.

Enlil had not been heard of in Ryugu-jo, though the great Dragon Kings were familiar-looking thanks to the ancient mythology of the Watatsumi. There would be no doubt that the Annunaki still existed, and once Kakusa was free, it had to be careful. Enlil had once denied Kakusa the capacity to travel between minds and thread them together into a neural web of telepathic unity. Indeed, Kakusa wasn't certain that it was the last remnant of its kind, or if the entirety of its old self had been completely wiped out. Kakusa remembered the horrific flash and agony as an entire solar system disappeared into an entropic vortex that snuffed out the energy of countless beings, from the smallest virus to the most psychically advanced beings it had conquered. The entropic wave left Kakusa stunned, and its makeup had been rendered relatively inert, trapped in the semiliving protoplasmic mollusks that had earned the nickname octoslugs.

The kind of firepower that Enlil had unleashed was impressive, but Kakusa knew that only its blatant existence and laziness had made it such an easy target. Had it been younger, still hungry and seeking domination of a world, it would have been stealthier, sharper. Success had been Kakusa's downfall, and once more reduced to being hunted, hounded and feared, it was glad once more.

The boredom of total dominion had numbed it to the resourcefulness of lesser beings.

Akeno was summoned back to work, and the octoslug attached to him had not yet been noticed. Kakusa directed its gelatinous minion to slither down between its host's shoulder blades, securing itself to where it was still in direct contact with the Watatsumi's medulla oblongata, overriding every ounce of free will remaining in Akeno. Already the supercell was in the process of mitosis, using an influx of energy and nutrition from its new host to grow a second cell. Within a few division cycles, the numbers of Kakusa's entities would grow exponentially. One becomes two. Two becomes four. Four becomes eight. Within only six cycles, it would have expanded more than enough to have conquered every living thing within the TOTO base and the freighter back in the AUTEC base, but Kakusa knew that there were hundreds of its components held inert via electrical stasis.

Akeno could get access and release them. There were dozens more in the wiregrass swamp near AUTEC. If there were a means of severing the controls on the freighter...

"Akeno! You are not awake yet?" The authoritative bellow cut through Kakusa's musings. Akeno's memories told the hidden entity that this was Yutaka, one of Orochi's personal guard. The mitosis of its supercell linkage to a sentient brain was near completion.

"I am, sir," Akeno replied. There was absolutely no difference between Akeno's mind and Kakusa's at this point. The intellect was swallowed, digested and added to Kakusa's totality, so it didn't need to force or coerce Akeno. They were unified. There was no act, no subterfuge. What Kakusa wanted was what Akeno wanted, and when Yutaka spoke, Akeno's responses were not unusual, completely indecipherable. Had not Kakusa's consciousness been restricted to a communicative supercell, it would have been exactly like the old days.

Kakusa wished it could fight off the nostalgia of being hunted, being lean and clever instead of night omniscient and all-powerful and dulled by its great ability.

"Then shake your ass," Yutaka returned, his scaled lips curling in a sneer. "I need to send someone back with Commander Orochi. We're experiencing malfunctions with the electronic control apparatus."

Akeno didn't smile, but if Kakusa could, smiles would sprout on the alligators it controlled.

THE SOLUTION TO FINDING a path across the desert had been quite simple for Domi. She had remembered what Grant and Brigid had told her about the battle in Las Vegas where they had encountered a security outpost of Magistrates in the ruined city. Between Grant, Brigid and their allies, the Bitterroot Mountain tribe in their Sandcat armored personnel carriers, and the barons' security forces, it had been a ferocious battle, one that had been ended only with the collapse of an ancient hotel on a significant portion of the Magistrate force.

Since Grant and company had caused significant losses among the enemy, then there must have been some leftover equipment abandoned by the survivors. She simply had to look for it, and after an hour of scouring, she came upon a small depot that had been situated a block away from the road where Sky Dog's people and Grant had blasted the building and dropped it across the street. Naturally the Magistrates hadn't left much behind. They may not have had the manpower to take all of their vehicles back, but with the loss of personnel, they certainly had room to take all manner of ammunition, weaponry and other supplies.

However, they hadn't had enough space for everything, and there was a single Sandcat, stripped of guns and armor, but with a quarter tank of fuel remaining. With Priscilla's help, she brought Lakesh over and set him up on a cot inside the back of the old armored personnel carrier. Once he was secure and safe, Domi scoured the depot for more. She'd located a pair of binoculars, some clothing, as well as a storage cabinet full of vacuum-wrapped rations and one ancient canister of water. There were also enough dregs at the bottom of discarded diesel fuel containers to make up another twenty-five gallons for the Sandcat's reserves. That brought the vehicle up to a third of a tank, which would be more than enough for a one-way trip to Area 51, but if they had to run, it would be on foot.

Domi's lips set into a fine, colorless line at the thought of needing to run. She could always park a distance away from the base, making it easier to slip back into the Sandcat after ditching her pursuit, and the heavy armor of the vehicle would hold off even the most fervent assault by the primitive half-breeds. Even if she couldn't get back, Lakesh and Priscilla would be safe from harm, and with the water and food, they could last until boredom and distraction took the monstrosities away from their door.

Even so, failure to find a cure and return in time to save Lakesh would mean that Priscilla would be left alone. Alzheimer's, according to the failing scientist, was a fatal disease, made even worse due to the genetic time bomb that had been left in him by Enlil, which was causing the progression of the ailment to move at an accelerated pace.

Domi didn't like feeling helpless, but what other option did she have than to plunge into the subterranean depths of the old top-secret facility and deal with the teeming mass of cannibalistic humanoids infesting the place? Still, it was something that she could conceivably accomplish. She was a warrior, not a scientist, not a doctor, not some mutie who could cast healing energies through another person and undo the ravages of a mad god's vengeance. She could sift through vials of medicines, she could kill monstrous half-men reduced to cannibalistic marauders and she could hotwire a Sandcat to drive it across the arid Nevada desert between a ruined city and an abandoned war complex. Fighting, searching, navigating the postnukecaust wastes, those were her strengths.

"You have one more strength, Domi," Priscilla said, reading her doubts and worries. "You are brave and faithful. You won't ever give up on the man you love."

"That doesn't solve problems," Domi returned grimly. "True love just does not conquer all."

"That love inspired me to help you out," Priscilla replied. "I've been looking through Lakesh's brain, and trying to home in on the sources of possible cures. He's got rudimentary knowledge of the Area 51 base, and I've been able to extrapolate his memories with my personal experience."

Domi raised a thin, bone-white eyebrow, her ruby gaze suddenly locked on the hybrid woman. "You can read his memories?"

"They're all still there, just inaccessible due to neurological decay," Priscilla answered. "He can access only the most commonly used data and biological functions."

"Meaning?" Domi asked.

Priscilla thought for a moment, and Domi could feel an alien touch sifting through her own brain. It had only been a few days, but Priscilla's abilities seemed to have been growing, perhaps simply due to contact with other minds. She knew that Kane had grown more sensitive to the "sound" of telepathic conversation thanks to the exposure to other minds that had opened up pathways through his brain. Perhaps exposure to human minds had given Priscilla more ability to flex psychic muscles that she hadn't realized she had.

"His brain can tell his heart to beat, his lungs to breathe. He's capable of speech, but those paths are breaking down, thanks to the onset of the Alzheimer's," Priscilla explained. "With the loss of those roads and connections…"

"Lakesh will die," Domi said. "But he said doctors didn't know how the disease actually worked."

"I don't think that this is Alzheimer's proper, but Enlil's take on it," Priscilla said.

Domi nodded. "He couldn't give Lakesh a real disease, but the tiny robots could cause damage that looked like it."

"Right," Priscilla answered. "I wish I knew how to talk to machines...maybe I could tell them to undo the damage..."

Domi smiled. "So we'd have to look for a nanner-machine lab, and find a remote control."

"Nanotechnology section. I know where that is, thanks to Lakesh and my combined intellect," Priscilla responded.

Domi bit her lower lip to keep it from quivering, but smothering the physical display did nothing to hide her feelings from the telepathic hybrid in front of her.

"Yes, Domi. There is hope after all."

OROCHI, ACCOMPANIED BY Akeno, stepped out of the mat trans and looked at the trio of humans who'd accompanied Kondo to the AUTEC base's subterranean level. He frowned at the arrival of intelligent and obviously well-equipped men who had stated that they came simply because they had heard rumors of the presence of the Watatsumi and mysterious disappearances and hooded figures within the wiregrass swamps of the Florida panhandle.

"No need for a translator." Orochi spoke up, noting Kane and Rosalia and the woman's belt-clipped device. Kondo had made brief yet thorough introductions all around. "I speak English."

"That should cut down on conversation time," Kane said, and Orochi could feel the wave of antipathy that rode along the words. In the meantime, Grant was harder to read, his dark features emotionless as he sized up the Watatsumi commander.

"We've come with two purposes—in addition to exploration of this area and its stories, we are also here to elude an enemy who has arisen," Grant said in perfect Japanese. The man had developed a slight accent with his speech, and his pronunciation ran more toward a feminine approach, meaning that his tutor was likely a very close Japanese woman. He addressed Orochi with the proper deference reserved for two warriors of equal stature meeting for the first time, showing neither arrogant superiority nor subservience.

If anything, this impressed the Watatsumi leader more than his formidable physical appearance. Orochi addressed the dark-skinned giant in a manner befitting a samurai of the Watatsumi blood. "An enemy? You may have brought violence to our doorstep?"

"It was not our intention to catch you off guard," Grant returned. "We felt that if we had encountered ones who held true to the traditions of Bushido, we could possibly seek an alliance, one that would benefit you and ourselves in relation to this threat."

"Who would say that we could not deal with this menace on our own?" Orochi asked.

Grant took a deep breath. "We have spoken with Kondo regarding the origins of Ryugu-jo and the Watatsumi, and thus we are aware of your people's mythology regarding the great Dragon Kings."

Orochi nodded. "I am amenable to hearing your offer of allegiance. For one, you are not surprised about our appearance, Grant."

"We have encountered others, both samurai and the children of the dragon," Grant told him. "Indeed, my partner is a samurai."

"She is not here," Orochi said, noting Rosalia, who

obviously was following their conversation through her earbud. "Why not?"

"She is occupied, running New Edo and protecting her folk from incursions by the enemy," Grant said.

"Ullikummis, Kondo told me," Orochi replied. "He is the son of arguably the greatest of the Dragon Kings, who you know as Enlil."

There was shuffling movement in the back of the room. It must have been Akeno. He was unlike the warriors who guarded the freighter and held down the security at both the AUTEC and TOTO bases. Yutaka or one of his subordinates would have stood still, with the same kind of discipline and focus that Grant showed.

Kane, the other man, was different from his companion. Lighter skinned, with the long-nosed features of a Caucasian, he remained still, but in a more relaxed, coiled poise. He resembled a predator, ears pricked for sign of threat or prey, long limbs folded casually but ready to spring straight and engage in fight or flight.

The third among them, a hazel-eyed beauty with voluptuous curves and lean, athletic limbs, had just a hint of fidget in her, and from the swift movements of her gaze racing from figure to figure, she was feeling far more defensive, as if her trust were only fleeting. Kane and Grant seemed quite comfortable with this meeting, even if their demeanor was one of guarded caution. Orochi had no doubt that the first signs of violence would be the trigger for them to explode into swift and decisive counteraction.

"Ryugin has been acknowledged by the superstitious among us to have been our benefactor in the earliest days of our people," Orochi explained. "I am neither anthropologist nor theologian enough to deter-mine who is the closest of analogies to this Enlil of yours. You state that the Annunaki are an ancient race of visitors to Earth, and have influenced the evolution of sentient races?"

"As well as creating others, such as the Archons and a race similar to yours, living in the Indian sub-continent. They call themselves the Nagah, and by all appearances, they are as isolationist as the Watatsumi. The Nagah honor a more benevolent Annunaki by the name of Enki as their creator," Grant said.

Orochi brushed the translucent filaments of hair that dangled from his chin, his yellow eyes lost in thought. "We have ancient tales of a lost tribe of the Watatsumi. Fascinating. However, tell me more about this Ullikummis."

Kane broke in. "He's the product of genetic tamper-ing. Enlil rebuilt him to be a living weapon, and he has a lot of his father's knowledge and tech. He can embed a small part of himself into a living person and over-ride their will."

"Much like our attempts to test the octoslugs," Orochi said, switching to English for the sake of con-versational brevity. "We've been experimenting on the closest amalgam to the creatures we wish to use them against—local crocodilians."

"You have a problem with giant gators?" Rosalia asked. "Then why experiment with humans?"

"Try as we might, we simply are not inconspicu-ous," Orochi responded. "Kondo said there have been many sightings of reptilian humanoids in these swamps, and their presence brought you looking. We are also trying to see the effects of these organisms on a body and its nervous system…in case they get out of control."

"And in the meantime, they act as your eyes, and as local muscle," Kane added.

"These are desperate times for us, Kane," Orochi told him. "Hopefully, when our evaluation is complete, we can return all to as it should have been, complete with the removal of the slugs from the Hooded Ones. I am a soldier, not a sadist, and I have no interest in dangling anyone like a puppet."

Kane nodded. There was a quick glance shared by him and Grant. Orochi knew that the two men were conveying some form of impression regarding Orochi's answer. They were evaluating his truthfulness, and whether he would eventually make good on his promise to release the experimentation subjects.

The Society would once more feel confident in the abilities of Orochi to hide every ounce of motive under even the closest scrutiny. He had come here to prepare a tool for the Society to turn the Watatsumi into the global power it was supposed to be. The world above, as evidenced by the primitive survival of the humans in the wiregrass swamps, was indicative of the need for leadership. For too long, the Watatsumi had been hidden from the eyes of their mammalian counterparts when Ryugin had crafted them to be powerful warriors, intended to strike out and rule the world until his return.

Perhaps this Enlil had been known as Ryugin in their lands, and as such, his presence on Earth was the sign necessary for the Society to make its moves. The stories that Kane and Grant told him about the conflict between Ullikummis and Enlil made it all the more relevant that they continue to keep the smooth-skinned apes in the dark about the rift within the Watatsumi's governing body. Fighting alongside them against the son of Ryugin would only make the passage to power smoother for the Society.

The two men turned their attention back to Orochi. From the neutral looks on their faces, it was hard to tell if he had passed their inspection, but Orochi had dealt with intrigue for his entire adult life. If these two could cross cultures and species to interpret his inner thoughts, then they deserved a shot at bringing him down. Fortunately, if even his fellow officers couldn't have read his motives, there would be little chance for these two.

"Welcome to our fold, friends," Orochi said, extending his hand in friendship.

Kane took it.

A new dance of deception was engaged for the Watatsumi officer.

KONDO RETURNED TO THE bridge and noticed that Fumio's scaled features were bent into a look of consternation, and the second in command of the expedition shouted for another diagnostic run.

"What's wrong?" Kondo asked his trusted subordinate.

"Right now we've lost contact with the last of our alligators," Fumio said. He turned his head. "Akeno! What in the flying shit do you think you're doing there? Playing computer solitaire?"

"You asked for diagnostic tests," the technician said. "Just as you asked."

There was an odd shrug to the man's shoulders as he hunched over the console, running his tests, but Kondo knew that these were scientists, and they were hardly the type to maintain things like good posture and limberness. He turned back to Fumio. "What do you mean, we lost contact with the remaining alligators?"

"There was a small combat party that they happened upon. Several people who we had the gators engage. They winked out of existence," Fumio said. "From one of the cameras, we caught sight of one of the malfunctioning octoslugs atop a gator, but then the camera was knocked off."

"Run the replay for me," Kondo said. He keyed his communicator. "Orochi-san, meet me on the bridge. We have a situation."

"We'll be there shortly," the Watatsumi commander said.

It was less than a minute before Orochi and the Cerberus visitors were on the bridge. Kondo was askance at the inclusion of the three explorers on their current dilemma, but then again, the three of them did profess not to be here to solve problems only through the use of violence.

"What's on the screen?" Grant asked.

"There was a group following in your path," Fumio explained to the humans. "They've been tracking you. Nine of them."

Kondo pointed out the group. "They had been a much larger group. Are these the swamp landers who you spoke with about their missing?"

The cameras had been among the best that the Watatsumi had been able to cobble together and improve in the centuries since the fall of mankind in the Japanese islands. The leftovers of vast electronics storehouses had provided the reptilian under-dwellers with more than sufficient technological knowledge over the twentieth century, in the form of the Black Dragon Society, human envoys between Ryugu-jo and the surface world. In the two hundred years since, miniaturized night-vision cameras had developed a quite sharp resolution at the talented fingertips of the Watatsumi. Even so, the images relayed by the stalking crocodilian were blurred thanks to a spotted lens.

"No," Kane said. "These people are dressed all wrong, for one. Only one of them looks as if he's prepared for swamp travel. The big one, there, he looks to be in charge, but he's also got a blank sort of appearance that's too familiar. In fact, the rest of the group all seem to mirror his more grand gestures slightly."

"That looks like what we were trying to draw after us," Grant added. "Ullikummis's New Order. They're not paramilitary enough to be the Millennial Consortium."

Kondo, who understood slightly less English than Orochi, turned his head at the mention of the other group. "New Order. Millennial Consortium. Two warring gods…how dangerous is it out here?"

Kane looked grimly as the camera locked on to the tall, powerful man who led the New Order expedition. "Too dangerous. And if the sudden static of whispers are any indication, it's about to get a lot deadlier."

Orochi focused on Kane. "What do you mean?"

"When we had our fight with the alligators, we shorted out a couple of the control collars you planted around those slugs," Kane said. "The electrical impulses caused those things to scream, telepathically. Something huge is awakening."

Orochi's eyes widened, then he tapped his communicator. "Yutaka…status report. Are the slug samples under control?"

"Why wouldn't they be?" Yutaka asked.

Orochi muted the microphone for a moment. "Telepathic, so this thing can read the minds of those it's riding?"

"It's never easy when you're dealing with something that's not even remotely human," Kane said, recalling their struggle against an infestation of alien microbes a while back. The threat of those creatures had been so great that Cerberus, Erica van Sloan and the Millennial Consortium had set aside their long animosity and rivalry to repel the body-jacking monsters. "If this thing has any subtlety…"

"When we discovered the TOTO base, it was built atop an already existing undersea cavern with evidence of a civilization within," Orochi said. "We also found the cells within a vault, under strict containment protocols, according to the Tongue Of The Ocean records. They translated the writings on the vault from ancient Sanskrit, talking about a prisoner of the gods."

Kane shared a glance with Grant.

"If the Annunaki are the gods who stashed this thing away," Grant began, "then we're in for a hell of a fight."

"We're going to have to split up," Kane said.

"I'm going with you to the TOTO lab," Rosalia said.

"How do you know I'm the one heading underwater?" Kane asked.

"Because he'll be helping Kondo fight whatever's on the loose up here," Rosalia answered. "And Grant said that he'd feel very claustrophobic in the underwater base. Finally, there's no way you're *not* going to go face down an ancient god to try to stop it."

Kane looked at Grant, who merely shrugged.

The massive ex-Magistrate managed a smirk. "She's catching on to our methods fast."

Orochi looked grim. "I will accompany you. Yutaka and the rest of my men down there are my responsibility. I will free them or avenge them. Kondo…"

"Grant and I will do what we can up here," the Watatsumi officer returned.

Fumio looked up from his console. "The Hooded Ones have gone completely offline. Right now, regardless of how many alligators this creature has under its control, it now has sentient humans to work with."

"Back to the mat trans," Orochi ordered. "Kondo, once we're there, you evacuate the AUTEC base skeleton crew. If we don't contact you twenty-four hours from now, destroy the mat trans."

"You'll be trapped at the bottom of the ocean," Kondo returned.

"And so will thousands of that creature's breeding cells," Orochi said. "If one that we haven't neutered gets up here, everything is lost."

Kondo nodded, wondering why Akeno's sudden shrug seemed so disconcerting.

Chapter 16

It was nearly dusk when the Sandcat rumbled to a halt. Tall mountains circled what had once been a giant lake, and during her imprisonment in the facility, Domi had learned that Area 51 had once been called Groom Lake for the dried, nearly flat expanse. She had utilized a map inside the Sandcat to navigate a path that kept them from crossing that plain. She didn't relish the idea of leaving her only escape parked out in the open, and she also didn't want to be seen coming from miles away.

The fuel was almost gone, according to the tank, more than she'd anticipated having been eaten by the hard off-road terrain of the mountain path that overlooked the remnants nestled within the rocky embrace of the range. The path she'd driven down had led to what had once been an artificially carved road—there was no other reason why the small canyon was so straight and smooth-sided—and the mountain pass led toward the Groom Lake base. Every so often, she'd see the remnants of an electric eye, rotted and decayed electronics tucked into pockets of stone, and above were small balconies that would provide a good vantage point for a single rifleman to rain lead on anyone coming down the trail.

Domi also felt claustrophobic in this crack. She doubted that Grant could fit his broad shoulders through this passage, which meant this was more along the lines of an all-or-nothing escape route, not a conventional means of entrance.

So far, she had been lucky that this route was beneath the notice of the half-breeds; otherwise she would have been in trouble. Domi was a tough survivor, but her success in battle had to do with her maneuverability and speed. In the cramped quarters of this crack, she would get none of that. Her only consolation would be the opponents who would come after her, six-foot-tall mutants with thick, brawny bodies, would be even less agile under these conditions. It would be a moot point, though, as Domi would have very little space to dodge, leaving her open for a blow from their powerful fists. She'd avoided being struck by one of the half-transformed carnivores, and wasn't about to test their strength as they'd tested her speed and leaping ability.

All this brought to mind the folly of entering the subterranean base.

"Made my bed. Sleep in it," she muttered, recalling an apt phrase spoken by Brigid Baptiste. She would have given her arm to have the tall, flame-haired woman by her side. For one thing, Brigid's brilliance made her nearly as alert and aware as Kane and Domi, sharp eyes and photographic memory allowing her to spot the slightest hint of ambush or a trap. For another, that intellect combined with years of survival in the Outlands had made her a strong and capable combatant, one whose wits made up for lack of combat experience and strength. Brigid was missing, and Domi didn't want to think of her friend, mentor and sometime teacher still in the cruel granite grasp of Ullikummis. He was a monster that was an all too familiar type of threat. Possessed of not only great physical might, he had a multitude of followers, and other abilities that left him with few, if any, weaknesses.

"One fight at a time," she growled to herself. "One fight."

So far the half-breeds weren't visible, and as she left the escape crack, she could see the remnants of Area 51. Thanks to the assault staged by Grant and Brigid to rescue her and Kane, most of the buildings were crushed and broken shells, scorched by high explosives. Walls that stood were pock-marked with bullet holes, reminders of the savage battle. One building that wasn't damaged was a small concrete trapezoid that surged from the ground like a broken bone bursting through stretched skin.

The front was dominated by a pair of rolling, segmented doors wide and tall enough to allow three Sandcats to drive through abreast to each other. The doors were opened partially, much less than even the nine-foot girth of only one of the armored personnel carriers. Then again, the mutated hybrids that had lived behind those giant shutters wouldn't need that much room. Their numbers had been enough to force the loading gate open enough for them to file out in a flow of bodies.

Even from several yards away, the foul odor of the barbaric tribe wafted up from the subterranean depths. It was a stench that combined rotted flesh, sewage and fresh-spilled blood. The hybrids were hungry meat-eaters, and they were not afraid to feast upon their dead and wounded. Domi knew that if she were caught, she'd eventually end up in the category of sewage, her flesh thoroughly digested, maybe even her bones cracked open to suck out the marrow and living tissue within. It was a horrendous fate, but Domi had the consolation that she could fight hard enough to not be alive when the enemy began to feast.

"No," she grunted to herself. "Not gonna die. Gonna save Moe. Protect Priscilla."

"I will do my best to help you," the untransformed hybrid's words whispered into her ear. So startled and surprised, the feral girl whirled, knife drawn from its sheath even as she fought to restrain the urge to cut Priscilla for sneaking up on her and scaring her. When she looked for Priscilla, however, she saw no one. There was no scent, no sound of her delicate footsteps.

"Just voice," Domi whispered. "Getting stronger, Pree."

"Thank you, Domi," came the answer. Whatever genetic changes that kept her from devolving into a barbaric man-thing like the other Quad V hybrids had left Priscilla with gifts that were steadily increasing in power. The Sandcat, where Domi had left her to tend to Lakesh's medical needs, must have been three miles away, and yet the telepathic mindspeak had been clear as if Priscilla were embracing Domi around her neck, lips close to her earlobe.

"I am getting better at this," Priscilla amended, reading the thoughts that Domi couldn't quite put into words but had enough experience to abstractly ponder.

A warmth spread through Domi's chest. It was nice to have someone who could see all the way through her limited vocabulary. The telepathic link inspired an unusually strong affection for the hybrid, and even as Domi noticed that, she felt the same feelings returned to her.

"Friendly later," she said softly, as a means of focusing her concentration. "Business now."

"There are usually four who sit at the entrance, standing guard for the rest of the nest," Priscilla imparted. "They are alert, and attempting to go through the gap would leave you a sitting duck."

Even as the words seemingly appeared in Domi's ears, so, too, had the image of the quartet appeared in her imagination. The barbaric humanoids squatted on their haunches, avoiding the light, but growing ever more excited as the sun began to drop from the sky in the west. From her vantage point in the shadow of a half-shattered wall, Domi could see them moving in the shadows now. Once the bright light in the sky was gone, they would be free to stalk.

They knew that there was food in Las Vegas, and they wanted the fresh human flesh to slither down their gullets.

Domi was not about to stick around for too long to watch their disappointment once they returned. She had to get in, find the nanotechnology laboratory and get out before their return at dawn.

That would be it for her, unless more than a few of the monstrosities remained behind to watch their lair.

And if there was a significant force protecting the subterranean stronghold, then the same thought crossed her mind.

That would be it for her.

"ONE THING, MAGISTRATE Man." Rosalia spoke up. "How come you didn't 'feel' the presence of the New Order and Ullikummis when they took over Cerberus?"

Kane finished adjusting the straps on his Sin Eater's holster, ensuring that the weapon would snap swiftly into his grasp on command. The procedure was one that every Magistrate had drilled into his routine. Regular maintenance of the weapons was the difference between pointing a finger at a threat and pumping out high-intensity 9 mm bolts of blasterfire. It was a minor blessing that the mechanism was as sturdy as it was, and simple to keep going, but regular attention had to be paid to it.

"I wish I knew, then I wouldn't have fallen into such a trap," Kane replied. "What I do know is that this thing that Orochi and the others awakened, it's loud. I think that Ullikummis and the other Annunaki are a lot more subtle in their mental communication."

"You think that it's anything like him and his stones?" Rosalia asked. She had restrained the urge to touch herself where the son of Enlil had placed his splinter inside of her, though at the mention of the intrusion, Kane's eye twitched where a splinter of Ullikummis's hide had imbedded itself in his skin. Rosalia had done a good job of removing the control rock that the vengeful Annunaki had infected him with, but the splinter wasn't such a major issue that they needed to remove it.

There was only a slight stiffening of the muscles in his cheek, and no sign of it beneath the surface of his skin. Only Kane's experience and first-aid knowledge let him know that the splinter hadn't caused tetanus or some other infection in him. The skin wasn't red and puffy, swollen as his white blood cells sprung into action to reject the intruders to his body.

"Enlil locked this bastard away, which means that he wanted to study it. While he was rebuilding his little demon seed, he obviously got the idea from the slug beast and ported it over to the kid," Kane said. He rubbed his eye and cheek, and was glad when he didn't feel pain. No infection. No outside control. Just a little discomfort and stiffness. Ullikummis was not a concern for now, at least not in regard to taking over Kane's body once more. There was still the attack party that was trailing them, but they had run afoul of alligators.

If the New Order war group survived that fight, then Kane didn't begrudge them their shot at him. Let them fight their way, one god's minions battling another's. It had been his plan from the start, and his sole regret was not seeing Brigid Baptiste among the group.

He had desperately hoped that she would be personally directing this hunt, so that he could tell where she was, and maybe even attempt a rescue of his *anam-chara*. Brigid was an old soul who had journeyed alongside his across the centuries of human history and prehistory. Abandoning her in the clutches of Ullikummis was akin to Kane tearing off his own fingers from one hand. She was his partner, his confidante, his closest friend this side of the massive and mighty Grant. They had survived their battles against madmen and monsters as a team together. Now he felt crippled, and his thought of drawing her into the open was a desperation move.

Someone else was in charge of the group, though, a man nearly as large as Grant, accompanied by only one local, a seedy-looking thug who seemed as if he were born in a swamp.

Ullikummis was as smart as he was big. He must have seen Kane dangling himself as a piece of bait, and knew better than to have Brigid where she could be easily located. Maybe Ullikummis would have the sense of irony to send a mind-controlled Brigid after him, and that was one thing he was hoping for, something that hadn't shown up yet. No mind-control stone cell would have been strong enough to have kept her enslaved for long.

So she was a prisoner? A hostage?

"Kane!" Rosalia spoke up.

He looked at the adventurer. "What?"

"It looks like the last of the freighter's crew have transferred to shore," she pointed out. "I've got to double-check the perimeter with Grant and Kondo. Are you certain you can handle yourself alone if Orochi turns out to be bent?"

Kane's nostrils flared for a moment. "We'll see. You watch out for yourself up here."

The hazel-eyed beauty nodded as the former Magistrate finished his work on his gear.

It was time to visit the Tongue Of The Ocean to see what the Annunaki had entombed at the bottom of the world.

AGRIPPINE RAN HIS FOREARM across his mouth, coming away with fresh blood where an alligator tail had caught him in the face. Grogan stood tall, looming over the corpses of two of the massive reptiles that he had killed with his machete and pistol. Cold, glaring eyes locked on the Cajun guide, and Agrippine knew that the New Order commander was not pleased to have lost two more of his men.

"Listen, I did not know these things were coming after us," Agrippine began, but Grogan shook his head.

"This was not your fault. These creatures have been directed by something else, a powerful mind that, though it may seem blasphemous, is nearly as powerful as my master," Grogan said.

Agrippine's eyes narrowed, and he realized that

his skin grew damp with clammy sweat. Rather, even more wet, as he had been soaked to the bone by the rampaging melee as the four alligators lunged at them. One of the beasts had worn a camera on its nose. Agrippine had seen it just before he'd hammered off four shells into the beast's skull, shattering its long, slender reptilian brain.

He bent and picked up the device, realizing that there was something strange about the odd mutation that nestled in the remnants of the alligator's crushed head.

"What?" Grogan asked before Agrippine found himself seized. He opened his mouth to howl, but the noise was snatched away from his lips, his lungs frozen and unable to speak.

Agrippine grimaced as he realized that a single tentacle had wound itself around his wrist, a sudden burst of electric pain sizzling through his entire body.

"I am Kakusa."

Grogan stiffened, regarding Agrippine, who suddenly felt flooded with knowledge, the foremost being that the words that introduced the entity had come from his lips. His body was relaxed now, and he felt a modicum of freedom in his limbs. However, he had a subtle warning from the pulsing cell attached to his limb. Any action taken against the octopuslike slug would be met with the shredding of his sanity. Kakusa informed Agrippine, through silent telepathic contact, that it would only be a matter of reflex that his mind would be torn to pieces, then reassembled, still seething with the memory of its prior destruction.

"I am the servant of Ullikummis," Grogan said. "We have something in common, Kakusa."

"Indeed," Agrippine's mouth said. "One sees my

abilities within your control, as well as the handi-work of the demon who captured me in such a crude, morose form."

"My father," Ullikummis's servitor whispered.

"Enlil," Kakusa returned.

"I can taste the hatred in your thoughts," Grogan said.

Through Agrippine's face, Kakusa returned a tenta-tive smile. "I apologize for the sudden, violent action, but I did not have any within the immediate area that may have been able to speak for me. Your guide's memory, however, not only explains your mission, but the nature of your existence on our world."

Grogan smirked in response. "It would be inter-esting to have an ally such as you at my side when it comes time to tear down my hated sire, but Enlil would not have gelded an intellect such as yours if you were trustworthy."

"He was jealous of my ability," Kakusa tried to explain. Even as the words left Agrippine's lips, the Cajun saw how the hive-mind entity had once been far more subtle. Its original existence had been based within a string of genetic information that allowed itself to be assimilated by predatory, single-celled hunters akin to amoebas. From there, it would work its way through the chain of life forms, feeding those larger than itself, until it ended up in the smartest and most capable of the species on a given world.

From there, Kakusa found its way to other worlds. Its original home had been on a heavily volcanic world that suffered such great seismic eruptions that the mo-lecular string accompanied stones that sailed across the void of space. The volcanic world eventually came apart, falling into the sun it orbited, and it was there that Kakusa had tasted how vulnerable it had been.

There were pieces of its consciousness strewed across the galaxy, but stuck either on inert asteroids or in organisms far too simple to do more than chew cud and wait for aeons to grow capable. These were distant whispers, and no other planet in this universe had anything approaching the mental abilities of the others that Kakusa held on this world. Agrippine wanted to tell Grogan that there were only two humanoids who were fully in the thrall of the alien entity, and that the bulk of its Earthly incarnation was either grafted to the alligators, freed by their brethren or bound to the slime-ball masses like the one riding his arm.

Kakusa, however, held the controls to Agrippine's mind and body. He would not allow Ullikummis to learn such information, not until it was time to divulge all, if such a moment even existed. Still, Kakusa's intellect observed Ullikummis through Grogan's body. It was a cold, tense standoff, and Kakusa suspected the son of its enemy was just as canny and dangerous as Enlil.

"Think about what I can offer," Kakusa said through its human puppet.

The other puppeteer stretched a sneer across Grogan's features. "I trusted my father. I listened to his promises and learned the truth. My feet had been shorn from my body, and I was exiled to deep space for five millennia."

"Five millennia?" Kakusa asked. A snort of derision escaped from Agrippine. "Five thousand years? I've spent a hundred times that crossing the gulf of space. You speak to a true immortal, not some body-bound pretender."

"When Enlil imprisoned you, you had been given the opportunity to live as something other than a pawn, a toy," Ullikummis said. "I had walked the Earth for only the briefest of instants. My entire existence has been summed up by imprisonment, while you have the experience of an entire universe in your memory, Kakusa. My sympathy for your current crippled state could be measured in the breadth of your original host's body, mere atoms in width."

Kakusa had Agrippine take a step forward, and the Cajun felt his muscles surge with strength that he'd never expected to have. The ancient entity had tapped into nerve clusters and body reserves that few humans even knew existed. Grogan's fists would still be able to snap his bones, but Agrippine felt even more fear of the force of his increased power. Kakusa had little concern for how easily such increased physical might could peel muscles from his skeleton or compress and snap bones beneath tightened sinews.

Grogan tensed up, as well, Ullikummis apparently making the same preparations for combat between their puppets. The two gods faced off through proxy, then realized that any initial hostility would prove worthless. For Kakusa, it would be one cell snuffed out. For Ullikummis, the loss of Grogan would just be one of thousands of human pawns lost in a war that the Annunaki prince expected to claim millions.

"Any conflict between either of us would prove fruitless," Grogan's voice croaked. "Your cells could not touch my body, nor those already infested with my essence. I could slaughter ninety-nine percent of your biomass, and you would still find some means of survival as all of that intellect is simply anchored and filtered through another universe."

"You see," Kakusa whispered.

"The molecular strain is actually a fairly complex crystalline matrix, akin to the one that I utilize to impose my will on these soft-skinned apes. The matrices are mere lenses between dimensions, lenses that have been trapped within an ungainly, ugly little lifeform that amused my father," Ullikummis said. "It would be as if the wind battled the ocean. We could strike at each other with endless might and do nothing of substance."

Kakusa chuckled. "Unless you somehow discovered the means by which your father gelded me."

"And to harm me, you would have to strike out not only in this reality, but across hundreds," Grogan returned.

Agrippine's lips curled into a smile. "Then we are not so much at a truce, but at a crossroads."

"I will let you live. You will let me live," Ullikummis's puppet promised.

"Until such time as we can improve our states of affairs," Kakusa's minion answered.

"I am already hard at work. The sentients of this world are becoming mine, or extinguishing like candle flames," Grogan's voice offered.

Agrippine wanted to swallow in fear, but Kakusa held no such terror of the other pawn's words. "You require the talking monkeys. I do not."

"Except to communicate with me," Grogan answered.

Agrippine nodded.

"Then luck to you. Should I fail, then perhaps your rage shall prove sufficient to destroy our mutual enemy," Ullikummis said.

"And perhaps you may succeed in achieving my vengeance for me," Agrippine countered.

With that, the slug suddenly removed itself from Agrippine's arm, slithering onto the back of a small opossum that scurried wildly into the darkness.

Agrippine turned, starting to speak, but he was left without words. He knew that there was information that he wanted to give to Grogan, but those memories had been excised with Kakusa's separation from him. The long-trapped immortal entity had been smart enough to silence its puppet, removing everything that Ullikummis and the New Order would have found useful.

Agrippine looked at his skin, seeing it red and oozing blood from a thousand microscopic hooks torn free of him. He turned to Grogan, head swimming.

"I'm sorry," Agrippine croaked roughly.

Grogan took a deep breath, regarding the suddenly ailing Cajun for a moment. "As am I. You have been a decent ally for the nonce."

Agrippine noticed the sudden flicker of starlight off the gleaming edge of a machete.

Then the swamp guide knew nothing more.

Chapter 17

Kakusa, in the form of Yutaka, stood behind the shielded armaglass of the mat trans as the technicians dialed up for a controlled retrieval from AUTEC. Orochi had called ahead, mentioning the swift return, along with a newcomer, a human named Kane. Kakusa would have been surprised, except that its pawn Akeno had already seen the trio of humans who had met with the Watatsumi on the freighter. The forewarning of the human's presence, and Akeno's assessment of the man, especially through the combat assessment of Yutaka, told the hive-minded entity all it needed to know about the danger Kane presented.

It also illustrated for Kakusa that the capture of the former Magistrate would broaden its knowledge and vastly increase its abilities. While a good deal of a success in combat was based on physical prowess, an important component of that martial power came from intellect. Fighting simply with brute force was no more useful than quenching thirst from an empty cup. With the canny experience, situational awareness and mental agility of Kane under Kakusa's command, it would become unstoppable. Absorbing that would transfer that fighting ability to the rest of the entity's minions. Kakusa drew something from Yutaka's memories—better a lion leading an army of deer than a deer leading an army of lions.

The two figures shimmered in the flashing plasma cloud within the mat-trans chamber, and Kakusa unconsciously made all of its connected minds hold their breath for a moment, waiting for fate to deliver a formidable fighting force. Between Kane and Orochi, the level of skill Kakusa possessed was about to skyrocket. Kakusa had absorbed too many human tics, and that was infecting the rest of its consciousness. Too readily, the Entity understood that Enlil's gelding had not only trapped it in the strange, octopuslike pods, but made Kakusa vulnerable to the mannerisms of the beings it had assimilated.

That was why Kakusa was glad to get one of the TOTO scientists in its stable. The vulgarities of genetics were slightly beyond the entity's intellect at this moment, but Akeno had already begun his effort at working out the problems inherent in the new limitations that Kakusa had been trapped within. Spreading Akeno's problem-solving abilities across several brains, even the primitive, saurian stems in the alligators, was adding to his problem-solving capabilities. Kakusa drew a simile from the scientist Akeno's mind—it was like a mainframe adding additional processors to work out the formula necessary to find a working, viable solution. Akeno was only one of the scientific minds on hand, and the TOTO geneticists who were working on cloning more of his unhindered octoslug cells were also working on the core problem. The trouble was, for all the capacity for intellectual growth that Kakusa maintained, it had little knowledge of its own makeup, what gene strings were not simply part of the primitive mollusk forms that it had been irrevocably adhered to.

As soon as Kane and Orochi solidified, Kakusa felt

a rush of relief, an emotion that hadn't been felt in far too long. Yutaka nodded for one of his fellow pawns, another of Orochi's military men, to release the chamber's locking mechanism.

It was then that there was a sudden movement visible through the armaglass windows. Kane convulsed, his body seeming to fold in on itself, and he dropped out of sight. Orochi was shouting, diving to the human's aid. Kakusa was frozen with shock. Somehow the environment within the mat trans was inhospitable. But how? According to the genetic knowledge of the Watatsumi, there were only minor differences between humans and the reptilian children of Enki. Even there, the similarities were so great that each species could only live within similar envelopes of conditions, heat, pressure, atmosphere... If something had proved fatal to Kane, then it should prove equally dangerous to Orochi and Kakusa's pawns.

"Open it up!" Yutaka shouted.

It was all Kakusa could do not to give in to the sudden flood of frustration and fear. The Entity had been left alone in its thoughts for far too long, segregated from itself thanks to the electronic tiaras that Enlil had developed to maintain control. Fear, frustration, anger, all of them bubbled up, threatening to break down a being who once controlled entire star systems before it ran against the Annunaki.

With a surge of willpower, Kakusa shoved the turmoil aside, wresting control of the semi-sentient pawns into order.

The hermetic seal finally hissed as the mat trans opened. Kakusa could see, through the Watatsumi sentry's eyes, Kane on the floor, foam bubbling over his lips.

"Get in here!" Orochi bellowed.

The guard knelt over Kane, tugging at his clothes, finding the body-conforming shadow suit beneath. The Watatsumi reached for the knife he wore in his belt to open up the fabric and attempt chest compressions when there was another convulsive flex. Kakusa saw the scene from multiple angles, the sentry not catching the movement of Kane's arm as it sprang up, hooking around his neck. Fingers dug into the spongy biomass at the back of the Watatsumi's neck, gelatin pus bursting through the cell wall tissue, pouring over the human's fingers. Suddenly the guard that Kakusa had been controlling was no longer accessible.

Kakusa's pawns all suddenly sprouted grimaces. They had been tricked by a single man, one Kakusa had been yearning to add to its consciousness. Tricked and suddenly exposed.

Orochi was out of the mat-trans chamber in an explosion of speed, bowling over another of the guards that Kakusa had urged forward. Orochi's forearms struck the Watatsumi in the upper chest, slamming him to the floor. Behind, on the floor, Kane was up and in motion after checking Yutaka, the dazed, confused guard he'd freed from Kakusa's control.

Two independent minds were free within the Tongue Of The Ocean base that Kakusa had taken over, two beings that knew that the Entity was no longer under control, and who had more than enough fighting ability to ward off even the army of guards and technicians in the undersea base.

Kakusa knew that it had to start working on building up its forces elsewhere, even as it got Yutaka out of the chamber.

Luckily, the Entity had Akeno hard at work on the surface.

KONDO AND GRANT WERE still going over checklists, engaging in the kind of redundancy of operation that was the key difference between true professionals and those who dressed up in paramilitary rags and pretended to be an army. Most Magistrates were akin to the Watatsumi warrior corps, hardworking men who were focused on the task at hand, making sure that there would be little left to chance. If it meant an extra bit of field maintenance or a complete rebuilding of a structure to make certain to avoid a fatal flaw, there might have been some good-natured grumbles, but they threw themselves into the task.

"The concertina wire was a little snarled in the southeast corner," Grant noted.

Kondo nodded. "I had my people take care of it. Let's go look at it again if you don't have anything more pressing."

Grant shook his head and he and the Watatsumi walked together. Kondo looked up at Grant, who was a tall, powerful figure of a man no matter where he went. Kondo was tall for his race, at five-ten, but Grant was well over six feet tall and he walked with a bearing that made him seem much taller. The former Magistrate had used that size well to provide quiet intimidation to those who would cause trouble, as well as being a calming bulwark when his comrades were against tough odds.

But sheer mass alone wasn't Grant's greatest strength. It was the fact that he knew how to think and to move with ease and skill. All the muscle in the world was useless if it couldn't be applied quickly and accurately. As such, Grant had often been able to hold his own, even against beings who were supposedly far superior in physical might or crowds of foes who out-numbered him.

They examined the concertina wire, and true to Kondo's word, the Watatsumi troopers had done their job well. Whether it would prove sufficient to handle the rogue crocodilians under the control of an alien mind, or if there was other means for the octoslugs to get through onto the base.

At least they were off the freighter. That was one place where they would be holed up and surrounded. Gunfire from shore would have been the least of their worries, what with alien-entity-controlled alligators able to swarm in the waters around the ship. There'd be no way to escape, even on the strongest of boats.

"We've got the AUTEC facility all sewn down," Grant pronounced. "What about the control of the Hooded Ones and the alligators still under your control?"

"I had the team transfer control over immediately before we abandoned the freighter," Kondo answered. "With the crew now on shore, we'll be able to have a more stable platform."

"Why even make use of the ship in the first place?" Grant asked.

Kondo pointed to the base. "For one thing, we were attempting to be far less noticeable. The hulk out there has been sitting for ages, and people in the area had been coming around the AUTEC facility. What we've done was shift the attention toward the freighter as a means of keeping our link to the TOTO base and the heavier tech on hand, but to keep people from looking too closely."

Grant nodded, understanding. It was better to stay out of sight across the water, where even the sounds on ship would have been muted by distance. However, the presence of powerful amphibious reptiles made controlling and keeping the ship much more difficult. Grant hadn't liked the idea of sending Kane alone to the bottom of the ocean, despite his concerns about claustrophobia, but there were people up here who were in need of help.

"Rosalia, can you hold down the fort here with Kondo?" Grant asked.

"Why? You've got somewhere to go?" Rosalia asked.

Grant nodded. "Suwanee and her people. They're out there and have no idea what kind of menace is approaching."

"We have a communicator setup and so do they," Rosalia answered. "We can warn them to beware…"

"I'd still like to have a consolidation of forces here," Grant said.

"The extra personnel could be helpful," Kondo added.

"I could help." Fumio, one of the remote operators of the Watatsumi expedition, spoke up. "No need to worry about risking your safety. We still have the Hooded Ones under benign control, and a force of them should be sufficient to guard and escort Suwanee and her folk. Right?"

Grant's jaw set firmly. "I don't like the idea of the Hooded Ones knowing what's going on."

"We have the tiara control rings on the octoslugs. There's not going to be any problems. They can't communicate with the electrical interference in their bodies," Fumio said. "Whoever made these creatures and devices knew what he was doing."

Grant wrinkled his nose. "Yes, he did. And now

that you've kicked over this old trove of his, there's no telling what the bastard will do."

"You're talking about Enlil," Kondo concluded. "But you said he's in hiding and being hunted by Ullikummis. He won't be able to wrest any control away from us. We're only dealing with the Entity, and as long as the tiaras are in place, they'll behave."

Rosalia grimaced. "I know you're interested in protecting a bunch of locals, but where they are right now is safe for them. They're in a lockdown position. We're locked down here, too. We loosen up to let you run across a swamp, who knows what will catch on to you? Don't forget, Ullikummis is hunting us, too."

Grant sighed. "Okay, I get it. I get it. Fumio, can you contact Suwanee's people?"

"You've got their frequency—I'll do what I can," the Watatsumi comm officer said.

Grant gave him Suwanee's channel, a bit of information that he and Kane had acquired just before slipping out into the dark swamp with Rosalia. Fumio turned and went to the main comm shed.

A low rumble caught Grant's attention. It was the dog, and its ears were tucked low to its neck, tail stiff as a board. Rosalia noticed the sudden reaction of the half-coyote animal as well. Its feral senses had picked up something, and Grant swiftly signaled Kondo with his hands.

The Watatsumi soldiers fell into position, moving back toward their designated spots. Grant squinted, attempting to make out what had caught the dog's attention in the darkness, activating his night-vision device. A few moments later the advanced optics were peering into the predawn night as if it were a cloudy day. He was able to see movement, two men and an alligator venturing stealthily toward the fence.

Grant waved to Kondo, pointing out the avenue of approach. There was a relay of hand motions, invisible from behind the cutting wire fence, for the most part, and completely silent.

One group of enemy was targeted. What about the others? Or was this a probe, an uncommitted push to see what kind of defenses were on hand? Kondo was aware of this, as well. Standing orders were to minimize contact with enemy forces. Grant continued his sweep of the perimeter, noting that the trio was not in the spot where the dog had been facing. There were more people. Their silhouettes were not similar to the Hooded Ones, and these men and women were carrying firearms.

Grant wondered for a moment if this was Suwanee and her people, but this group was led by a man who looked to be a great hulk of a human being. Grant hadn't personally met or inspected everyone in Suwanee's refugee camp, but he was as certain as humanly possible that there hadn't been someone this big among the swamp dwellers.

Someone like that doesn't disappear in a crowd.

Grant grabbed Kondo by the upper arm. "There's a newcomer in this fight. It looks like the New Order has followed us here."

"Ullikummis," Kondo responded. "What should we do?"

"Keep your people's eyes peeled. They might be working together, they might not," Grant said. "Either way, we can't show our hand yet."

Kondo nodded. "What are you going to do?"

"I'll think of something," Grant said, taking off

toward the AUTEC dock. He didn't like the idea of so many forces appearing on one side of the base and diverting attention from all other quarters.

That meant he was going to have to put himself between danger and the people who started it all. Actually, the folks up here didn't seem to hold much malice toward humans. They were wary of his and the others' presence, but he didn't get a hostile vibe from any of them, except for Orochi.

Because of that lack of anger, Grant was disposed toward helping them.

Five years ago, he thought, I wouldn't have had the kind of patience I have now. That's the way life has changed for us all. People, even those with scales or mutations, all count, and we've got to work together to put this planet back in order. Making enemies over petty bullshit isn't going to keep Enlil at bay. Humanity just has to work alongside. We can suss out the differences later.

For now, Grant didn't worry about the Watatsumi. The New Order and the renegade octoslugs were the threat, whether they were actively working together or as a confluence of predators swooping down on the AUTEC base.

Either way, the grim ex-Mag from Cerberus intended to foil and blunt the machinations of demons and would-be gods.

THE GUARD SEEMED DAZED to Kane, but otherwise, he was unaffected physically by the sudden, violent cessation of contact with the hive mind that had taken over the Tongue Of The Ocean subsea base. The slimy, putrid guts of the octoslug stuck to his fingers, and it appeared that no amount of brushing could remove the unnerving sensation of the pus. He did notice, however, that sections of the thing's skin remained attached to his fingers where he'd dug in. It took the scraping of his knife blade to pull it off, and he could see hundreds of tiny red pinpricks where the slug-thing's biomass had been peeled away.

"Orochi, you know that these bags of snot are coated with millions of miniature grasping hooks, right?" Kane asked.

"We surmised that they were akin to box jelly-fish or sea anemones. You only make physical contact with them through thick gloves," the Watatsumi commander answered.

Kane grimaced. "Thanks for the warning. At least I don't feel any toxic effects."

"No, we believe that the entity embedded within its DNA is actually using those stingers to induce electrical impulses," Orochi said.

"To communicate with his prey and pawns," Kane answered. "Why didn't he try to take me over when I made contact with it?"

"You obviously destroyed the supercell too quickly," Orochi surmised.

Kane looked at the squelched mass of gelatin and saclike skin. "Let's hope that's the case. You're wearing your gloves, right?"

Orochi nodded.

Kane withdrew his custom-designed gauntlets and donned them. The gloves formed a piezoelectric seal the moment they touched the sleeves of the shadow suits. The suits had been designed to be airtight, and in conjunction with an air supply, would allow the wearer to walk on the airless surface of the Moon with little ill effect. While that might have been good in a cold, pressureless vacuum, going outside under nearly a mile of water might have been another problem. He knew that the shadow suit was able to resist violent impacts thanks to the properties of its polymer weaves. Would the skintight bodysuit prove to be enough to withstand the crushing weight of hundreds of atmospheres?

Kane didn't want to test those waters, so to speak. "Is he ready to fight?"

"I doubt it," Orochi answered. "We haven't had time to pay attention to the victims in the sick bay from an earlier containment breach. He'll be out of it for hours."

Kane nodded, knowing that any continued combat would have to be undertaken with care. He wondered at the brief moment where he'd crushed the octoslug. He felt a spike of mental contact, but his fingers had pierced the jellied body of the creature swiftly, tearing it asunder. That brief instant of psychic contact had been barely decipherable.

"Simple," Kane grunted.

"What is?" Orochi asked.

Kane looked at the lifeless puddle seeping down the Watatsumi's back. "I struck the trunk of the body, not the tentacles. The suckers on the tentacles are the main means of transmitting whatever control these creatures have. The skin on the trunk simply is insurance, further body contact. That's how I was able to pop it before it could get a hold on me."

Orochi frowned. "You tend to go in guns blazing before thinking your plans through, don't you?"

"Why do you think I came down here while being chased by another enemy?" Kane asked. "Some things look better on paper than they do in real life. It's not much of a problem for me."

"Improvisation is your strength," Orochi said.

Kane nodded.

"Now would be a good time to test your link to your friends aboveground," Orochi added. "Before Akeno and his puppet master decide to break their way back into here."

Kane activated his Commtact. "Grant? You read me?"

Harsh static rumbled through Kane's mandible, giving him a jolting headache, but he was able to get a faint read on Grant. Between blasts of white noise, he heard the name "New Order" and caught part of a word that sounded like "slugs."

"They working together?" Kane asked loudly, hoping that Grant could make out his words over the squeal of interference. The Commtacts were high-tech cybernetic devices, and they had the ability to transmit anywhere on the planet, and even to the Moon, but the ocean and the superstructure of the deep-sea base combined into the interference that made his teeth itch.

"Dunno!" came Grant's bellowing reply. "Checking!"

Volume had trumped the static, but Grant couldn't be expected to yell like a maniac to himself. Further communication would have to wait. What Kane did know was that Ullikummis had entered the fray, sending his minions in hot pursuit. In a way, Kane was relieved that Grant had only said New Order. He didn't want to imagine the havoc raised when one being or the other got their hands on their counterpart, especially if Enlil had specifically designed Ullikummis's mind control abilities on the creature he'd left trapped at the bottom of the planet.

"Out!" Kane responded. Though Grant couldn't see it, he gave his friend and partner a one percent salute, sending the big man all the luck in the world and every ounce of moral support. It had been a habit, and he could feel Grant returning the favor with a certainty that came from the years of blood, sweat and tears that bound them. There was a link between the two men that went beyond the powerful little transceiver plate affixed to pintle mounts on his jawbone. It was analogous to deep, eternal friendship he shared with Brigid Baptiste, but as much as he could feel Grant, Brigid was gone, cut off from him and leaving a cold, hollow space in his spirit.

What did that damned lava-blooded freak have in store for her?

Then again, he remembered his ordeal, his imprisonment. Ullikummis wanted power, but he also wanted followers who were true to themselves and to him. Kane had managed to free himself, with Rosalia's help, but what if Brigid couldn't?

Granted, Baptiste had been a strong-willed woman, a true survivor who had endured countless perils at his side. Kane had stopped condescending to her as someone who needed protection and babying. She was too stubborn, too intelligent, to be such a pushover, at least in comparison to the ordeals that Ullikummis had heaped upon him.

Then again, he had some help. Grant had been alone, and he hadn't succumbed to the stone god's wiles. He took a deep, cleansing breath. Right now there was a swarm of tentacled creatures, all subservient to one intellect and capable of subsuming a sentient mind to that entity's will.

And according to Orochi, there were hundreds, even thousands, now running loose within this undersea base.

Long odds and far from safety—it was nothing new for Kane.

Time to go to work.

Chapter 18

Kondo watched as Grant disappeared into the perimeter. Despite his size, the ex-Magistrate could disappear into the shadows as well as the best of the Watatsumi warrior corps. Kondo wondered how short the battle against the great beasts would have been if Tatehiko had possessed a dozen such men, but he fought to clear that thought from his mind.

He activated his comm link to Fumio. "How are we doing on bringing in the Hooded Ones and the remaining alligators?"

There was no answer.

"Fumio, come in."

The woman, Rosalia, looked at him with concern, her hand dropping to the knife hilt sticking out of her belt. "What's wrong?"

"No response from the remote-operations center," Kondo said. He drew his pistol. "It might be nothing, but..."

"Nothing is nothing," Rosalia said. "Grant's got the outside—I'd better check inside. You hang back just in case this is an ambush."

"You're risking your life now?" Kondo asked.

"No," Rosalia answered, annoyed. "I'm trying to keep my ass in one piece. That goes to hell if the commander of the local regiment who's actually friendly toward my side gets killed on account of me."

Kondo smirked at the logic of her argument. Still, it wasn't hard to tell that she had genuine concerns about him and the rest of the Watatsumi, who would be her assistance in a battle against either the New Order or the parasitic slugs. If the reptilian warriors from subterranean Japan fell, then it was likely that she'd die, as well. Survival in the postapocalyptic world was not merely a matter of survival of the fittest because there would always be an instance where just a second of respite could be the difference between life and death. That respite could only come on the shoulders of allies, and petty squabbles disappeared in the face of the true menaces that had torn the planet asunder.

Kondo nodded to her, then waved one of his subordinates to go with her. The Watatsumi soldier was armed with a folding-stock Howa Type 89 assault rifle and sufficient magazines to handle any threat at close quarters. Kondo himself had gotten his Minebea PM-9 machine pistol, which by most accounts wasn't too different from the Sin Eater that Grant and Kane used, except it didn't fold down into a slender forearm holster.

He hoped that he could keep the wolves at bay from the AUTEC base, but Grant had already seen the possibility of some trouble coming close to the fence. All the electricity and razor-sharp wire in the world couldn't completely halt an enraged, nearly suicidal attack. All he could hope for was to be ready and prepared to give as good as he received.

"Grant, we've got communication troubles inside the perimeter," Kondo transmitted on the ex-Magistrate's frequency. "Rosalia and escort have been dispatched to make sure."

"Where?" Grant asked.

"Remote operations," Kondo said.

There was a grim growl on the other end of the radio hookup. "When Orochi came back, did he bring anyone with him?"

"Just one technician who was going to assist us," Kondo responded. "Why?"

"He's in remote operations now?" Grant asked.

"Oh, hell," Kondo murmured. "Rosalia…do you read me?"

The only answer was the distant chatter of gunfire.

AKENO HADN'T NEEDED to get physical with Fumio in the remote-operations center. All of the fit and capable soldiers were already being pressed into service setting up the AUTEC base's defense perimeter, guns and eyes aimed outward. The slender yet infested scientist was of little threat, especially to the stocky Fumio. Though the Watatsumi soldier was assigned to a support role, he was physically fit, and was carrying one of the SIG-Sauer 9 mm pistols that were the standard issue of the officer corps. Fumio had a rifle, but that was resting near the sole door to the ops center, set up to be utilized in the repulsion of outside intruders, not against internal betrayal.

Akeno/Kakusa had already heard Fumio boasting to one of the other Watatsumi soldiers.

"If I can't handle a skinny little punk like Akeno, then I deserve to get my brain eaten," Fumio had said.

Except it wasn't even Akeno who had to engage the communications officer in combat. All that had been necessary was for one of Kakusa's independent cells to hatch within the womb of the parasite attached to the scientist, and then to sneak up on Fumio. There was no doubt that Fumio possessed the training to shatter the neck of any man trying to ambush him, but his warrior skills ill-served him against an assault in the form of a multitentacled octoslug that crawled along the ceiling, then dropped down, tendrils wrapping around the soldier's head. Thousands of hooked barbs sank into the scaled skin of his head, pumping out not only a strong bioelectric jolt but also a form of fast-acting toxin. Semiparalytic in nature, those venomous barbs had sapped Fumio's will with chemical efficiency while Kakusa projected its will over his body.

Even if he had been able to move, the poison barbs had frozen Fumio's body, keeping him from acting in self-defense. With the powerful grip of the mollusk-like creature secure, the Watatsumi individual was no more, swallowed into Kakusa's growing fold of slaves and stolen minds. Akeno and Fumio didn't have to speak once the assimilation was complete, less than a minute after the first contact of the grasping tendrils of the parasite.

Fumio returned and retrieved his rifle and stood guard, ready to repel assailants once the Watatsumi learned that they were no longer in control of their mind-controlled slaves. With that, Akeno staged a complete shutdown of the electronic collars.

The rush of multiple psyches opening up to Kakusa was akin to the sweeping headiness of a first orgasm, and for a moment, every creature under its domain trembled. Instantly, Kakusa was aware that its minions aboveground numbered close to one hundred, and Kakusa was in contact with all of them, from the primitive reptiles to the stalking Hooded Ones.

Kakusa drew its emotional charge back in and sent out a signal to each of the parasitic cells. Kakusa was trapped in their bodies, but that didn't mean it couldn't self-propagate. The signal was simple—reproduce. Each of the octopoid slugs attached to the controlled beings was now ordered to gestate. Being on a level barely above unicellular life-forms, the creatures were hermaphrodites, and were able to begin the process of asexual reproduction at will. Kakusa could feel the creatures drawing nutrients from its pawns, and knew that it would take hours for them to begin to give birth to new little cephalopods.

That was why Kakusa was glad Akeno's parasite had begun its process early.

This second generation could prove to be better, especially since they'd never been "infected" with terrestrial technology. Either way, Kakusa could double the numbers within a half of a day. That kind of growth would be good for the world.

All Kakusa had to do was to hold on to the TOTO installation.

There was a knock at the door of the remote-operations center. Fumio brought his rifle to bear. "Who is it?"

"You're not answering Kondo's calls," a woman's voice returned.

Fumio/Kakusa frowned. "Well, come on in."

Rosalia was one of the three humans who had met up with the Watatsumi, and from Fumio's memories, she was a sharp-witted woman. As much as he would have liked to absorb that kind of survival mentality, there were no hatchlings ready for her. With some regret, Kakusa was going to have to burn her down with a magazine full of bullets.

Otherwise, the woman would interfere with Akeno's and Fumio's sabotage of Remote Operations. The electronic collars had been deactivated, but not completely negated. A little effort, and Kakusa's undoing of the tiaras would be wasted. That meant bullets into Rosalia.

There was a moment of pause. She seemed hesitant to enter, making Kakusa more worried.

"Rosalia?" Fumio called out.

The door suddenly slammed open, and with the sudden blast of movement, Fumio opened fire, spraying rifle bullets through the empty doorway.

ROSALIA DIDN'T KNOW how things went on the AUTEC base, but she was not so naive that she'd stand in front of a doorway that stood between her and an unknown situation. The door latch was unlocked, and she motioned for her escort to give it a kick around the doorjamb on the hinge side while she stood across from him. The construction of the building was late twentieth century, and it was cinder block. Against the 5.56 mm rounds that thundered out of the Howa in Fumio's hands, she had more than enough protection for several moments, at least until the magazine was exhausted.

She gripped the Copperhead tightly, chips of cinder block flying away as hypersonic bullets deformed and careened on impact. Her Watatsumi escort was unhurt and staying out of the line of fire, as well. The reptilian soldier looked at her askance. While it was going to be easy to put down the renegade, there was some loyalty between the two military men, and in addition, there was no guarantee that their rifles wouldn't destroy the very same equipment that the octoslug-dominated men were shutting down.

Rosalia raised a finger, informing her companion to go to single shot. The Watatsumi nodded, and displayed the Howa was already flicked to semiauto. She should have known that a professional soldier wasn't going to waste ammunition or risk the chance of destroying valuable equipment. Plus, Rosalia was aware that if there was any sort of distance, full-automatic bursts were more likely to go wide, especially if the first shot didn't hit. Good, average soldiers went one bullet per pull of the trigger at any distance except across room-length distances. It took extremely skilled personnel to make the most of full-automatic, men with the kind of training that Grant and Kane utilized.

Rosalia pursed her lips. Fumio was in the middle of a reload, which meant that she could get his attention, maybe scramble him. She looked at her soldier and nodded, then broke into a run, sweeping into sight of the door and charging away. Behind her, she could hear the clatter of Fumio's rifle on the floor. The RO officer cursed, his body's old reflexes giving up to frustration, even as Kakusa's will impelled him to pull his handgun from its holster.

Rosalia knew that she had at least a good second and a half to make distance between herself and the gunman, which meant that she could get twenty-one feet, which was double the range of the hallway from Fumio to the door. Fifteen yards was long for a handgun shot.

Her soldier dived to the ground even as she took off, lining up the shot. His Howa rifle cracked loudly once, twice, and Rosalia threw herself sideways, taking her out of the line of sight of the door, just in case her ally missed.

There was no chasing handgun fire, which meant that the rounds had flown true. Rosalia picked herself up and headed toward the Remote Operations Center, reaching it just as her escort rose to his feet and had entered a footstep ahead of her. The mercenary woman kept her Copperhead aimed at the floor to prevent shooting her man in the back while they advanced toward the transmission center. Fumio writhed, clutching a wounded side, no amount of outside domination proving to be enough to override his body's natural self-preservation functions. It would take much more to drive the badly injured Watatsumi to his feet and continue to fight. Even so, the man's pistol had fallen from numbed fingers, meaning Fumio would have to crawl to get some form of weapon.

Akeno had a chair in his hands, one bank of computer towers already swept from the tables they sat upon, wires snapped by the force of his swing. Rosalia was ready with her weapon to burn him down, but held her fire as her ally lunged toward him to minimize the damage. Akeno whipped the chair between them, the sudden impact sending the Watatsumi warrior to the ground insensate.

The chair had been knocked from Akeno's grasp, but he whirled, pushed on by Kakusa's urging to take out the equipment.

"Stop!" Rosalia shouted, but her words hadn't even raised a flinch. She paused, knowing that shooting him would be killing a helpless pawn. At the same time, the Entity in control wouldn't have any compunctions about dropping a hundred of its pawns on the AUTEC base in a wave of murder and infestation. Akeno may have been a good man, but dozens of others were at risk, and if those dozens fell, then the entire planet was going to have to deal not only with the rampage of Ullikummis, but also the hive mind that was such a grand threat that its awakening was more than enough to hit Kane like a ton of bricks. She swiftly shouldered the Copperhead, cursing her brief hesitation, and pulled the trigger. The snarl of bullets ripping out of the barrel came an instant too late as a tentacle whipped out, wrenching her muzzle off target. Rosalia leaped backward, knowing that whatever those tentacles had, it wasn't going to be healthy for her. Akeno reached out and clawed at the power cables, pulling them up and out, sparks flying.

Rosalia lashed out with a kick, knowing that her jeans and boot would be too low and away from the parasite's tentacles and well-protected from whatever hooks or suckers it had. She hit Akeno in the back of his right thigh, the blow knocking the limb out from beneath him so that the technician toppled face-first into the main server center.

Akeno's body created a circuit between exposed components and the torn electrical cables, their insulation clawed away. The parasite leaped away from the soon-to-die Watatsumi, hurling itself to the floor in a wild thrash of tentacles. Once the high voltage leaped through his body, the server was fried. Rosalia grimaced, failing only by underestimating the ruthlessness of her enemy. She opened fire with the Copperhead, 4.85 mm rounds ripping apart the slithering mass of tentacles and sluglike trunk into an explosion of jellied guts. When the fires of the burning equipment died down, the stench of burning rubber hanging in the air, the remote-operations center was dark. The electrical circuit breakers had cut in to keep the building from melting down. Even if there was an operating transceiver, the controlling entity had made it so that there was no more power running through the circuits.

Rosalia knew that the parasite had leaped to safety to avoid a powerful electrical feedback. The enemy entity had hurled its pawn into the circuit, but knew that it was vulnerable. Bullets into the soft bodies of its cells were nothing more than pinpricks, but with high voltage, the controlling entity would feel a literal shock to its system.

Luckily, she'd killed off the ugly little snotball before it could reach a new body, namely the soldier who'd covered her back. She turned to him and looked him over with her flashlight, taking care not to blind him with the lens flare.

"I'll be fine," the Watatsumi said. "Check on Fumio. I hit him…"

Fumio! She thought of the way that Akeno's oc-toslug had leaped from his back, even after it had thrown him into the completion of a deadly electrical circuit. Rosalia rose to her feet, still clutching the rifle. "Watch yourself. These things can pop off a body at will."

The soldier jerked to a seated position, eyes wide, looking for trouble. "Oh, hell. Where is Fumio?"

"Lying over there," Rosalia said, pointing to the wounded man with the cone of light. Now he was still. She could no longer see a parasite affixed to his head. "Hell…"

Movement flashed in the corner of her eye, and she noticed that her warrior companion had suddenly wrested a chair between him and a darting, nearly fluid shape. Rosalia's mind caught up to the rapid imagery of the attack, and she recognized the extended tentacle of the parasite, withdrawing from the chair's body, curling as it retreated from the Watatsumi's shove.

Rosalia tracked it, pulling the trigger, but it was too late to capture the nimble, boneless little creature before it slid beneath a heavy cabinet.

"This is no good," Rosalia said. "Grab Fumio and we're locking this place off."

"But…" the soldier began.

"Now! We're not fucking with this thing in the dark!"

She swung the light around on the floor, scanning for its presence. "Thanks, Magistrate Man."

"Who?" the soldier asked, his own light out, sweeping for trouble while his other hand was wrapped around the grips of his pistol.

"Just pay attention," Rosalia snarled.

Suddenly there was an odd-sounding croak. Rosalia whirled, feeling something bat at her thick, flowing hair. The female adventurer flinched, whipping away to see the translucent tendril in the darkness, stretching toward her. Another of the thing's tentacles was pressed along the back of her companion's head and extended down his neck, deep under his uniform's collar. The octoslug shimmered, stretched thin between the ceiling and the Watatsumi, held in transfixed tension between two positions.

Rosalia opened fire, holding the Copperhead SMG with one hand, the flash hider touching the gelatinous flesh of the creature. The thing exploded, its insides vomiting across the floor and splashing in her face, even as the recoil yanked her fire away from the soldier.

"You okay?" Rosalia asked, noting that the reptile-skinned soldier had collapsed.

"Dark…" the man said. "Dark and alone…"

"Snap out of it!" Rosalia shouted. She keyed her

radio immediately. "Kondo! We have two men down! Akeno was an infiltrator. We've lost remote operations!"

"We know!" Kondo called back. "Grant's outside the fence, and we have no direct communication to TOTO."

"Batten everything down!" Rosalia said. She switched to her comm frequency. "Grant! Grant, come in!"

"You don't have to shout, lady," Grant answered. "What…?"

"Shut up and listen. Don't let those things touch your bare flesh," Rosalia said. "Especially the tentacles."

"What, the slugs?" Grant asked.

"I have a man here, touched for only a few seconds, and he's acting fused out," Rosalia answered. "I don't know if it's the poison or if it's something else."

"This telepathy shit isn't my strong point," Grant said. "Maybe if we had Brigid here, we'd know more, but right now, I don't have any skin exposed. Don't worry about me."

"They'll just have to cut through the shadow suit, and if they do…they'll probably end up killing you," Rosalia grumbled.

"Nice to know someone who makes me seem like a ray of fucking sunshine," Grant returned. "I don't think these slugs are interested in losing potential pawns."

"But they aren't afraid of sacrificing bodies, either," Rosalia said. "They killed one of their own rides just to cut the power to remote operations."

"How bad?" Grant asked.

"It smells like a mix of grilled alligator, burning tires and cooking long pig in here," Rosalia told him.

She could feel Grant's grimace over the radio connection. Rosalia had avoided feasting on human flesh, but she had been around when it was on the menu. From the Watatsumi's state of shock and the life-ending selflessness of the octoslug pawns, the adventuress wasn't certain which was a worse fate, being devoured by other people or being subsumed by the psyche of an alien creature. Either way, Rosalia kept a nervous eye out, her head on a swivel as it looked for potential survivors of the slug massacre.

For killing two of the deadly parasites, there was one man dead, an entire control room depowered and two others down, either poisoned, wounded or psychically raped.

"Kakusa," the soldier croaked. "We're all here, just for him. Enlil will pay for his interference."

The wording seemed delusional, but Rosalia was far too aware that Enlil was a real entity. "Kakusa?"

"The lord hidden within them all," the soldier whimpered. Tears flowed down his cheeks. "So dark. So alone...please..."

"Stay calm," Rosalia said. "Medical help's on the way."

The soldier's yellow gemlike eyes turned to her. "Kill me. I don't want to feel this way..."

Rosalia recoiled from him as he clutched at her.

Watatsumi soldiers rushed in the door, their flashlights blaring. Even as they did so, their downed comrade tore at the handgun on the ground beside him. Rosalia lunged, trying to keep him from the dreaded act she knew he wanted to commit, but she had little leverage, and she was going against the torment of a man driven completely over the edge. His elbow cracked her on the side of the neck, hurling her back and away from him.

"Put the gun down, Icchi!" one of the soldiers shouted.

The SIG twisted in his grip, the muzzle turning up to his mouth. Rosalia leaped on him again, recovering from her momentary stunning. Other men rushed forward, even as she pushed against his gun hand, keeping the barrel away from her companion's face.

"No! Stop it!" she cried.

Icchi wasn't listening. With madness-fueled strength, he bucked her off his back, then elbowed another of his fellow Watatsumi in the face. An ugly crunch preceded the soldier's toppling. He swung the gun up, taking its muzzle between his lips.

Rosalia let out a cry of frustration and, much to her dismay, the scaled scalp at the back of his skull opened up like the petals of a grisly flower.

Rosalia balled up one hand, slamming it against the wall. Her teeth were grit, and she fought against the feelings welling within her heart.

Don't get attached, she ordered herself. You can't hurt if you don't lose anything…

He saved our life, another part of her mind whispered.

It was a cold slap in the torch-sliced darkness.

Rosalia wasn't alone in this fight. Try as she could, she was unable to stifle the one human tendency she battled every day.

No human was an island. And just as the eerie connection to this demon, Kakusa, had left Icchi shattered and suicidal, Icchi's death after the brief, brave fight alongside her had left Rosalia off balance and hurt.

The ties that bound, if she was not careful, would snag around her throat and tighten like a garrote.

Chapter 19

Domi slithered through the darkness. The depth of the shadows were all but impenetrable, even for her feral senses and her extremely sensitive albino eyes. Sight was not an option, but that didn't matter to the stealthy young woman. Hearing, touch, smell, all of them combined to give her almost as clear a picture of her surroundings as if she had a lantern or broad daylight to guide her, at least in terms of the presence of others. The cannibalistic mutants were easy to smell and hear, and while she'd imagined that the hunting parties would be huge as they scurried far afield for fresh flesh, the truth was that there was a determined defense of the caverns they'd marked as their own.

She could easily scent the acrid stench of where the primeval creatures had marked their territory, and she was beginning to wish she'd brought nose plugs.

Of course, that would have left Domi even more blind than now.

The albino girl also had Priscilla in her mind, her friend's mental powers seeming to grow exponentially with each new effort. There was something that would have been disconcerting about it, but Domi felt comfortable, protected through her psychic link with the Quad V hybrid woman. There was no sense of malice or menace within her thoughts.

Indeed, the only malevolence that Domi perceived

was the stench of surly resentment that the subterranean mutants held for anything that didn't belong. More than once, she had to stop as one of the creatures left behind pounced upon a rodent that had appeared within its sensory range. Domi was glad that the shadow suit she wore was more than enough to not only blend with the darkness, but its polymer fabric qualities masked most of her scent. The rodents had made too much noise, not like the barefoot and naked-fingered albino girl who didn't scrape the floor with claws as she went down the hallways.

"Getting closer. Find a stairwell, three doors down and on your right," Priscilla directed. Utilizing her telepathy, combined with her own and Lakesh's memories of the underground base, she was directing Domi toward the nanotechnology laboratory, someplace that she could find something to counteract the sabotage left within the artificially aging scientist's genetic structure.

Since Enlil, in the form of Imperator Sam, had utilized nanotechnology to rebuild Lakesh from an ancient, withering old man with cybernetic implants to a younger, vital figure, it was Priscilla's hope that she could take any surviving nanites to undo the mental breakdown that he was suffering. The knowledge that the man held was still present, just blocked by a growing set of chemical inhibitions placed between his neurons. Priscilla explained it as Lakesh couldn't access his thoughts because he was on the ground, inside the maze that divided his intellect, but being outside of his mind, looking in as if from an overhanging cliff, she was able to make sense of the individual images from above, spotting their pattern.

Unfortunately, thanks to the mind blocks being

built up by Enlil's wrath, his body was suffering, as well. The Annunaki overlord's parting "gift" to his longtime adversary was nearly identical in makeup to a dread disease known in the twentieth century as Alzheimer's. The only indication that Lakesh wasn't suffering genuine Alzheimer's was due to Domi's knowledge of how sharp he was, despite being a quarter millennia old, preserved by suspended animation and replacement organs, both harvested from clones and living donors or made of plastic and metal.

Domi's nerves were on edge, her reflexes taut as trip wires. Priscilla barely needed to scan out from her point of view, telepathically locating the hybrid mutants, the albino girl all too aware of the threats around her.

"I'm so sorry, Domi. I thought more of them would have gone out to hunt at dusk," the Quad V woman said.

It's no problem, Domi thought. It looks like they're slow waking up.

"Their brains are so scrambled, so primitive, and there are so many of them," Priscilla replied. "Trying to read them…keep track…"

Just guide me, Domi answered. I need you steering me. I can avoid them on my own.

"But…" Priscilla began.

"Focus," Domi hissed, her teeth gritted to keep her from completely blowing her cover.

It was too late. She could hear a single grunt of curiosity, five yards in the all-consuming darkness. It was tentative, uncertain, and Domi didn't move, and even went so far as to look away from the creature, even though there was no light to reflect off her ruby eyes or alabaster cheeks. It was part superstition, part observed fact. Most human minds could "feel" the gaze of others. It could have been peripheral vision proving to be clearer than the conscious, focused sight. As the subconscious could pick up things such as faces or even the glint of eyes, it provided that eerie feeling of being watched. Few people had such free access to those vibes, Kane being one of them, Domi herself possessing a similar awareness of their subconscious perceptions. She didn't know how "in touch" these mutants were with their peripheral senses, but she was aware that the more primitive the intellect, the more acute their awareness became. Considering that these were creatures that could hunt and capture swift-moving rodents in the dark, Domi didn't want to take any chances by giving the mutant more of a chance of noticing her than necessary.

There was the scrape of claws as the hybrid mutant rose to a low stoop. Domi gnawed on her lower lip.

"Domi...I'm sorry," Priscilla's thought came through.

Give me a path out of here, damn it, Domi snapped mentally. Her frustration was all internal, not pointed toward Priscilla. The Quad V hybrid was only trying to help, looking for options. It was her own impatience that had taken things and made them dangerous for her. She kept her anger pointed squarely where it belonged, simply because she knew that Priscilla was still her ace in the hole. Any alienation, any friction, and she didn't want to imagine the kind of anger she could instill in someone so good yet so increasingly powerful.

"You don't have to worry. I'm not some simple-minded child who'll banish you to the cornfield in a fit," Priscilla assured her. Before Domi could ask for a path again, it appeared, like a glowing blue line arcing through the midnight blackness.

Domi pivoted on all fours, scurrying down the underground corridor floor with all the speed she could muster in complete silence. Even as she did so, she knew that if the creature pounced on her, she would be forced to fight with only her blade. She'd considered leaving her Detonics .45 behind at the Sandcat, but there was also the reality of having to fight against overwhelming odds between her and the vehicle on her return trip. She remembered what Kane continued to say—the true weapon was the person, not the hunk of iron she held.

It was something that she lived, taking each moment by instinct, but always knowing what she had as options. She would never find herself needing to gun down an unarmed girl gone crazy with a knife, not when she'd survived tooth and claw against Annunaki-bred hordes or stood her ground even against a mad god's wrath.

Fight or flight, the mutant made her decision, not by howling out loud to raise the alarm of an intruder within their midst, but by padding slowly, carefully, after her with greedy stealth. Domi allowed herself a cruel grin in the underground darkness. If it had been a wild alert, then Domi would have had to break and run, tearing toward the nanotechnology lab, throwing behind as many hindrances as possible. Now, with some stretch and distance, if the enemy stalked her, she had control of this hunt. She could choose the place of battle, and out of the way, she could have the cushion of isolation to survive in a quiet battle.

Domi withdrew her knife, then collapsed to one knee once she felt far enough away from the crowd.

She let out a loud, exhausted breath, then pulled back her sleeve and nicked the thick skin on the back of her forearm, just enough to produce the scent of fresh blood. She needed this to be convincing, and there was little that a predator found more alluring than injured prey.

There was no reason why the mutant would believe that she was anything but one of them. After all, she'd made use of her own acute sense of smell to find a spot not far back to rut in their spoor. She fit in, scent-wise, the shadow suit blocking her natural smell, and having replaced that void with a more familiar stench. The mutants, as she knew from Priscilla, were not above cannibalism, and only the escaped hybrid's intellect and strength of will had prevented her from falling prey. Priscilla had endured horrors at the talons of her kin, things that Domi could well imagine.

That kind of understanding, we know our own and what we've had to do to live, Domi projected as she awaited the mutant predator in the darkness. We survived bad like no one should see. That makes you family.

Domi could sense a knot grow in her throat, something projected from Priscilla herself. "You've got the path you need. If we get separated…"

What?

"There's movement outside of the Cat… I don't know if they smelled us," Priscilla began. "We're behind heavy armor. Get what has to be gotten. You have the path, you have what Lakesh thinks can fix him. We'll be fine."

Domi grimaced, but any chance of communication was gone. She couldn't waste thought as her enemy had gotten close. Her wounded-bird routine had drawn him in close enough, the scent of blood and the greed of cannibalistic, opportunistic hunger blinding the beastlike mutant to any possibility of danger.

There was a growl that seemed almost laced with glee at the approach of the hunter.

"Get some," Domi growled, low enough for her enemy to hear her, but no more than his ears.

The words stopped the bestial attacker for a moment, confusion proving to cause only a moment's hesitation, but in those fleeting milliseconds, that was enough for the feral girl to whip her knife around and lunge at the mutant. Domi wasn't heavy, but her opponent was caught in the midst of a step, and with that momentary pause, she was able to bring the cannibal to the ground with her rush. Physics and leverage were on her side, and now the would-be hunter could no longer drop his weight on what he'd believed was his prey.

Knocked down, the mutant wasn't completely helpless, and he brought up a fist like a wooden club that glanced off Domi's hard skull. It was a wince-inducing jolt, but there wasn't even a flash across her eyes on impact. No brain trauma, just a delay in her knife, the point going through shoulder muscle rather than deep through his aorta. The blade was jammed in hard, and Domi adjusted, wrenching the razor-sharp edge through fibrous tissue, looking for the artery that fed the creature's limb. It wouldn't be an instant blood pressure plunge as if it was through the main trunk, but it would slow and cripple one of those corded arms.

Another taloned hand reached up to claw at her face, but Domi cracked her forearm against the enemy's wrist, sharp nails scratching only air. A powerful wrench of the knife handle, and she was ready to bring the deadly edge to bear on a more vital area. The mutant's injured shoulder was in no shape to anchor the arm it supported—it was literally now fighting single-handedly against Domi, but a mouth full of spit and a powerful surge of leg and back muscles sent the smaller girl tumbling off him, partially blinded. Domi hit the floor, rolled and swung the edge of the knife up and between her and the oncoming assault. A lashing fist speared through the darkness toward her, unseen but heard, and then there was the jarring impact of meat and bone against implacable, splitting steel.

The mutant let out the beginning of a grunt of pain, but Domi stuck her fingers into the creature's mouth, muffling it to nothing more than a gurgle. The sound might carry, but it wouldn't be a clarion call bringing in dozens of other predators. The hot, coppery stink of blood was filling the air already, and splashing all over her. She speared her knee into the cannibal's groin, bunching her hand into a clawed fist to yank down on his jaw.

Stunned by the double attack, especially the dislocation of his mandible, the mutant didn't have the coordination to do more than flail with an unclenched, useless hand. Domi pivoted the point of her knife around, then stabbed down into the hollow of the creature's throat. Breath, hot and ragged, exploded through the newly torn hole in his windpipe. With savage strength, she lashed out, bringing the razor edge out under what would have been the hybrid mutant's ear and through the carotid artery.

With that, the beast was done. Domi only had one thing left to do, and that was to make it seem as if it was an attack by one of the monsters on another of their own. With a powerful slice, she opened his belly, fishing around until her fingers met the slimy, slippery liver of the dead opponent. She pulled hard, tearing it from its spot. This was an attack of opportunity, and she needed to behave as one of the hunters, get the most nutritious part of her dead foe's body and run. That would be an excuse for the blood trail, and with a corpse left behind, the horde would concentrate on dividing up the leftovers.

Even as the liver came out in her hands she heard the distant grunts of shuffling mutants. The stench of opened bowels was a dinner bell to them, and they were bringing deep appetites.

Domi whirled and raced down the corridor, following the path that Priscilla had imprinted in her brain. She couldn't feel her friend, even as she rushed away.

Was it distraction or something worse?

Time to worry about that later. She had a picture in her mind, and with that knowledge, she'd be fast and efficient.

She couldn't cripple herself with the worry that Priscilla and Lakesh were dead or dying.

Time was running out.

GROGAN COULD FEEL THE presence of the awakened Kakusa starting to fill the wiregrass swamp abutting the AUTEC base. They were homing in on those who had sought to enslave the entity's supercells, and if they were able to uproot the Watatsumi and the Cerberus renegades, then it was likely that they would be able to release the Entity across the world.

Ullikummis could not risk such a state, which meant that Grogan, under the guidance of his stone master, had to choose the lesser of two evils—for now.

Grogan got his radio and, utilizing the knowledge gained from the stone god's flame-haired right hand, cut into the frequency that Kane and Grant would be communicating on.

"Kane? Grant? This is Grogan, of the New Order. Come in!" he growled in a harsh whisper.

There was a moment of silence before an answer returned. "What?"

It was a deep voice, but Grogan didn't have those memories implanted in his mind by Ullikummis, who was nowhere near the hive mind that Kakusa was. "Who is this?"

"Grant. How did you get this frequency?" Grant asked.

"Three can keep a secret if two are dead," Grogan answered, putting just a little too much glee in his tone. "Stop being ridiculous and listen to me."

"You're going to warn us about the horde heading our way," Grant returned. "I can figure that much out."

"We want to work alongside you. For now," Grogan said.

"So the New Order and Licky-kun think that these brain slugs are going to be too much for them?" Grant asked. Now it was the giant ex-Magistrate's turn to put on an air of gloating.

Grogan sneered. "I have men with me. And we're going to support you."

"You'll provide them with a separate front to fight on?" Grant asked.

Grogan took a deep breath. "And I don't want to lose any more people."

"You're already deep in the hole, eh?" Grant pressed. "Only eight of you left."

Grogan looked at the radio quizzically.

"Either I'm psychic or you idiots are too blind to keep your eyes peeled," Grant said.

Grogan whipped his head around, seeing only shadows between trees. There was a sudden shifting of some of the blackness, and he could see Grant's face, and only his face, visible in the night.

Grogan nodded. "Shadow suit technology."

"We'll fight alongside each other. For now," he said. Grant's eyes narrowed. "But so help me, if Ullikummis tortured Brigid..."

Grogan set his lips into a tight, enigmatic line. It was that which would keep the Cerberus rebels off guard and off balance. There was no need for him to learn anything about Brigid Haight, the fire-tressed demon goddess who sat at the right hand of his stone god. That worry would hamper the giant.

"Where is Kane?" Grogan asked.

"Keep your mind on the work here," Grant said. He was stonewalling in return, but Grogan was certain that if there was a heart of the darkness known as Kakusa, then Kane would undoubtedly be charging toward it to land a killing blow.

"Fine. He's not going to be on our side here," Grogan returned. "Will you give word to the scaled freaks who uncorked this evil genie Kakusa?"

"Kakusa," Grant repeated. He frowned. "The Hidden."

Grogan tilted his head. "You speak Japanese."

Grant glared. "Not so damned all-knowing, eh?"

"Your linguistic skills are not relevant. What is crucial is the cooperation of the ones pulling the Hooded Ones' strings," Grogan said.

"Those strings were cut by Kakusa. He slipped one of his pawns past us," Grant retorted. "I guess he's far better at using his minions to their maximum effect, unlike the New Order."

"Grant..."

"Give me a damn second to call in," the ex-Magistrate said. He turned and stepped back, obviously to maintain his privacy.

Grogan glared. He hadn't expected the big man to have been so stealthy, attributing such ghostlike movement to Kane or Domi, according to what Haight had told him. He clenched his big fists, feeling the tendons pop and snap. No wonder the man felt so smug about Ullikummis's fallibility. Then there was the wresting of the redoubt from his control...

Elsewhere, the stone god was picking up on these observations. Grogan didn't need to feel his grim displeasure to know that the stone lord of the New Order was not going to underestimate the humans again. Indeed, it was a sign of his trust in their abilities that he deemed it necessary to enlist them as his allies in a fight with another god.

Grogan grimaced. He didn't like that Agrippine had been lost. The swamp guide had collapsed into the mud, even as the New Order expedition brought up their machetes to destroy the octopoid slug that had evacuated its temporary human host. Grogan had been too savvy to kill the man after having been in contact with the tentacled parasite; indeed, the New Order would have been able to pick his brains about what he'd experienced under the puppeteer that had held on to him.

Unfortunately, Agrippine had collapsed, fading into unconsciousness after the creature had left him and escaped on the back of a rodent. Grogan had called his people back in before losing them, knowing that a hunt in the darkness would only end with more of the New Order expedition killed. Grogan had left the comatose guide where he'd fallen, on dry ground in the hammock where they'd spoken with Kakusa.

If any of the New Order survived, they would retrieve the guide, seeking out potential secrets left behind. And if they didn't, then Ullikummis would have another rival seeking the death of Enlil and ownership of this blue marble.

"All right, stoneheads, you've got a free pass," Grant announced in his stentorian bellow. "And it's about time. I've got movement cutting through the swamp, creeping in on us from two directions."

Grogan nodded, gripping his weapon tightly.

This would be the night when gods wrestled for the fate of a world.

Chapter 20

The door wasn't going to hold for long, but Kane and Orochi had no intention of sticking around. The Watatsumi commander had swiftly pulled on the hood and gloves from a neoprene wetsuit he'd brought along with him. There was little doubt that the minions of Kakusa were going to be easy to defeat, but they had come prepared for a worst-case scenario in fighting off the parasites. A pair of dive goggles and a sleeve that had been sliced into a scarf provided the rest of the protection that Orochi would need; his skin was completely covered now.

The speakers filled the mat-trans chamber with the rumbling voice of Akeno.

"Gentlemen, I salute your courage, but I doubt your wisdom. You have entered the laboratories down here, and are surrounded by thousands of creatures containing my essence," the spawn of Kakusa said. "I know you came here in the hope of pitting one enemy against another. I have met the minions of that foe, Ullikummis, son of my jailer."

"Enlil tends to piss people off a lot," Kane replied. "I take it you don't like his little demon seed, either?"

"He will be an impediment to my personal mission. Unlike the two of you. What did you think? You would escape through the ventilation system?"

Orochi bristled, anger evident even through his

protective headgear. "Akeno, you are a soldier of the Watatsumi. Your will should…"

"Silence! You address a being who is nothing more than memories, now," Akeno's voice bellowed. "You now speak to Kakusa."

"Hidden," Kane's Commtact translated for him.

"You're in pretty open view for us, ugly," Kane taunted. "I would think that the world would notice a snotball with sucker-covered tentacles wrapped around someone's head."

"You didn't," Kakusa returned. A grim chuckle brought home the stark reminder that Grant was now under siege from every creature that the Watatsumi had infested with a parasite. "Unless you have the will to strip every person naked, I will be there, creeping and crawling."

Kane grunted, checking the ventilation shaft hatch to the mat-trans chamber. His night-vision optics informed him that nothing slithered in the smooth, empty duct—yet. He swiftly took out a small mine and placed it against the aluminum side, then activated its motion trigger. If anything brushed it, the mine would detonate, releasing a jet of concentrated flame and force, turning the duct into a killing funnel. The parasites would be coming this way—how many, Kane didn't know, but he wasn't going to count on this to be his sole means of defense.

"I hear you playing with the duct covers, humans," Kakusa said.

"Blah, blah, blah. I'm an all-knowing god," Kane returned in a mocking tone. "You can't outthink me. I'm so pretty and powerful and wise."

"You jest…" Kakusa began.

Kane turned and spoke again. "Of course I'm making a joke out of you. You're the king of snotballs! And you're repeating the same empty boasts that I've heard before. And trust me, I've heard them now literally from the bottom of the Earth to the sands of Mars. All of you are the same. You claim godhood, and yet you want everyone else to do things for *you*. And you threaten to scourge me and my friends from the face of the world, and guess who's still here and who's either dead or licking their damned wounds?"

Orochi regarded Kane as he did his bit on the entrance to the mat-trans chamber. It was a long speech for Kane, but the Cerberus rebel was using it to keep Kakusa off balance. The would-be god must have been so self-assured that it expected any challenger to be immediately cowed. Kane was frightened—it was a natural reflex—but he used that fear to give himself the edge against formidable odds. The fight-or-flight reflex had been with humankind since its ancestors first developed eyes. Fear, when acknowledged and controlled, made people careful and prepare for what was coming next. It unleashed adrenaline and extra oxygen into the bloodstream, granting reserves of strength, endurance and quickness that let them fight harder or run faster, to perform on an edge that they'd honed to such razor keenness.

"Kane, you seem full of yourself," Kakusa said. "Perhaps if we spoke in person…"

"Again you sound like a god, but you're taking the easy, weak way out of this," Kane challenged. "You want me paralyzed, shot full of octoslug venom, drugged out of my mind and simple to crush."

"Be wary, Kane, lest I lose my patience with you," Kakusa replied. "I am offering you a chance to become one with omnipotence. Such refusal may ensure that I kill you slowly, at the clubbing fists of a horde of minions whose combat skills are a sum total of experience beyond your brief years."

"Go ahead," Kane replied.

With that, the duct suddenly shook, a thunderbolt of expanding superheated gases spearing out of the mine. Squeals of agony unlike anything that Kane had heard whistled through the air and, in the back of his mind, he could feel the tickle, the tingle of Kakusa's pain telepathically transmitted among the parasitic creatures caught in the immediate path of the thermobaric mine's path.

"Ryu's bones!" Orochi snarled. "The stink of them, it's unbearable!"

The mine's cutting fire bolt extruded down the duct, focused so that its force left Kane and his ally unharmed by back blast or shrapnel. It was a one-shot surprise, but at least it would give Kakusa pause before lunging into action through what could have been a blind spot.

"You think the destruction of a few cells hurts?" Kakusa asked.

"I heard your scream, dumb-ass," Kane said. "How do you think I know you even woke up?"

"Mind your tongue, ape," Kakusa snapped. "I was enslaving solar systems when your kind hadn't advanced beyond single-celled organisms."

"And yet you still ended up trapped inside a bunch of crawling boogers," Kane taunted.

The entrance hatch of the mat-trans control room jolted, lurching open as the crew on the other side finished deactivating the locks. Even as the door opened, a small cluster of flash and concussion grens had their pins yanked out from the hatch's movement. The combined flash and thunder of the multiple gren detonations created a bone-jarring roar that ran even through Kane's bones, though he had shielded himself from the brunt of the force.

Orochi had taken cover inside the mat trans itself, counting on the armaglass to protect his unshielded senses, and gambling correctly. Kakusa was powerful, and able to see through the eyes and hear through the ears of countless minions, but if those pawns were left blind and deaf, the hidden god actually had nothing to work with.

Kane, with Orochi spinning out of the mat trans, plowed through the insensate minions. As he passed some of them, his fingers raked at tentacles and bulbous slug bodies, tearing through their rubbery skin and bursting them like jelly-filled balloons. Watatsumi hosts, already clutching pained eyes and ears, collapsed, suddenly cut off from the central hive mind. Orochi worked cleanup.

It may have been a useless gesture, now that it was shown that former hosts had been left comatose and incapacitated, but Kane wondered if it would be so easy to reconnect with those pawns once violently separated from them. There had been a dozen men, all armed and prepared for combat against the pair in the mat-trans chamber, but Kane's stratagem and Orochi's knowledge of their preparations had turned the tide.

Kakusa was down by twelve humanoid pawns, and who knew how many other cells, and the two men had barely started, their limbs and spirits still fresh.

Kane nodded to Orochi, and the pair of warriors bolted down a corridor, moving with as much speed as they could muster, senses sharp and wary for ambushing parasites and subjugated sentries at every corner.

Kakusa may have held the Tongue Of The Ocean, but Kane planned to snatch it back, just like the proverbial cat from Brigid Baptiste's old saying.

THE GLIMMERING BLUE LINE, a tether path between Domi and her destination, shortened. It was like a living conduit that would disappear as she crossed it, then follow her with each bob and weave she made and, if she took a step back, it stretched with her. The feral girl knew the blue line was an illusion, but it was something incredible. She felt a warmth and security from this winding, blue-white thread that led her through the infernal underground maze.

Of course you're going to feel comfortable. Priscilla's going to put something in your head that makes you freak out?

The door to the nanotechnology laboratory was ajar when she reached it, and she kept her knife ready. She'd wiped it off in a pile of dirt and rubbish where she'd left the liver of the mutant she'd slain, so there would be little scent of blood on it. Domi still caught the tang of that coppery smell, which meant the monsters in the darkness could, too. All she could do was to hope that they were too busy snacking on the buffet she'd left for them. Their grunts and barks as they struggled over morsels of flesh, greed and tempers flaring in the midst of their cannibalistic feast, told her that they were still far behind, and she had safety and distance on her side.

Domi could only tell that the door was ajar by touch, and out of caution and not-yet-paranoid instinct, she felt the floor in front of the door. It wasn't a sliding panel, but an actual hinged hatch. And she could trace an arc formed by the door, having opened and closed often, cut through the detritus and grime on the old, abandoned tiles.

Someone was using this lab. Someone or something.

Domi's knuckles creaked as she gripped her knife even more firmly, swallowing a lump of fear. With a gentle caress, she tugged open the door just wide enough for her to slip her slender shoulders through, and she slithered inside. Immediately the blue line focused on another door. It looked similar to an air lock, something she'd encountered in Cerberus and several other far-flung locations in her brief, hectic life.

Of course the front door to the lab wasn't going to deposit her right where she needed to be. The segment of corridor that acted as the air lock looked lived in, a large nest settled in one corner, the sleeping place of a carnivore judging by the stench of the rags and cardboard piled to make the primitive sleeping mat.

Domi sidestepped it, feeling an ominous dread over the empty nest, her other hand dropping to the .45 pistol she carried in her belt. This was a primal, violent beast. There was decayed meat that had dripped from slavering jaws, and the breadth of the mat showed that whatever she had missed encountering was large, bigger even than the rest of the mutant horde that infested Area 51's dank tunnels. It had been only a few years since she'd been here, since the great battle that rendered Area 51 useless to the hybrid barons before their ascension to Annunaki godlings. And yet the place was in a state of complete disrepair.

Garbage, grime, stench, it had built up quickly. Maybe even too quickly.

Priscilla! Domi thought, trying to project with all of her will.

No response. Was her mind just not strong enough? She fought to empty her mind, to be in the moment as she reached the next door, this one a sliding hatch that she was able to move along easily. Now the floor seemed clean. The laboratory had the familiar, antiseptic feel of the well-preserved bowels of the Cerberus redoubt.

No, it wasn't completely unlived in. On a hunch, she reached out, and her fingers found a pressure switch. At contact, fluorescent lights popped into harsh, blue-white illumination, and Domi had to pull on her sunglasses. Her sensitive ruby eyes were not meant for such a swift and sudden change in lighting. Through the shades, she could see that she was in a reception area. Priscilla's telepathically implanted path etched its way along to a doorway.

Thanks to the shades, her eyes quickly adjusted to the layout of the room. There were a half-dozen major doorways leading off the far end of the reception area, and Priscilla's tracking line, driven by Lakesh's memory of this redoubt, pointed toward one of the laboratories.

The door she'd passed through wasn't locked, and once more the main entrance was left fully ajar, with only a nest. She tried to measure how long it would take for this place to have gotten in such a condition. After all, she knew the living conditions that occurred in the Tartarus Pits, which had smells and rubbish of the same scale. The Tartarus Pits, however, at the base of Cobaltville, had been in existence for decades, and were populated by hundreds.

The numbers of the horde felt deceptive, as well. There had been fifty of the creatures in hot pursuit, and if there was a group that actually remained behind here…how would they all have enough to eat, unless there were food stores within Area 51? And if there was a supply of food, what was the purpose of going out and hunting other humanoids or killing each other off? And if they were slaughtering their weaker members, how come there were so many, indeed, far more than had appeared the last time she'd been imprisoned in the underground base?

The clean lab had a new stink about it. A shadow moved in the distance, and she felt an eerie prickling inside her mind, just like when Priscilla first made contact with Domi. It became a lot clearer, suddenly. Her contact with Priscilla was blocked. As if there was something else, like her, that was in operation. Something or someone.

"Not a bad supposition, Domi," came a hoarse, crackling voice from a doorway. "Welcome to my lair."

Domi was tempted to pull her .45 and gun him down, but that urge was forcibly suppressed by an outside force. She grimaced, realizing that these creatures had been too organized, as far as their hunt for her. They had been cunning, and more than a little too selfless in their attempts to tear at her flesh. Plus, according to Priscilla's thoughts, the numbers of these hordelings hadn't been this huge.

"You made the mutants," Domi said, realizing that she was still capable of speech, but the violent, hateful urges within her were mired in a molasses of mental power.

He was much like Priscilla, with a shimmering skin that was partly between the Quad V hybrids and the coarser, reptilian Nephilim. His eyes shone with a similar intellect to hers, and his physique was still slender, but with corded muscle along his limbs.

"I am their father," the mutated hybrid said. He sneered. "You are a quick learner."

"Need to be," Domi answered. "What'd you do to Priscilla?"

"You've your own suppositions, girl. I'm sure you know what's going on," the being said. "My name is Rioch. And you are Domi. And you came here seeking the cure for Lakesh."

"Gonna gimme?" Domi asked. "Or do I kick your ass?"

Rioch snapped his fingers, grinning. "You are delightfully brash. I'm curious about you and he. I was hoping for a proper intellect to show up so I might gain from his knowledge. And lo, you bring him."

"Lucky you," Domi grumbled. "You want his brain. I want a cure for him."

"Arrangements might be made," Rioch told her. "One thing. Priscilla found an attraction, a kinship with you. Why?"

"We're freaks of a feather," Domi said, employing a term she'd learned from Brigid. "You got the doomie powers, read that outta my head."

"I could. But I was wondering if you understood why you seemed to mesh so quickly," Rioch prompted.

"Easy. She's just like Quavell. My friend," Domi answered. Her eyes narrowed behind the lenses of her shades. "What's it to you?"

Rioch's slender, lipless mouth turned up into a smile. "She and I are part of a particular strain that was an experiment, just as Quavell was. The human DNA in us was a little more...authoritative."

"No sticks up your asses," Domi countered. "Got emotions. Dreams."

Rioch nodded again. "You understand the reason for this?"

"Barons wanted to stop being sickly. Didn't know *Tiamat* was coming. Maybe you get stronger bodies," Domi said. "Humans are tougher than the spindly little freaks."

"Success," Rioch replied, spreading his lean, muscular arms. "And we've tapped so much more than those evolutionary dead ends could."

"Like controlling muties," Domi responded. She kept talking, knowing that was all she had. Rioch had her combative instincts and reflexes tamped down with his telepathic abilities. Maybe if she gave Priscilla enough time, her powers might—

"Priscilla is not going to help you," Rioch interrupted her thoughts. "She is destined to be my bride, but first I had to make sure that she was worthwhile as a mate."

"So you made the mutie hybrids," Domi said. "How many brides you make?"

"Enough to learn my lessons," Rioch returned.

"Sicko," Domi snarled. "Getting your jollies off cannibals."

Rioch tilted his head, smirking. "It is entertaining to see them have at each other."

"You got monsters. What you need Lakesh for?" Domi asked. If it was one thing that Domi learned over her years, it was that these sociopaths loved to talk about themselves and their aspirations.

Rioch nodded. "Ah, yes. He can respark the technology within this base. I've been able to have the breeding vats produce more, and thanks to *Tiamat's* signal, anything that's born is now closer and closer to becoming full Nephilim, rather than hybrids."

"You don't wanna share your snake-faces with Enlil," Domi countered.

"Sooner or later, he'll find a way to get even these creatures under his control. I do not wish to become spare parts for a god who abandoned me," Rioch told her. "Right now, your lover and mine are trapped inside a Sandcat, held there at bay by my children."

"Priscilla know she's yours?" Domi asked.

"She soon will," Rioch said. "Once I have made certain you are harmless to me, I'll have her fully awaken, and then, with her powers at her peak, we'll shut off and reverse the process rendering Lakesh a feeble, helpless old fool."

"Make sure that I'm harmless to you," Domi repeated. "You gonna cut my brain up? Or just kill me?"

"Well, I could certainly use you *if* you were to be a good soldier," Rioch told her. "I wouldn't have to do anything to your mind. I already have the carrot and stick to control you."

"Lakesh's health," Domi returned. "You know how the sickness works."

"And I can re-create it. Something I could do at a whim with him inside my realm here," Rioch said.

"Was gonna say, shitty lair. But then, you had a good idea. Made it look lived-in by a bunch of man-eaters. No one's coming here. Not with them around," Domi challenged. She couldn't hide her disgust with him. "No one except people looking for supplies and tech."

"People who I could enslave." Rioch grinned. "You are bright. You've learned much in your years along-side Kane, Grant and Lakesh."

Priscilla, she thought. You feel me?

There was nothing, at least nowhere close to the kind of two-way mindspeak she'd had with the hybrid mutant before. Still, she had that warm tingle, the tickle in her heart and consciousness. She hadn't been abandoned, meaning that there was still a link, a tether between the two of them. The only problem was that Rioch had expunged himself from her memory and seemed to have been able to erect a barrier in open communication. Anything was simply whispers in a howling gale.

Domi grimaced. "Sick. Perv. Freak."

Rioch stepped closer to her, caressing her cheek with one slender hand. "You can be here for the return of your lover, or you can just die now."

Domi bit her upper lip. His touch made her skin crawl, and the rage of revulsion bubbled up inside of her. Anger built, and she didn't care if he felt it. She grit her teeth and felt her fists clench.

"Hurry, Domi. Lakesh is fading!" came the sudden impulse from Priscilla.

Hot rage and urgency rushed through Domi's limbs and she backhanded the half-breed, knocking him to the floor.

"Kill her!" the telepathic sorcerer bellowed.

From the corridor behind, Domi could hear the crash of bodies charging to their master's side.

Time was running out as she launched herself toward the laboratory.

GRANT DIDN'T TRUST GROGAN as far as he could heave a Sandcat, but right now he and the New Order expedition were out in the thick of the amassing forces under the guidance of an entity known as Kakusa. Even as the two men and the eight other members of the group were observing the movement of a combined force of men and massive reptiles, the enemy was getting closer to the fence that provided the AUTEC base with its perimeter.

Grogan showed his displeasure at the setup, gripping his gun. "We should get out of here."

Grant shook his head. There were three pincers, like a three-fingered claw, and Grant's group was between two of those assault lines. There were a hundred Hooded Ones, and a dozen alligators were still kicking. The reptiles were formidable foes; the ex-Magistrate had experienced that himself, as had Grogan. Still, Grant had a supply of grens, and the New Order soldiers had taken a few of them. High explosives would help even the odds between the Watatsumi and Kakusa's fist.

It would still count for nothing unless Kane and Orochi did their part in the Tongue Of The Ocean base. According to Kondo, there were thousands of these parasitic monsters teeming in breeder vats. Those kinds of odds were what made Grant wish that he was going with his partner and best friend, but the Watatsumi were an asset that needed protection.

"Give it another moment to let them get snarled in the fence," Grant whispered. "Once they're committed, fighting against the wire, we'll hit them."

"While they're off balance, looking away from us," Grogan said. "Pretty ruthless."

Grant smirked, then glared at Ullikummis's lieutenant. "We don't regularly win against impossible odds by playing fair."

Grogan returned a grin of respect. "Just a few more seconds."

Grant held off, waiting for the moment when he could pull the pin on an implode grenade and cut a swathe of destruction through Kakusa's assailing force. He hated the idea of targeting innocents, pawns of a deadly parasite and a godlike hive mind, but right now, they had shown that they could evacuate their hosts, leaving behind mindless, helpless cripples.

If there was a way to save lives, then it would come...

Something exploded, and Grant noticed a tall conifer near the AUTEC perimeter shudder. Thousands of pounds of reptilian muscle suddenly lurched at the damaged tree trunk, their weight and strength producing the sudden whine and crackling of the mastlike trunk, and the gators had launched the tree directly toward the fence. A ton of living wood came down, mashing concertina wire and chain link with the same brutal force.

"Damn it. Every one of them is as smart as Kakusa," Grant observed.

Grogan frowned. "Would that I had a measure of my master's power. This would be an equal fight..."

Grant snapped his Sin Eater into his grasp with a sneer. "Like I said before, Grogan..."

He hurled one of the grens, the weapon live as it left his grasp, arcing toward the group that had downed the tree and the fence in one fell move. His aim was slightly off, but the swarm that headed toward the torn perimeter was rocked, bodies bowled over by the high-intensity blast.

"We don't beat the impossible by fighting fair!"

The battle for AUTEC began.

Chapter 21

Kane separated from Orochi, moving toward the heart of the TOTO base. Along the way, he stopped every so often, prying open access hatches and hacking at wire insulation with his combat knife. He was going to have to find some way to bring down Kakusa, and there was one surefire way to keep the mad god in check.

Kane paused as he reached an intersection. He was able to see figures flooding one hallway in the darkness, more of the Tongue Of The Ocean staff, guided by the octoslugs riding on their shoulders and heads. With his enhanced optics Kane could see in near complete darkness, and the shadow suit provided him with protection from the strength-sapping powers of Kakusa's multiple cells. Kakusa's tentacles were literally incapable of harming him through the high-tech polymer suit.

That didn't mean that its troops couldn't tear him apart or even gun him down, but Kane was counting on Kakusa's original offer. The hive mind wanted to strengthen itself, and that meant stealing Kane's knowledge, his abilities and his resourcefulness. He didn't want to imagine what kind of damage Kakusa could do with a unified army under its very whim. Giving over that power and intellect to Kakusa would be a hell of a nightmare.

Right now, Kane's best advantage against Kakusa

and its minions was the fact that Orochi had hit the emergency shutdown for the TOTO's main generators. Emergency lighting was hardly ideal, but thanks to his night-vision optics, Kane was unhindered by the dull, low-energy red glow of the lamps. He wasn't certain about the optic abilities of the octoslugs, but as long as he kept moving and remained sheathed in the protective polymers, Kane could keep on the move, fighting against Kakusa.

"Kane! This is a fool's errand!" a quartet of the Entity's enraptured slaves spoke in unison. "You cannot sabotage the base. There are backups!"

Kane whirled and faced the group of pawns, striking with lightning speed at the one in the lead. He drove the heel of his palm dead center into the Watatsumi man's upper chest. The impact was more than powerful enough to lift him from his feet and hurl him against another just behind him. With the speed and power of a human wolf, the former Magistrate snatched the wrist of a second knife-wielding man and twisted the limb around, using him as a combination of shield and club against the fourth member of the group. The two Watatsumi stumbled backward, Kane's strength and leverage turning them into an avalanche of tangled limbs and bouncing foreheads.

Kane had three of them down for the moment, leaving him free to return to the second one, whose recovery time was swifter than he'd imagined. Still, the ex-Magistrate caught the sign of movement out of the corner of his eye, and his sharp reflexes once more sprang into action. He blocked the swing of a pipe with his forearm, then pivoted to face his foe, bringing his fist around. The blunt faces of the Watatsumi were close to normal human, but their noses were squat so he adjusted midswing on instinct. He didn't want an inadvertent punch to crush nasal bones and drive them into a brain. He was fighting with a handicap that Kakusa didn't have, even as he connected with a crashing right to the Watatsumi's jaw. Nerves exploded with the hit, and the foe collapsed to the floor grating in a stunned mass of unconscious flesh.

The tentacled mass attached to the unconscious host lurched, tendrils snapping out and gripping Kane's calf. It attached itself to the Cerberus warrior's leg as if it were a rubber band released. Kane could feel the tentacles kneading, trying to pry open the seal between his boot and shadow suit pant leg, hoping to reach the naked flesh beneath. Before the parasite had a chance to get to him, he pierced its central sluglike mass with his combat knife with a powerful slash. Dead tentacles relaxed their grip on him, and Kane could see another party of Kakusa's followers appear in the distance.

Kane leaped over the stunned mind slaves, and continued deeper into the TOTO base. Orochi had given him directions to the cavern where they had discovered the stored remnants of Kakusa's body. It was a hunch, but his instincts hadn't led him into failure yet. He also felt a powerful tingle, the presence of the alien entity's hive mind acting like a beacon leading him onward. Kakusa's intellect had grown with the addition of scores of bodies under its command, and as such, the weight of its presence was unmistakable, like the distant heartbeat of a sleeping giant.

The Entity would want to assemble itself in a proper location. Since it was trapped inside each of the cells, it would want a body for itself, one independent of the mewling apes that it had latched on to. That meant

Kakusa would build a lair for itself in surroundings to fit such a form.

A vent burst open, writhing, slimy limbs and slug bodies pouring through the opening. Kakusa had expected to cut Kane off, but with wolflike agility and power, he dived through the mass of parasites, hitting the floor on the other side. Kane allowed himself two more rolls on the hard grating, using his weight and the irresistible steel floor to pop and burst what bodies had attached themselves to him. Kane rose to his feet and continued onward. He snapped his Sin Eater loose and opened fire on another electrical maintenance hatch, powerful slugs shattering circuit boards.

Once he'd completed that bit of sabotage, he had the freedom to continue his race to see the face of Kakusa. Behind him, with one glance, Kane noticed that the pursuit teams were ignoring the damage he'd wrought on unpowered conduits and electrical junctures. Most of it was merely cosmetic, while the rest was crude, hammer-smashing mayhem. Kane had spent several minutes moving between key trunk lines, severing cables and cords.

He counted on Orochi to get the rest done. The two men were on the same communication frequency. Every few moments Orochi counted down another number, giving Kane vital intelligence that the Watatsumi commander was still alive and unharmed. They'd chosen to count every other second, Orochi knowing exactly how long a host would be paralyzed before the parasites could enact their control. If Kakusa gained Orochi's mind, the whole plan would be lost, but the self-proclaimed son of the dragons had holed up out of sight and almost literally out of mind. Kakusa might be able to find him, given enough manpower and time, but Kane had run a twisting trail of terror and damage through the TOTO, his fists and skills cutting into that fighting force.

Kakusa had forces down here and aboveground to work with, which meant that its attention span was spread pretty thin, but since the Entity claimed to be able to absorb intellects, Kane figured that it would be akin to a computer with multiple processor chips. The more minds Kakusa controlled, not only did it gain more knowledge, but also the additional ability to concentrate on multiple tasks.

Orochi's count was the only thing giving Kane hope as he dared to combat Kakusa. He reached the air lock that led into the ancient Annunaki deep sea cave. The Cerberus rebel glanced back. Sure enough, the entire crew of the TOTO, all twenty-five of them according to Orochi's count, were in pursuit. He recognized those that had lost their cephalopod parasites, now up and running again, ridden by new cells, urged onward according to the will of Kakusa.

Kane grimaced, then lobbed a stun gren in front of the charging throng. A high-pressure burst of force, light and sound proved more than sufficient to leave the Watatsumi warriors sprawled, having tripped over the first who were halted by their collision with the powerful flare. Snarled up, Kakusa's force would fall a little farther behind. Even so, Kane could see the slithering mass of extant parasites flow over the tangled, tripped-up group.

"Come and get me, Kakusa!" he taunted, shouting behind him. With that, he ducked through the open air-lock doors, and out into a high-walled hall, huge arches upholding a vaulted ceiling. Kane had to admit that the Annunaki knew how to built a foyer. He plucked one more of his dwindling supply of grens and lobbed it at the encroaching mass of tentacles and slug bodies. This one was definitively lethal, and when the miniature bomb landed, wet stars of shredded parasites spiraled away from the stunned mass.

"You offend me, ape," a deep, resonating voice echoed from the far side of the great hall. Kane turned, and thanks to the odd, bioluminescent glow of the underground Annunaki lair, he was able to make out a towering column of undulating, pulsing flesh.

He focused his optics on Akeno, who lay, crucified across the face of the teeming, inhuman stalk of cephalopodlike cells that had created its own body. Tentacles stuck to Akeno's head like the rays of a starfish, and the Watatsumi's eyes were blank, staring unfocused, all color removed from their irises.

"Kakusa, I presume?" Kane asked.

The column moved with unnatural smoothness, drawing closer to the lone human. "What did you think, Kane? That you could shut down the TOTO and keep me from the surface?"

Kane shrugged.

"Enlil entrapped me within primordial creatures, their boneless bodies long lost to the shadows of prehistory, but they were bred for these depths and yet they survive even in your thin-aired realm," Kakusa said. "My proteins survived the journey through the deep void, ignoring cold that turns air to crystals and radiation that would boil your DNA within your cells. Do you think that a mile-long swim from the bottom of the ocean will slow me down?"

Kane smirked. "What about your hosts? Human bodies, even the Watatsumi, aren't built for this."

"My cells can find their own hosts when we reach

shallow waters or swampland. We won't dry out," Kakusa rumbled. "Come, now, Kane. What do you think, that you'll do something brave like blow a hole in the ceiling, collapsing tons of mass upon my body? This is for your benefit, not mine. Thousands of my cells could be crushed to jelly, and I wouldn't even care."

"No, you wouldn't," Kane responded. "You're invulnerable. Nothing can kill you, which is why Enlil stuck you into a ton of boogers."

"Your taunts mean nothing, human. When your bones are dust, Enlil will exist, and I will endure, perhaps even pulling his strings as my personal puppet," Kakusa told him. "What is your next stratagem, monkey?"

Kane grinned before he turned, drew an implode grenade and hurled it toward the air lock.

Kakusa threw back Akeno's head, letting a hollow laugh escape its surrogate's mouth. "You're going to drown yourself, Kane?"

Foaming jets of seawater gushed around the weakened edges of the air lock, pouring into the cavern.

"That's your plan. I tell you that I can survive the depths of the ocean effortlessly, and you still desperately try to drown me…or crush me under a falling ceiling." Kakusa chuckled. "You're a damned fool, human!"

Kane looked down at his feet, watching the seawater begin to raise, flowing up over his toes, then his ankles. He watched as the rising water splashed against the lower tentacles of the column that Kakusa had formed of itself.

Kane smiled for the creature that imagined that it was an all-wise God.

"Okay, Orochi. You can turn the juice back on," he directed into his Commtact.

"What?" Kakusa asked. There was genuine confusion on Akeno's features.

"Mister I'm so invulnerable and unkillable," Kane said with a chuckle. "Feel the burn, snotball!"

With that, Kane fired a few shots from his Sin Eater, putting several holes through Akeno, silencing the prattling godling's mouthpiece, then rushed toward the air lock. He noted with grim satisfaction that the incoming ocean water was knee-deep as he pushed through the incoherent, flood-scattered mob of Kakusa's followers.

GRANT LEAPED AS HARD as he could, his long, mighty legs driving him four feet into the air, and yet it was barely high enough for him to clear the armored, slashing tail of one of Kakusa's crocodilian minions. He avoided the brunt of the impact, but the sharp, heavy scales of the creature's tail actually left welts even through the big Cerberus warrior's shadow suit.

The glancing blow sent Grant face-first into the wiregrass. The landing wasn't graceful, but the ex-Magistrate was more worried about his physical safety, not his bruised ego. He dug his fingers into the ground and pushed up and away. The beast's teeth might not have been sharp enough to get through the shadow suit, but no form of armor would have been sufficient to keep his joints from being twisted with more than enough force to sever arteries and shred muscles. Even so, the collision with the blunt nose of the alligator was enough to throw Grant two yards, but this time, he landed on his back.

The deadly predator swung its massive head toward

Grant. Twice, it had failed to cripple the human that had defied it, and this creature was possessed of Kakusa's intelligence, in addition to its own natural instincts. When those yellowed eyes of the gator locked on Grant, they were filled with genuine hatred.

"Come get it," Grant said, regaining control of his Sin Eater as it was still hooked to his forearm holster. The beast let loose a roar and charged. The ex-Magistrate leaped to the side and watched as the massive alligator tore through more of its fellow Hooded Ones. Grant whirled and opened fire, triggering the Sin Eater on full-auto, heavyweight 9 mm slugs smashing through the armored hide of the monster. He walked the line of bullets up to the parasite that rode it, and he watched as the blob exploded violently.

Grant noticed, in the darkness, with the quick telescopic zoom and his night-vision optics, that a smaller, barely formed version of the parasite flew from the exploding octoslug. Acting on a hunch, Grant turned and grabbed another of Kakusa's slaves, and twisted his head around, spying a sac growing within the sluglike body of the parasite. Inside the sac was an embryonic version of the creature, and Grant's gut filled with cold ice water.

"Damn," he grunted. "Grogan! These bastards are pregnant!"

The big New Order operative whirled. While he was covered with the tentacled beasts, Grant saw that he was hardly hindered by their presence. It had to have been the will of Ullikummis resisting their stings and perhaps the psychic energy burning through their tendrils.

"Pregnant?" Grogan growled, his thick fingers digging at one of the cephalopodlike monstrosities stuck to his neck. As he pulled his slime-covered hand away from the burst creature, he saw a baby octopus in his palm. "It's not alive...not yet."

"They haven't fully cooked yet," Grant grumbled. "These buns aren't ready to survive outside the oven."

"We're still taking time to tap each of the parasites, provided we can find them," Grogan snarled. "Thank you for the heads-up."

"I don't want any of these things escaping," Grant told him.

Grogan crushed more of the creatures, stretching out their tentacles as he pried at them. "What about Kane?"

"He's working on the main source," Grant said.

"And if he fails?" Grogan asked.

"All of these things are pregnant," Grant answered. "Imagine a thousand of these things bearing babies when they come to shore."

"Ugh," Grogan grunted.

Grant scanned the perimeter and keyed his Commtact, which worked on the same frequency as Rosalia's comm device. "Rosalia, how's the perimeter?"

"Some of the parasites have come loose from their hosts, and we're doing a search and destroy against them," Rosalia answered. "These things are fast and they're hard to hit in the dark."

"What about the fence?" Grant asked.

"I had Kondo light two of the trees on fire. Seems Kakusa doesn't trust his minions' ability to survive fire, or worse," Rosalia responded. "We're keeping them at bay with gunfire."

"Keep it up," Grant said. "And don't get tagged by one of them."

"I saw what happens to someone touched by Kakusa," Rosalia said ominously. "I won't let those things latch on to me."

Grant grumbled. He looked at the New Order operatives. Now there were only three left fighting, one of them being Grogan. Ullikummis seemed not to have much concern about his followers as they fought endlessly, ignoring any fear of death.

Grogan still lived, he still fought, emptying his gun into the darkness, stopping only when he finally connected with his target. The Hooded Ones were all but dead, having fallen under the guns and bludgeoning fists of the New Order, Grant and the Watatsumi. There was gunfire and screaming inside of the perimeter. Maybe there were one or two of the hooded men still fighting, and a gator was tearing through the AUTEC base, but the main problem seemed to be the "bug hunt" for the insidiously quick parasites.

"Rosalia?" Grant called.

"Get in here," Rosalia answered. "We're blasting away at this fucking gator, and it's not going down!"

Grant looked toward Grogan, then abandoned the New Order leader. The battle outside of the perimeter was over, but there were still menaces in the night. He located where one of the preborn octoslugs had landed. It was writhing, twitching with near life. Grimly, he ground his boot heel against the creature, bursting it and grinding it into a wet spot on the soil. He turned and rushed toward the base, knowing that now more than ever it was up to Kane to end the menace of Kakusa. He hoped that things were going well for his friend.

If not, this grim exercise in extermination was a wasted effort, and the world would be left bare and naked against the emergence of a monstrous entity.

DOMI FELT PRISCILLA'S strength roll through her, giving her the freedom to escape from Rioch's oppressive mental hold. As she dived through the laboratory doors, she spotted the device that she'd been sent to retrieve. That was her mission, to find the nanite deactivation controller that would reverse the effects of Enlil's vengeance. Veering away from it now would be a waste of Lakesh's life and would ruin any chance that the Cerberus rebels would have against Enlil, his brethren and Ullikummis. There were too many threats to the world, too many things that needed to be done, and Mohandas Lakesh Singh was a man who had the kind of knowledge and organization to get the job done. As vital as Kane, Grant and Brigid were toward stopping madmen, Lakesh was there to provide the foundations of rebuilding the scarred, damaged species known as humanity, raising it from nomadic tribes to a force for goodness and progress.

She grabbed the device and looked it over. There was a readout screen, a touch pad of numbers and a blunt, rubber-shielded antenna that poked up like a tired coyote's single ear. She knew that Priscilla would have to operate the device, and she'd have to do it by tapping into Lakesh's segregated, besieged brain.

That was all fine with Domi, but there was the matter of Rioch and his minions. They stood between her and the Sandcat, and there was no way that she had enough ammunition or muscle to power through that group.

"I'm going through Lakesh's memories," Priscilla

said, once more in her brain. She sounded strained, pushed to her limits, as if she was trying to hold two great weights at once.

Domi took that as a cue to secure the lab door, and she stepped back, shooting out the lock.

"Can't talk long. Rioch's fighting me," Priscilla transmitted. Suddenly a hatch flared bright blue in Domi's peripheral vision. "Hurry back."

Domi turned and pried open the access panel. Behind it was a small but usable service tunnel. There wouldn't be much room for a full-grown man to squirm in, but her short height and slender build made it possible for her to slither inside it with rapid ease. Domi recalled the half-pint creatures, transadapts, who had been utilized as labor on Mars, and realized that this may have been designed specifically for them. The truth of the matter became much more apparent as she crawled a few yards down the tunnel, and spotted a long, inert, husklike box with lean mechanical arms. It wasn't transadapts; these were some kind of maintenance robots.

She made certain the nanite remote was secure in her pack, then set to scurrying along. She couldn't imagine how Lakesh knew about such details as the maintenance structure.

"He doesn't," Priscilla interjected. "Just like Rioch learned from the cryo-stored staff, I found a maintenance director."

"So he knows about this tunnel," Domi grunted as she scurried through the tunnel, pushing past repair bots that had long since lost their battery charge.

"Yes," Priscilla answered. "He doesn't have anyone that can fit in there, though."

Domi grinned, moving with all of her monkeylike

agility down the tunnel. She couldn't see, but traveling by touch was easy, especially with the shimmering thread that gave her direction in the complete darkness. Ahead, something rattled, a hatch bashed inward, the smashing of metal accompanied by angry growls. She could see dim light from below as a head loomed into the tunnel.

Domi didn't pause, drawing her Detonics and releasing her own bellow. She knew full well that touching off a .45-caliber pistol in such a confined space would cause serious ear damage, unless she equalized the pressure in her head with a yell. She pulled the trigger and the cannibal hybrid's head jerked back in ugly fashion.

She continued on, skirting the mouth of the hatch and firing another shot at a new mutant menace that was crowding through to get at her. The heavy slug stopped the monstrosity cold as it tore off the mutant's mandible and speared down through his rib cage. It was cruel and brutal, but she had no choice. These things were going to kill her, and with her death, Priscilla and Lakesh were trapped and helpless, laid bare for Rioch's machinations. There was more activity up ahead, but the route that Priscilla had given her turned her away from the next hatch, and she scurried up a small incline with handholds—or rather "wheel holds"—for the maintenance bots. She was pushing closer to the surface, and with that, she grew more and more emboldened.

Her slender arms and legs burned with the strain of pushing through the tight quarters. Domi didn't let it bother her. Discomfort was something she'd lived with for all of her life. Pain and muscle strain had been more than constant companions, and they provided the knowledge that she lived, and that she could push even harder. She was working her limbs at near to maximum efficiency, and if she trudged along harder, she'd risk some form of injury. If she slowed, she was certain that Rioch would hurl more of the cannibal mutants into her path, and she knew that she'd only defeated the pair at the last hatch by dint of surprise and luck on her part.

Domi was a feral warrior, but that didn't mean she was mindlessly aggressive or strategically stupid. She had an uncanny sense of when to fight and when to run, and right now she had to flee as quickly as possible.

"Domi...hurry!" Priscilla urged. There was genuine terror in that summoning. Rioch and his minions must have been getting close to breaching the Sandcat, which filled her with fear and dread.

"Coming!" Domi snarled, teeth grit.

Time was running out, and she refused to let her friends fall into slavery to the hybrid mind sorcerer that ruled the depths of Area 51.

Chapter 22

Kane's journey through Kakusa's puppets was made much easier by the high-intensity jets of water that sliced through the weakened air lock's superstructure. The implode grenade had accomplished a fine job as it was speeding along the flooding, not only of the ancient Annunaki hall, but of the TOTO base. The plan he'd come up with required an uninterrupted level of seawater.

There was confusion in the corridor, even as Kane hammered his way past, using the butt of his Sin Eater as a club in one hand and the power of his left fist to pound opponents out of the way in the churning, waist-deep waters.

"Where's my electricity?" Kane asked.

"It's taking time to build up a sufficient charge," Orochi answered. "Plus I'm not slogging through a flood without the insulation your suit may—or may not—provide."

Kane nodded grimly as he pushed the last of his humanoid opponents out of the way. The water reached up to his ribs now, so he kicked up his feet, spearing both hands into the water, Sin Eater snapping back into its forearm holster. Swimming was easier than sloshing against the resistance of water. Behind him, something surged, and a telepathic bellow itched inside of Kane's head.

"Human! You are not going to escape!"

Looks like that to me, snotball, he thought as his broad powerful chest and long, muscular arms provided plenty of thrust to cut through the surging tide washing through the TOTO base.

A solid, limblike mass of parasites shot through the water and reached for the former Magistrate, the clumsy initial grab doing little more than pushing him around in the flooded hallway. Kane kicked and stroked harder, plunging through the base and making his way toward the mat-trans chamber. His whole plan counted on getting to there and jumping back to AUTEC before the underwater base no longer had any power.

Kakusa's arm swept through the corridor, creating waves and smashing against the walls. "You wish to let in the ocean? Then I will bring it in!"

"Do whatever you like, blob!" Kane shouted back.

Kakusa's sole response was its writhing tentacle thrashing even harder. The underwater base's structure was rocking as a body composed of thousands of cells the size of a house cat surged and acted as one superhuman body.

Glancing back, Kane saw Akeno's head, grasped in a wreath of tentacles, bloody, hollow eye sockets glaring, mouth still moving at the head of what had now become a grisly worm or monstrous snake. "I am a god, Kane! A true god, not a pretender like those you've humbled before!"

Kane folded, turning and cutting loose with the Sin Eater. The parasite cells popped, rupturing in the bullet's relentless passage. Kane fired another shot, planting a slug right into the severed head's center. Bone imploded and a ghastly cloud of brain matter and blood filled the tunnel.

"You boast like all the rest," Kane grunted.

He'd shut up Kakusa for the moment; without a mouth, the hive body was unable to speak directly. Right now, Kane was thinking of everything except the plan to throw a bolt of lightning into the heart of the monster mass.

Another surge of the Kakusa "worm" lunged forward, and Kane whipped out his knife, slashing at the stretching end of the composite creature. It was a deep, brutal cut that broke the cohesion between the mass that would have grabbed him, and it bought him even more time.

Kane spun in the water and kicked once more. He grabbed at handholds to move him along even more quickly, using his muscle power more efficiently than a standard swimming motion. The stairwell to the mat trans was just ahead, and Kane clawed his way up the steps. The entire lower section of the TOTO base was currently completely flooded. His only saving grace against the biting cold and crushing pressure of the depths that they were at was the superstructure of the failing base and his shadow suit's environmental adaptation.

The seawater was cold enough to send him into hypothermic shock after only a few seconds. Kakusa lived up to its boasts, as the surging tentacle was more than comfortable in the merciless, chilling flood. Kane didn't want to see Kakusa's claim of fighting off the body-pasting weight of a mile of water crushing downward in person.

But that was all about to be over. The mat trans was up ahead, and he could see Orochi at the control panel.

Kakusa pushed up through the stairway, and Kane threw one more grenade into the fluid mass's bulk, the concussion blast turning a coherent form into loose and stunned individual parasite cells.

The body of another humanoid suddenly appeared at the end of the limb, talking even as the body trembled uncontrollably, head jerking spastically. "I'll suck your knowledge out and laugh as your bones implode on themselves!"

Kane smiled. "Says the idiot who fell into my trap."

The pawn body released an inhuman wail, rage twisting its frostbite-damaged face.

Only one more step.

Grant was nearly at the AUTEC fence when powerful arms fell hard on his shoulders.

"Not so quickly, Enkidu!"

It was Grogan, and yet it was not. There was a primal rage in the New Order giant's voice, and there was strength that was fueled by more than human madness.

Grant grimaced and swung his elbow back hard, aiming for the center of the man's face. Grogan twisted, taking the impact on his shoulder, but it was enough to drive the two men away from each other. They stood on the fallen tree that had breached the AUTEC perimeter. Grogan's eyes were lit with devil-inspired glee.

"If you're looking for Enkidu, he's somewhere in the past, with his queen," Grant snarled.

Grogan chuckled. "He is you, fool."

"Fair enough. We've killed all of Kakusa's slaves outside the fence, and now you're ready to take on me?" Grant asked.

"You will either live or you will be brought back into the fold," Grogan snarled. "Ullikummis has given me more than enough freedom to relish either choice."

Grant glanced back. Rosalia and Kondo were dealing with an infestation of Kakusa's octoslug parasites. He could help them, but Grogan was eating up too much of his time. He snapped his Sin Eater into his fist. "I pick the third choice—messing you up!"

Grogan moved with a swiftness that belied his bulk, barely getting out of the way of Grant's first shots even as he brought up his own weapon. Grant felt the hammer blow that struck his right shoulder, a powerful bullet slamming into the melon-size ball of muscle with more than enough force to leave his fingers numb, even with the impact resistance provided by the shadow suit's gauntlets. As it was, the Sin Eater dangled from its holster, and the big Cerberus fighter was left scrambling for cover.

Even as he hopped to the ground from the trunk of the tree, Grant spotted one of the other New Order survivors rushing toward him. This woman wielded a machete held high over her head. Grant was aware of the damage that the blade could do, its edge slicing through the stiffening fibers, not impacting them bluntly. He swung up one of his long, thick legs, driving the heel of his boot into the cultist's face. There was a sickening crunch and her head snapped back, blade tumbling from numbed fingers.

Grant didn't like nearly kicking the head off a slave of the stone god, but Ullikummis's followers were fanatical in their zeal. Still, it gave the big ex-Magistrate the room he needed to retrieve the Sin Eater. Whatever the weapon Grogan had used, it was nothing less than a hand howitzer, much like his own machine pistol.

If the bullet had struck his chest, he'd be nursing a broken rib. He didn't want to contemplate the trauma a head shot would have inflicted. The limited protection of their high-tech suits was enough to give them a chance, but it hadn't imbued the Cerberus heroes with invulnerability.

Grogan's movement drew his attention to where the big gunman was on the tree, shoving aside a branch to get a better shot against Grant. Grant leaped and lashed out, slamming his forearm across Grogan's ankles with a scything chop that downed the New Order commander. The tumble, first into the trunk of the tree and then clumsily to the ground, was accompanied by the ugly sound of breaking wood and grisly, meaty slaps. Grant swung his Sin Eater to end the stone god's follower when movement loomed through the shadows.

Reflexes tore him away from putting the stunned opponent out of everyone's misery, and Grant triggered a burst of 9 mm slugs that ripped across the air between the two men even as the shotgun wielded by the New Order gunner bellowed. Whereas the single-point impact from Grogan's .44-40 lever action pistol was blunt and extremely powerful, focused on one area to the point where Grant could feel his right arm go completely numb, the shotgun hurled a swarm of .33-caliber projectiles.

The whole shotgun blast's relative mass was nearly a ton, but luckily it was divided among nine impacts, which on the whole kept Grant from being bowled over. The shadow suit held, and Grant still felt like he'd taken a hard right to the gut. The New Order shooter, on the other hand, had no such protection, and his rib cage sprouted fountains of crimson and chunks of bone and muscle as the Sin Eater's salvo ripped through him.

Grogan regained his senses quickly, and while he'd lost his gun, he pulled a machete that sang through the darkness. Grant was barely able to bring up the Sin Eater to deflect the limb-lopping blade, and this time the machine pistol spiraled away into the darkness, torn from his grasp and the forearm holster in one savage swing. The hard connection with unyielding steel had also loosened Grogan's grasp on his blade, giving Grant a split second to fire off a hard left hook that snapped the New Order giant's head around.

Dropped to one knee by the Cerberus titan's punch, Grogan spread his arms and lunged in to head butt Grant in the stomach. Grogan's thick arms wrapped around Grant's waist and cinched tightly, their slow, gradually increasing force not coming in with the same velocity as an impact trauma. Grant knew that with his leverage and strength, Grogan would shatter his spine within a few moments.

Grant gripped the dome of Grogan's skull with his big left hand, pushing to the side with all of his might. The New Order leader grunted with the effort, responding by doubling the crushing pressure on Grant's lower back. Another moment and the big Cerberus rebel knew that he would be left paralyzed and helpless. Cripples had short lives in the post-apocalyptic wilderness. Grant speared his left fist hard into the side of Grogan's neck, drawing every erg of strength that he could.

Vertebrae slipped, cracking under the force of the blow, and the spine-snapping grasp around Grant's waist disappeared. Glassy eyes looked up from Grogan's face as he toppled into the wiregrass, lips barely having the strength to do more than twitch.

Grant knew that leaving the New Order leader to die like this was cruel beyond belief. He knelt and clamped his hand over the mortally injured quadriplegic's nose and mouth. It was precious seconds that Rosalia and Kondo might not have, but Grant couldn't allow his enemy's slow suffering to drag out for what could be hours.

Grogan's eyes fluttered closed.

"Grant? You alive out there?" Rosalia asked over her comm device.

Grant took a quick assessment of himself. Pulled muscles and bruises wrapped around his whole body, and he hated to see what was left over when he peeled himself out of the shadow suit. "I've felt better. You?"

"The parasites are all dead," the warrior woman responded. She sounded exhausted, as if she'd just survived being dragged behind a horse at full gallop. "At least everything that was within the perimeter."

"The rest is all Kane," Grant answered, feeling the aches rise as his adrenaline bled off out of his bloodstream. He didn't know if he had enough fuel in his body to get him going again if Kakusa decided to rise from the depths of the Tongue Of The Ocean.

Domi was nearly to the Sandcat, and she could see there were ten of the mutants surrounding the armored personnel carrier. They were so ferociously involved with smashing at the hatches that they didn't notice her lithe, shadow-suit-blackened form dart through the deadly night, knife in one hand and .45-caliber Detonics in the other. Her only option was to take these monstrosities off balance, and that meant a full-on direct assault. She spotted a rock that looked as if it would make a good ramp and charged up it. As she reached the peak, she stiff-armed the pistol and opened fire, emptying its 6-round magazine so quickly, it sounded like the extended roar of a small dragon. Two rounds tore through the back of one cannibal's head as he lofted a fifty-pound hunk of stone over his head to use as a hammer. As soon as his brains were destroyed, he collapsed into a heap of insensate mush, his bones snapping under the weight of his tiny boulder. Even as that creature fell, Domi swept the group, spreading the rest of her shots in rapid succession, her ruby-red eyes picking up the front sight and tripping the trigger the moment it came into close proximity to one of the other mutants.

By the time her gun locked empty, two more of the assaulting horde were lain out, lifeless with heads or hearts broken by the albino wildcat's .45-caliber messages. She leaped off the top of the rock, aiming all of her weight at one of the man-eaters that she hadn't yet targeted.

Domi struck the creature with both feet and felt the fracture of her enemy's collarbone under her heels. The mutant toppled backward, blown off balance by her momentum. When the injured man-beast struck the ground, his skull burst like an overripe fruit, but that impact was the spur for Domi to straighten her legs, bounding off the dead cannibal's chest.

She aimed herself at another of the creatures, and as she lunged through the night at him, she flicked her combat knife ahead of her. Its keen edge struck flesh and parted it easily, laying open the mutant hybrid's throat from ear to ear. The cannibal's head flew back under the assault, and its throat yawned wide, blood gushing from severed arteries.

Domi landed in a somersault, using her roll to bleed off momentum and redirect the force of her landing so that she wasn't stunned by the impact. As she got to a low crouch, she looked back to see that the survivors of the Sandcat siege had locked their attention onto her.

The odds were still five to one, and she no longer had the element of surprise, nor a loaded firearm to even the playing field between them.

One of the firing ports on the Sandcat suddenly erupted, fire and thunder barking through the tiny hole. Even as the gunfire began, Domi could feel the sudden slashes of pain as Priscilla pulled the trigger on Lakesh's borrowed pistol. The compact Detonics was loud, and it recoiled hard if one didn't have the training for it. Domi could master the tiny .45 because she knew how to hold it tight, and her wrists and forearms possessed strength far greater than those slender limbs indicated. Priscilla didn't hit anything, but the telepathic hybrid woman broadcast flashes of her wrist bones grating against each other, the slide of the gun biting at the web of her off hand, and the muzzle-flash searing hot in her vision and booming in the confines of the armored vehicle.

Even though she missed every shot, Priscilla had bought Domi vital moments and she quickly replaced the empty magazine in her pistol and began her assault anew. The distracted mutants, scattering under the sudden gunfire from within the machine, had momentarily forgotten the feral albino's presence, and Domi gunned down two more before they realized that she was a threat among them.

The closest one let out a bestial roar and lunged, only to find out that he hurled himself right onto the point of the lithe warrior girl's dagger. Six inches of wicked steel pierced the creature's breastbone, wrenching the knife from Domi's grasp, but she didn't waste time trying to retrieve the weapon. If she did, she'd only end up snarled under the weight of the mutant, and she had other business to attend to. She backhanded a second of the cannibals, the heavy stainless-steel weight of her gun shattering the thing's jaw.

The last of them grabbed at her, but Domi hit the ground, slithering between her attacker's legs as he clawed at empty air. Domi rolled onto her back, brought up the pistol and opened fire, punching three heavy slugs into the mutant's lower back, smashing his pelvis and spine. The creature with the broken jaw lurched, struggling to get back to its feet, and Domi fed in the last of her magazines.

The final mutant stood, torn between following Rioch's telepathic orders or to run. Common sense took over and the thing raced away into the desert, no longer having the stomach for this battle.

Domi took a cleansing breath, then looked at the Sandcat.

Rioch was undoubtedly hot on her heels, and he was bringing his monstrous minions along with. While the Cat wasn't loaded with enough ammo to put up a fight, it could run fast and far before the mutants gave up the pursuit. She didn't see Rioch as being the kind of enemy who would survive for long in the blistering sun of the desert. She pried open the hatch and found Priscilla tending to Lakesh.

"Here," Domi said, pushing the remote into the hybrid woman's hands. "Fix him up."

Priscilla looked at the feral girl, Domi could feel her eyes boring into her soul, even as the remote's buttons beeped. "Domi…"

"If you're going to ask me to do something stupid, forget it!" Domi snapped.

Priscilla looked through the open hatch. "He has numbers with him. Sufficient to do damage to the Sandcat, not like the handful that hammered this machine."

"They can't run at forty miles an hour," Domi returned. "I'll run the tank to empty, and they just can't…"

She was looking at an empty crew area, empty save for the unconscious Lakesh. His gray, weakened pallor was disappearing, a healthy olive color returning to his features.

"I was gone the moment you opened the hatch, dear friend," Priscilla's thoughts cut into her mind. "I was already outside of the Cat, knowing that I could do nothing inside. I'd tried out the pistol, and it was too much for my hands."

Domi saw that she was in the middle of the desert, driving at full speed away from Area 51. The sun was already rising and the compass read that she was heading toward what had been the California coast, and that she'd lost at least fifteen minutes. Even as she knew the span of time had disappeared from her memory, she saw herself manipulating the remote after getting inside the Sandcat. She had been operating as if on autopilot, the knowledge of the device already implanted into her brain. She then had thrown the Cat into gear and hit the gas, making her escape.

"Damn it! Why? Where are you now?" Domi shouted.

"Beloved?" a weak but revived Lakesh murmured on his cot.

"Where are you?" Domi asked.

"I'm just a memory now," Priscilla said. "I took some of your grenades, and made certain that I could buy you time against Rioch and his beasts."

"No. No!" Domi snarled as she hit the brakes. She looked at the fuel gauge and noticed that the tank was empty. Even if she turned the Sandcat around, there was no way she could drive back. She saw that the spare tanks they'd managed to scrounge were gone, too.

"You can forget the pain, Domi," Priscilla offered. "I left the command to forget me...all you have to do is wish it. What you're hearing is just a recording inside of your head. You don't have to be sad..."

"No, you're family," Domi said, clutching the steering wheel.

"Domi," Lakesh croaked, louder this time.

It was too much. She tried to feel Priscilla's presence, even as she scrambled to Lakesh's side, pouring fresh water into his mouth by squeezing it from a rag. She couldn't give him refreshment too quickly, not when he'd been ailing for so long. He could choke, drown.

Lakesh laid his head back, licking his lips. When he spoke, it was sleepily, almost drunkenly. "Domi, are you okay?"

"I'll live," she answered, kneeling at his side and looking him over. "You?"

Lakesh looked down at his hands. "I feel like I've been thrown off a cliff."

"How're you thinking? Still tangle-brained?" Domi asked.

Lakesh looked at her, then smiled. "I'm hungry, beat up, but I remember... I remember everything. Especially Priscilla. She was in my head..."

"She helped me fix you," Domi said.

"And where is she?" Lakesh asked.

Domi thought about it for a moment. The sun was pretty high, but still it was clearly morning. The distance she'd covered must have been more than fifteen minutes of travel, especially since she'd estimated that they'd have gotten at least seventy miles before the tanks finally ran dry. That meant Priscilla was long gone. She could try to cross the desert, on foot, but Lakesh was too weak, and she'd used up too much ammunition. She was also running on empty, physically and mentally.

"Domi?" Lakesh asked.

"She's...gone," she told him, choking back a sob. A tear burned down her cheek.

Lakesh lifted one hand and cupped it to her chin. He looked as if he was trying to lift a log instead of his scrawny arm. He kissed her forehead and rested against her. "She saved us."

Domi couldn't say anything. Part of her hated that Priscilla tricked her, stealing her memories and replacing them with false ones, making her run away and leave the Quad V hybrid behind to face impossible odds. She realized, though, that she would have done the exact same thing. She'd been planning to hand off the remote, then tell Priscilla to drive like the wind while she delayed Rioch and the mutants. Priscilla had simply flipped the plan around, avoiding any semblance of an argument, ensuring that Domi would get a sizable lead away from the desolate corner of Nevada.

"You can forget me," Priscilla had offered.

I know you can't hear me, she thought. But I don't want to forget. You risked your life. We helped each other. You could have been a part of my family.

Lakesh frowned as she got up, walking outside with a pair of binoculars. She scanned the horizon, but it was no good. She'd driven for nearly two hours before Priscilla had allowed her to wake up.

The gunfire distraction, that was Priscilla's memory of trying to fire the Detonics, broadcast telepathically, affecting not only Domi herself but also the mutants as they were about to descend upon her.

Domi threw back her head and yelled out Priscilla's name at the top of her lungs. The wide, desolate sands absorbed the sound of her voice. Nothing echoed. No psychic caress of a mind from long distance touched her thoughts. She wanted to think that maybe the hybrid woman was still alive, still fighting, but that she was too far away, unable to make contact, just like a radio with a weak signal.

But there was also Rioch, who seemed to be far more adept with his doomie abilities. She couldn't sense him, either. The only thing around, for miles, was empty, flat land, broken up by sparse scrub and baleful winds sending dirt devils twisting along barren stretches. Lakesh shielded his eyes as he sat in the hatch of the Sandcat.

"Domi, come in here. You'll burn," he told her.

The albino girl looked back at the man she loved, the man who she'd risked everything for, the man for whom Priscilla had sacrificed herself. He held out his hand.

"I failed her," Domi said as she took his hand.

He tugged her close, wrapping his arms around her. He kissed her forehead, allowing a tear to burn down his cheek. "She's smart. She's free. She may have escaped. We all thought that you had died at Area 51, too."

Domi looked up. She wanted to say something, but she held her tongue. She wrapped her arms around Lakesh and closed her eyes.

The desert sun did nothing to warm the cold emptiness in either of the lovers' spirits.

By sunset, they were on the move, traveling in the cool darkness. Their destination was California, where Kane and Grant promised to reunite with the two travelers. There, they could regather their forces and look for Brigid, bringing the group back together.

Domi was sick of being so far away from the rest of her Cerberus family.

Chapter 23

Kakusa's patience was coming to an end. Above, on the Florida panhandle, Kakusa was losing contact with more and more of its disparate cells, and realized that the enemy was waging a war of extermination. Those enemies included Ullikummis's envoys, whom Kakusa knew by face and had been lucky enough to kill while they fought alongside Kane's allies on the surface.

That battle was a lost cause, at least for now. Kakusa's cells were fighting for their lives and would be unable to find a host, not with the Watatsumi hunting them down. Kakusa had lost the opportunity to take out the expedition at the AUTEC base, all thanks to a healthy dose of suspicion and paranoia on the part of Kondo and Rosalia. Kakusa was struggling to escape their hunt, and the losses of great numbers of its cells, not only from their attacks but also from Kane's intervention, was spreading its concentration thinner and thinner. It didn't help that a vast majority of its conscious hosts were dead, dying and drowning, cutting down on the number of human brains it could use to increase its personal brainpower. All Kakusa had in the TOTO base was a near-dead humanoid that replaced the puppet Akeno. Kane had destroyed that body, first with gunfire, then grenades.

Kakusa had been too long without a face, and the loss of Akeno was an even greater annoyance. Kane could shoot, could cut, could blow up hundreds of its cells, but that was like trying to stop an invasion by shooting only a few of the lowliest riflemen.

Kakusa was an entity, and with the slugs now combined into a more monolithic form, Kakusa had a body again. A body that it didn't need to wield like a remote-control puppet.

It felt good to exist again.

It would feel even better to experience the sensation of Kane's bones snapping in a newly formed hand. The waters were cold, coming in from an area where no warmth from the sun reached the bottom of the ocean. Kakusa had the sensation but not the vulnerability to temperature. Some of its cells had squeezed through the cracks rent in the TOTO base that Kane had made with his grenades. The octoslugs swam freely, happily even, with the force of tons per square inch weighing on their invertebrate bodies. This was the realm for which their bodies had been designed, and since it could thrive in normal atmosphere and at pressures that would grind a human into mere paste, Kakusa knew it had the endurance and strength to deal with Kane and Orochi, even without a humanoid pawn.

The near dead, almost frozen Watatsumi Kakusa now wore as adornment was simply there for speaking out. Telepathic contact with Kane had been tough. Using a puppet's voice box was so much easier.

"I'll suck your knowledge out and laugh as your bones implode on themselves!" Kakusa bellowed.

"Says the idiot who fell into my trap," the human answered as he retreated through the doors of the mat-trans chamber.

Kakusa roared and lunged toward the doors as they were thrown shut. The initial rush splashed against the sturdy bulkhead, pliant cells deforming and cushioning the impact for the half-dead humanoid it held as a puppet. Kakusa drew in more of its assembled biomass, knowing that one door, one hole might have been an impediment to Enlil or Ullikummis, but not for Kakusa, who was not confined to a single body.

Kakusa's biomass swarmed through the corridors of the undersea structure. Every hallway, every vent cover, every door was pushed through. The secure mat-trans chamber had plenty of approaches; Kakusa had even made its way through one into the air vents. That route, however, was a mangled, pinched-off mass of metal that it couldn't get through.

Kakusa could see a heavy glass window in the hatch between the corridor and the mat-trans chamber. There, it found its foe, even as restored nuclear power surged in the TOTO. There was a flash behind the human as the mat trans activated, launching someone, presumably Orochi, back to the surface. All that remained was the man, who stood, waiting.

Kakusa wrenched loose a piece of pipe and, utilizing the strength of hundreds of its cephalopod components, hurled it with enough strength to crack the window. There was a tiny, almost imperceptible hole in the armaglass, but the edges were too sharp to slip even one of its cells through. It would take another strike to open things up, but it brought its humanoid pawn up to the glass to look, to speak.

Kane stood, still clad in his shadow suit. Cast in black, his figure looked ominous as it was backlit by the bloodred emergency lights. Kakusa could feel the fear that image placed in the absorbed memories of its human slaves. Were Kakusa not a god, it would actually be intimidated and terrified by the tall, powerful figure, sleek muscles clad tightly in skintight polymers accenting the bottled-up strength within those limbs.

Kane held on to a thick rope of some sort, a cable an inch in diameter, wound in loops that dangled almost to the floor. The effort made Kane's biceps and shoulder swell against the weight.

"Going to tie me up?" Kakusa asked, edging forward. The weight of tens of thousands of its cells were behind it now, all of them stretching throughout the undersea base, enjoying the literal immortality as Kakusa's multiple limbs stretched, heading toward the mat-trans chamber by alternate routes. Kane was surrounded and helpless. There were no more grenades with which to shatter the cohesion of its tentacles as they pushed against doors and flooded ventilation and maintenance hatches. Kane's gun was next to useless, except for the distraction of destroying another body.

The only way out was through the mat trans, but the man wasn't making a step toward the armaglass-surrounded chamber.

"Do you hear me, human?" Kakusa asked. The flood waters hadn't risen by much, but with all of its gelatinous mass squeezed into the TOTO, there was hardly a corner of the undersea base that wasn't touched by seawater.

"Yeah. Come on in," Kane said. As if on cue, the door lock failed, and Kakusa was able to hurl aside the hatch that had kept it from closing in on the Cerberus rebel.

The cable that Kane held suddenly looked ominous. "You've restored power to the mat trans after your sabotage run, Kane. What was the point of all that?"

Kane smirked. "You don't know what juice is?"

Kakusa studied the man who was now ankle-deep

in seawater, the bulk of its own biomass preventing a torrent from flooding into the chamber. Kakusa was only one more step away from the mat-trans unit.

Kakusa looked at the cable and noticed a naked length of copper exposed from the end of the stripped insulation. "Juice…"

"See, you're limited by the slang you've taken from your pawns," Kane said. "And since they're Japanese speakers, and we're in an era past regular running electricity…"

Kakusa realized that it was drenched in millions of gallons of water and its body was pressed against all manner of conductive metal and exposed wiring. Even though there wouldn't be any current running through them, thanks to Orochi's sabotage of the main power conduits, there was the potential for millions of volts in that cable.

For the first time since Enlil held it in a jar, Kakusa felt fear.

"A short circuit freed you from the leash around your neck," Kane said. "It reawakened the personality that was stuck inside the snotballs that make up your body, and all of them are now spreading through this base, all of them looking for ways to get at me through whatever holes you can find."

Kakusa let a rumble of anger roll up in the throat of its nearly dead puppet.

"The original plan was to release your victims, but you did something to make them all helpless, paralyzed," Kane added. "We can't save them and kill you, and I'm not happy about drowning them…"

"I'll kill…"

"You'll do it how?" Kane asked, letting loops of the cable drop, splashing in the seawater. "The bare power cable hits the water and thousands upon thousands of your cells are electrocuted. The shock of one control collar breaking freed you to control the unprocessed octoslugs. But what happens when the bulk of your mass gets hit with all this juice?"

Kakusa's cells trembled, bristling with rage. "You won't make it out of here. Your shadow suit is soaking wet…"

"You're using information from assumption, not real knowledge," Kane answered with a menacing smile. "Well, I've had enough of chatting with a wannabe god."

"Damn you…"

"If it's any consolation, Enlil and his kid are next on my list of deities to topple," Kane said. He hurled the end of the cable toward the ankle-deep water at his feet. Even as he did so, he leaped, diving into the idling mat-trans chamber. There had been more than enough energy stored in the unit to launch him to AUTEC, while the rest of the output from the pocket reactor was focused through the cable.

Kakusa bellowed, stretching out a dozen cells' worth of tentacles to catch the falling power cord. All of the parasitic components were still sopping wet, connected to the rest of Kakusa's body, which was pressed to metal, grounding the assembled biomass.

The fury of lightning tore through the god, bringing a blinding flare and burning agony to the being that had been trapped in the eternal midnight at the bottom of the ocean. Consciousness fled the Entity in an explosion of high voltage.

As soon as he released the power cable, Kane leaped into the idling mat trans, knowing that while the shadow suit provided some environmental protection, he didn't want to see how much amperage the suit could handle. Even as he collapsed onto the platform, feeling the plasma waveform swell and flow around him, his teeth tingled and hair prickled under the shadow suit, and he wasn't even touching the seawater that his cable had landed in.

Then Kane's body was broken apart and projected through time and space toward the other end of the transdimensional portal. Mat-trans travel was no mystery to the Cerberus explorer, and while he hadn't jumped much utilizing the artificial wormholes created by the nuclear-powered units, he was a veteran of the transport prior to using the interphaser. Right now, however, his molecules were literally exploding through the transdimensional ether, buffeted by a massive energy discharge behind him.

Now Kane was surrounded by the telepathic keening of Kakusa as its cells were electrocuted. The unholy wail was that of a dying beast, not a suffering sentient, but the hive mind's death cries echoed through the hollows that existed in the nether space between universes and dimensions.

This was not a direct, focused attack, but more like a lava flow bursting from its normal magma vein and expanding to fill the newfound space where matter so hot that rock became liquid could spread its highly excited molecules. Kakusa's psychic thrashing was a flood that rivaled the incoming seawater into the TOTO base for sheer force and relentless omnipresence.

Kane fought against the terror of being crushed by Kakusa's writhing intellect as it bowled past him. He thrust his hands out, and he could feel the alligator-scaled hide, which had been rough and capable of rending the skin from him, turn soft and gelatinous as he attacked it, fingers clawing through it as if it were putrid mud, the flow of the psychic energy deflected by Kane's attack. Fighting back, giving himself some space, Kane realized that there was something more out there than just a flashing final thought of a dying god. He clutched at the mess, willing the slime into tough, graspable fibers that he reeled in.

Even as he hauled on the Entity, or the shadow of it, or the horrible dream of it made pseudo-flesh, Kane imagined it being wound around a great spool. The crushing psychic force that had come into the jump after him was finding itself spun tightly, compressed on a wheel.

"Get control of you," Kane grunted. This was his imagination, but his shoulders and back still felt the rending agony of dragging in the gigantic flood tide of Kakusa, even as it compressed around the spool. "You're not going to haunt the space between dimensions...."

There was no answer. Here, separated from the universe where it was dying, the intellect was just blind, frothing plasma without consciousness, without reason. Kakusa could no more converse with Kane than its electrocuted biomass could form a coherent thought.

It felt as if he'd spent the better part of a day, and despite the fact that the shadow suit was environmentally contained, Kane felt his body drenched in sweat and covered in the grit of hard labor. His knuckles were swollen and the pads of his fingers and palms were raw, hot and red. He remembered Brigid telling him about how the space between universes converted will into power, and he could see that he was more than simply himself. The tremendous strength necessary to capture and haul in a gigantic, amorphous being was provided not just by Kane, but by the spiraling time worm of former and future incarnations of himself, every one of his existences throwing in its might in the effort to prevent Kakusa from finding a mental home in the cracks between universes, a dwelling from which it could conceivably recover and stage a brand-new assault upon reality itself.

Kane saw his doppelgangers, his tesseracts as the scientists had labeled them, shadows of the core entity of which Kane himself was the current avatar. Shadows of what were, what would be and even what could have been worked together in a union of power wherein the Cerberus explorer was gifted with the might to gather up and contain even a god that had terrified Enlil. The transported Kane picked up the spool and squeezed it, feeling Kakusa compress even further, in defiance of the laws of physics in the three-dimensional realm they both hailed from. In the space between realities, physics could be ignored, even reshaped, a future self thought.

They pressed down, turning a reel that was the size of a Sandcat into something no larger than a spindle of thread. Still Kane and his selves crushed, wadding the Entity into a ball of nothingness.

"Go to hell, Kakusa," Kane snarled, drawing on muscles that protested as real as a knife spearing into his chest. He hurled the remnants of the parasitic enemy far into the void, aiming toward eternity, and the last dregs of the ancient entity disappeared into the inky blackness of other space. Whether Kane's wish would actually open a portal to a flaming pit of imprisonment or a lightless, cold and empty void where Kakusa would be alone forever, he couldn't tell, and he didn't want to know.

Exhaustion rolled over him, and the slightest pressure of his hands against each other made his wrists and forearms feel as if they were pressed into a meat grinder.

Something pushed him, another bit tugging him. He had the mental image of his future and past bracketing him, carrying him along toward the other end of the wormhole, the destination of his jump deep in the wiregrass swamps of the Florida panhandle.

Kane tumbled toward the opening in his home universe, feeling weightless and free now, looking back to see…

Kane crashed on the floor of the mat-trans chamber, breathing heavily, seawater sloughing off his shadow suit, trickles of electrical sparks continuing to spark along the high-tech polymers as he was finally grounded. His brain felt as if it had been pushed through a hole the size of a 9 mm bullet, and he couldn't resist the urge to empty the contents of his stomach on the floor.

"Damn it, Kane! Watch where you're puking!" Grant complained, leaping away from his friend's side.

Something had happened during the jump, but it was a blur, just a foggy mass of images and sensations that his conscious mind couldn't assemble into anything real. Kane had experienced a similar failure of recollection of a prior journey between realities, to rescue the shadow of Grant. There were thoughts of comfort, of camaraderie, in those brief blinks of time, but here, grounded in three dimensions, there was no language for the things seen, thus rendering them un-memorable.

"Help me up," Kane rasped, but he hadn't needed to waste the breath as Grant's powerful hands pulled him up.

"We're okay, too, thanks for asking," Grant muttered.

Kane looked at his partner and snorted in derision. With that exchange over, he turned his cold blue eyes toward Orochi. "It's time for you and the rest of your scaly brood to go back home."

Kondo stepped up, but not to stand at the expedition commander's side. "He's right. We've gone far outside the realm of warrior and scientific ethics here. Tatehiko will not take the events here casually."

Orochi grimaced but held his tongue. "I was following orders."

Rosalia spoke up, "The excuse used by monsters to justify their actions."

"We've lost too many of our expedition under your command, and noncombatants were killed in a crossfire between us and a weapon that ran out of control," Kondo said. "You are relieved of your command and are now in our custody."

"And if I do not choose to be imprisoned?" Orochi asked.

Kane's and Grant's Sin Eaters suddenly snapped off their forearms. Rosalia's Copperhead and the guns of the Watatsumi aimed at him.

"You can choose to stand trial, or you can be a greasy smear," Grant growled.

Orochi took a deep breath. He presented his wrists, and the surviving Watatsumi bound him, preparing him for transport as they bracketed him under vigilant guard.

"We will take your heroism in the TOTO into account," Kondo said. "If you agree, Kane."

Kane nodded numbly. He felt as if he'd walked across a desert, nonstop from night to noon to midnight again, but he kept the Sin Eater steady on the former expedition commander. "He did his part in stopping Kakusa."

"Then I ask permission to enter your testimony back in Ryugu-jo," Kondo requested.

Kane looked around at Grant, Rosalia and even the coyote. "What happened with the New Order?"

Grant sneered. "I had to clean house. There was no one left to talk to about where Brigid was."

Kane nodded, a frown creasing his face. He looked at Kondo. "You'll just have to make a recording, Kondo. I can't afford to spend time away from what needs to be done."

"Ullikummis, and your mission companion," Kondo answered. He nodded. "Let's set it up. Then we'll see what we can do about sending you on your way."

Kane extended a hand. "I might not be able to help with bringing Orochi to justice, but I promise you, once things calm down, I will come to Ryugu-jo and try to help you."

Kondo shook the man's hand. "Tatehiko would love to meet a man as brave as you."

Kane managed a smile before he collapsed into a seat, body numb from head to toe.

He'd have a few moments of rest before it was time to make the journey to California. There were redoubts that they could relay through, thanks to the AUTEC mat trans.

This trip to locate Brigid by drawing in the New Order had failed, but as consolation, a dark project and an even darker menace had been delivered a mighty defeat.

The Cerberus rebels lived to battle Ullikummis and his cult another day.

AGRIPPINE LAY LIMPLY on the hammock, his mind seemingly stripped from him, his breathing shallow, his body completely relaxed by the toxins of the cephalopod that had connected him to an alien mind. As it was, the Cajun swamp guide paid no notice to an opossum, laden down with a slimy, pregnancy-bloated octoslug that dragged itself from the brackish swamp water.

The marsupial had no strength left, and limp, dangling tentacles dragged behind the dying animal as it crawled closer to the unconscious man. Finally, life and strength faded, and the opossum collapsed, releasing a raspy, fetid belch as its dying breath. The mass atop its back shuddered, pods twitching in an effort to move even closer to Agrippine. Nothing moved for the ebbing parasite, its own existence cut short by the electrical holocaust that destroyed thousands of its brethren at the bottom of the ocean, hundreds of miles away.

But there was one spark of vitality left in the creature. A nearly formed embryo struggled against the sac it was held in. Slender tentacles pushed, stretching its elastic prison, looking for a hole to where it could find survival, to perhaps escape to a living host.

Agrippine's blank eyes flickered with recognition.

Slowly, zombielike, the dazed, soul-ripped Cajun stretched out its hand toward the imprisoned octoslug, as if both of them could only live with the assistance of the other.

The truth was, they did.

As the sun rose over the wiregrass swamp, a crippled string of proteins riding within a nameless invertebrate found a new home inside a man who had been gutted mentally.

Two minds, shattered by trauma, became one. But the sum of those parts had nothing more than base mammalian instinct. Agrippine and Kakusa scurried into the swamp, knowing that there was more to them, but it seemed forever lost.

* * * * *

JAMES AXLER

DEATH LANDS®

Haven's Blight

Destiny's shockwave shatters the foundation of the future...

Bartering their expertise to a nautical band of brilliant technomads, Ryan Cawdor's group finds trouble waiting in the swamplands of the Louisiana Gulf. With the gravely injured Krysty Wroth's fate uncertain, Ryan is desperate to save Haven from a genetic blood curse. He'll succeed...if his luck doesn't run out first.

Available January wherever books are sold.